JILLIAN E THOMPSON

Dying For A Little Charm

A Clearwater Witches Cozy Mystery

Acknowledgments

My history inspired this story, and I drew on pieces of my childhood for it. However, I think Lilliann has a stronger foundation through her adoptive parents than many of us, myself included, have with our biological parents. Lilliann's trauma causes her to self-sabotage a lot of aspects of her life, including relationships. The fact that she chooses to try therapy and work through her trauma is a big step. If you have your own trauma or need help, there are a lot of places you can turn, whether it's a trusted friend or co-worker, a teacher, or a parent. There are crisis centers if you don't know who you can talk to or whom to trust. As a teacher, I let students know I care deeply about their physical/mental health. Trauma has a massive impact on society here in the United States, and we, as adults, cannot help children if we cannot self-regulate our own emotions and triggers. Find a way to help yourself if you are struggling, because somewhere out there, there is someone who will benefit from learning from you.

* * *

To my beloved sons, you are my greatest source of inspiration. Every time I put pen to paper or type on my screen, I do so with the belief that the most beautiful things in life come from the experiences we have. Through my writing, I share my experiences with the world, hoping to inspire others. I write because my mind is overflowing with thoughts and ideas that I need to capture before they slip away. Above all, I want you to know that I love you more than words can ever express, and my writing is just one of the many ways I try to convey my love for you both.

My beloved husband, I truly appreciate the unwavering support you have provided throughout our journey together. Whether I am immersed in work or feeling low and lethargic, you have been a constant pillar of strength, happiness, and affection. I am grateful for your unconditional love and encouragement. Your unwavering support has given me the confidence to express myself freely through my writing. I cannot express how much I value and cherish every moment we share. Thank you for being my rock, my joy, and my soulmate.

For my students: Remember, writing can be a powerful outlet and give you a safe space to express yourself. Through each character, I hope to convey various aspects of myself and inspire you to realize that with determination, anything can be accomplished. My time teaching you has enabled me to become a better writer, a more effective teacher, and a better person.

Thank you to the fantastic people who helped me improve this book from the first draft. Thank you, Shannon Massey, for being the best editor I could ask for and for coming in after I self-published, reading through it, and not only providing editing but also offering valuable feedback to help make this into a better book. I want to give thanks to @sugarphoenix on Discord, who helped me fine-tune the first few paragraphs of the book. I also want to recognize the beta readers who helped me make the novel more cohesive and fluid. Mariah Bell, for being the very first person to read this novel in its entirety and tell me where the little nuances needed to be repaired. Jonathan Taylor provided a lot of valuable feedback and called me out on things that someone unfamiliar with the culture and genre requires to know about magick and how it all works together. To the beta reader who preferred not to be named, who was by far amazing, caught a lot of little details that didn't flow, and helped me get this novel to the next level. She worked with me extensively over the last several weeks to refine and expand this book into something truly remarkable. I'm very grateful for her assistance with it, even if she decided that some of what I'd written was not her cup of tea.

Thank you so much for being my sounding board and inspiring me with some different ideas for Lillie and company.

Finally, thank you for reading my book, the first in the series for Clearwater. While my humor may not be for everyone, I hope you found some enjoyment in it.

Thank you!

One

The boxes in the backseat stared at me as I reached across to grab my phone from the passenger seat, attempting to grab it through my peripheral vision instead of turning toward it. Considering the ring earlier, I knew I should call Mom back, but I didn't want to talk to her yet.

I inhaled deeply, trying my best not to sigh again, my phone forgotten as the boxes filled my vision from the rearview mirror. *Truly, my life had been reduced to a total of eight boxes.*

Eight boxes.

Mostly, it was my clothes and the books I just couldn't live without. But seeing those boxes staring at me was like a ton of bricks landing on my head. I had truly, utterly screwed my life up.

It must be my luck to always screw everything up. Stop, I reminded myself; *you promised Ally that you would use positive self-talk. Fine, then, I was in a position to start over again because this was the way that I was going to make things right in my life.* I said to myself, reframing the negative thought. It didn't mean that I didn't still feel defeated by all the bad things.

Never in my life, even when I had found the adoption papers, had I felt so defeated. Heck, even when I was dealing with the most difficult students with constant name-calling and volatile behaviors during the last three years in public schools, it never felt like it did right now at this moment. It was like layering lava on top of smoking charcoal; it burned through me, red-hot.

The trees started to thin out as the town's city limit sign came into focus. Clearwater, Colorado, only had a little over seven thousand people living there, but it felt a lot smaller than that when you were living there full time.

I thought about the Violet Bite as I drove; it was one of the hallmarks of Clearwater, considering that it had been named after its signature dish, the Violet Death. Homemade pancakes, light and fluffy, covered in a sweet violet syrup, topped with lavender butter. It had been my favorite to eat when I worked at the Violet Bite every summer during school. It had been a great job for me, even during the summer I had to work with her. I'd learned a lot about how to read people and situations during that time, although it hadn't helped with my ADHD. I was always a bit distracted when it came to remembering things, so my orders had often been confused.

Luckily, most people were understanding. No one expects much from a teenager.

I wondered if they would have a position available for me over the summer. Yes, I knew I would be starting at the local high school in the fall, but I still needed something to do for money in the meantime. Working as a waitress was something that I'd done a lot throughout college too, but now I was better at not getting as distracted as I'd been as a kid. Maybe that would work in my favor when I ask about a position?

As I drove over the bridge into town, the sound of the rushing river waters greeted my ears. The trees faded into the background as the buildings came into view, and the sheer beauty of my hometown struck me. It was like seeing the sun for the first time after being blinded. At first glance, not much had changed, but at the same time, everything felt different.

Or was it me?

The sound of the water was soothing, and I almost stopped the car to take it all in, but a text notification interrupted my thoughts. It was probably my mom checking if I had arrived yet. As I rolled past the first few buildings, I searched for the sign of the Violet Bite. It was a rustic-looking building that had begun to show signs of wear when I left for college. I hoped it had received some tender loving care since then. The town was a tourist trap, with many visitors drawn to the hot springs, but the Violet Bite was a trademark of the town's hospitality, in my opinion.

As I approached, my car slowed down, and I marveled at how well-maintained the chrome panels of the Violet Bite looked in the fading sunlight. It was like stepping into the past, and I couldn't help but feel a wave of nostalgia wash over me.

Upon arriving at the parking lot, I found a vacant spot towards the back of the building. After turning off the ignition, I sat for a moment to observe my surroundings, anticipating a barrage of questions and concerns from the locals.

I wanted to compose myself before entering, as I didn't want to get overwhelmed and lose my cool. After a few minutes and a few unanswered and unread notifications on my phone, I felt prepared to head inside. Looking in the mirror, I did a quick wipe of my face with a wet nap to make sure that none of the tear stains were still visible.

I caught a whiff of myself and fumbled for the Lingering Ember perfume I always kept in my purse. Three quick spritzes should be enough to cover that I'd been in the car for seven days musk.

Running my fingers through my hair, I stared myself down and repeated my mantra in my head.

I can do this.

The neon sign reading Violet Bite flared to life as I closed my car door with my keys in my hand. I knew I had to fix the door, as it either slammed shut or refused to open without force. However, I wasn't ready to part with my car just yet. I planned to have it fixed when I had saved enough money, or perhaps my dad could help with some oil in the meantime.

As I approached the door, the clear glass bricks surrounding it gleamed in the fading sunlight and the glowing neon sign. The Violet Bite had been amazingly restored to its former glory, and it looked darn impressive. I felt a knot forming in my stomach as I opened the door; the bell chimed as I stepped into the restaurant.

All eyes turned toward me, but I quickly made my way to my mom's table, trying to avoid being the center of attention. I sat down in the booth, placing my purse and keys beside me before glancing at my mom. Her auburn hair had a touch of gray at the temples, but otherwise, she looked unchanged. That wasn't completely true, I determined, as I took in her face. There were crow's feet gathering at the corners of her eyes, and laugh wrinkles were beginning to form around her lips.

"Lilliann Luella King, it's about time you got here," she announced loudly, and I internally groaned.

Did she have to make it so that everyone focused on us?

"I sent you a bazillion text messages, and I'm sure that I left several voicemails as well."

It was just like her to exaggerate everything. There were not a bazillion text messages on my phone, and I'd spoken to her just outside of the last town I'd stopped in for gas. My mother excelled at being the town gossip; knowing everyone's business was her gain. So, if you need to capture someone's attention, you'd better know something about them, right?

"Mom," I whined. "Would you stop it? We spoke like twenty minutes ago… If that."

"No, no, no," she retorted. "Two hours at minimum, two hours, Lilliann. Anything could have happened to you in the last two hours, Lillie. Don't you know that I worry about you?"

I struggled to respond at that moment. I wanted to be a smart aleck and tell her something along the lines of that she hadn't worried about me for the last nine years, but at the same time, I knew that she did care about me, but had honored my need to be away from her and everything that I'd learned. It was unspoken between us about what happened to me being adopted, but I knew, in my heart, that she had loved me like her own child since I had come into her home. I was so lost in my thoughts about the past that I completely missed the waitress coming up to the table and asking for my order.

Mom cleared her throat with a sharp look at me, pulling me from my intense thoughts, and gestured towards the waitress with her eyes before I caught the fact that I had indeed been struggling with my ADHD again. I needed to get my prescription refilled soon. The waitress, because I still hadn't even looked at her, cleared her throat after a long moment of waiting and leaned her hip against the table as she called me by name.

"Lilliann, are you ever going to order?" The tone was whiny and overly dramatic, which seemed intentional because I recognized that voice immediately. Maddison McGregor, my nemesis from high school, was waiting tables. *Oh, this was good.* I was totally fine with not working at the Violet Bite if it meant not lording it over Maddison. The swift flash of us running around the tables passed through my mind before I smiled.

I turned to her; a brilliant smile on my face. Her blonde hair was tied back in a ponytail, and the purple apron was clean and freshly pressed, a rare sight given how busy the restaurant was. Her makeup was painted on thicker than Mom's attention-seeking and clunky red heels clicked against the floor.

Why would you wear heels as a waitress? I thought, before realizing that perhaps she was trying to call attention to herself, and choked on the laughter threatening to erupt.

"Oh, Maddison!" My voice was saccharine as I looked her over. "What a shock to see you here! Do you remember that time when you dropped the ketchup bottle in the lunchroom at the high school and you spent the rest of the day looking like you'd been involved in a bloody murder?"

I was going to enjoy this, at least while I could, because I just knew that she would find a way to turn it around and try to make me feel like the inferior one. I laughed as I reached for the menu that sat behind the salt and pepper shakers by the wall.

"It was so funny!"

Maddison floundered like a fish with my snarky retort. Her hazel eyes flashed with a mixture of annoyance and anger as she stammered.

"Well, um… you know…"

She tried to pull her words together as I opened the menu up to see that not much had changed. My regular was still there, a good old-fashioned hamburger with everything on it. "You weren't the best at holding onto things, if I remember correctly," she retorted.

I could hear my mother choke on her drink with the retort, and I shot her a nasty look. What's odd is I swore Maddison said she was leaving after high school and never looking back? Obviously, she hadn't.

I needed to drill my mom more about what happened in that situation, but I was ready to get her out of there before she said anything to me about Jack or the wedding.

"Sure, Maddison, it's always about me, isn't it? You were Ms. Perfect," I said sarcastically. "Anyway, I want a hamburger with everything on it and a little extra mayo, too."

I put the menu back, ignoring the flare of righteous indignation that enveloped my stomach as I looked good and hard at her.

"A chocolate milkshake sounds great, too. Please don't add any extras. I'd hate to have to talk to the manager." I smiled devilishly.

This was definitely the highlight of my day.

She rolled her eyes at me as she walked away, and I was giddy inside. *Who cared about working as a waitress if I could use it to lord over the 'perfect cheerleader'?*

Maddison was such a stuck-up snob in high school. When I was in one of my self-destructive tailspins, it was easy to be as nasty to her as she had been to me. Looking back, our rivalry was kind of ridiculous; it revolved around Alec, my high school love, and my friendship with her great-uncle, Mr. McGregor. I mean, I always hung out at his bookstore, and he was almost part of the family, in a way. Besides, we'd been best friends in elementary school until puberty hit. Then everything changed.

I glanced back at Mom, who was taking a sip of her tea like nothing had happened.

"So, what's going on there?" I asked inquisitively.

"Whatever do you mean, darling? How am I supposed to know?"

"Yeah, whatever. Give me the deets, Mom. I know you know."

She rolled her eyes at me before peeking over at the counter to make sure Maddison wasn't close by.

Mom sighed, as though she was uncomfortable with the idea of what happened to Maddison.

"Things didn't go her way when she left," Mom said simply. "It was a horrible situation, and even though the two of you don't get along anymore, something I still don't understand, her situation was very similar to what you just went through."

I watched her out of the corner of my eye as she walked around the tables in her high heels. She'd been wearing heels since the spring of our senior year when she joined the Violet Bite team, although I couldn't remember her wearing heels when we were running around the tables as we actively avoided each other. I remembered how she flashed her heels at school that spring before everything happened.

I wondered how bad things must have been for her to go back to waitressing when she'd sworn up and down in the hallways those last few weeks of school that when she left town, she would never work a waitressing job again.

I mean, it was pretty ironic to see her struggle, considering how she always assumed everything would be handed to her on a silver platter during high school, even though I knew that it was the complete opposite. The memory of Jack flooded my mind, causing the laughter to dissipate quickly.

I guessed that I could be kind to her, at least for a little while.

She came back over, carrying my milkshake and a metal cup with the extra in it. I smiled at her warmly this time as she placed it down in front of me.

Reaching out, I put my hand over hers as she went to leave the glass on the table.

"Hey, Maddison, I am glad to see you." I tried to be civil and kind. "We'll have to catch up sometime, yeah?"

Her shock was quickly covered by her normal resting 'princess' face.

"Why would we need to catch up, Lilliann? There's nothing to catch up on. I know all about your failed attempt with… what was his name again? James, Patrick, Marcus…" Her eyes glinted evilly as she stared down at me. "Oh, no, that's right. His name was Jack, wasn't it? Didn't he leave you standing at the altar while he ran off with some little tramp?"

Her words were a slap in the face, but she didn't stop there. Oh no, she had to dig the knife in a little deeper.

"Oh, right…" She gave me a little smile. "It wasn't a tramp; it was your closest and dearest friend. Quite a scandal for a senator's son, so he must have loved her a lot more than he loved you."

She withdrew her hand and walked away from our table, leaving me to glare at my mother. Anger simmered in my veins.

"Why did you have to share every detail with *everyone*?" I asked, emphasizing the last word.

Yes, Mom was the town gossip, but I hadn't expected her to tell everyone about Katie. Humiliation flooded my cheeks. I dropped my head into my hands to hide the tears prickling at the corners of my eyes. Mom's comforting hand enveloped mine with a gentle squeeze.

"Now, Lilliann, you know I didn't tell everyone everything." She tried to deflect the growing discomfort that was building in my stomach. "She probably looked up the information; it isn't like it wasn't public knowledge that your wedding didn't go as planned. Just like Maddison said."

I rolled my eyes. *Great, Mom, yes please remind me it's all over the internet.*

I can only imagine the kids in the high school looking up this information to start the new school year. They are going to have a heyday with me.

"Jack is a senator's son. It will remain newsworthy for a while. It will die down again when Jack marries what's-her-face."

I groaned, dropping my head to the table again and covering it with my arms. I did not need the reminder that Jack was supposed to marry Katie within the next year, something his father had demanded of him when he ran off from our wedding; at least that was what I'd hear in the rumor mill while I was in New York.

"Please, Mom, can we just drop it?" I pleaded, feeling overwhelmed by the situation. As I hid within my cocoon of safety, truly just hiding out in my arms, inside of the booth, I could feel the tension radiating off of my mom. It wasn't hard to notice her uneasiness from the conversation and the teenage drama between Maddison and me, as if it was going to be any different. We had hated each other in high school, and it seemed we would continue to harbor hatred for the rest of our lives. Through the small opening between my arms, I glimpsed her worried expression.

Seeking comfort, I reached out blindly for my milkshake, and my mother nudged it closer to me. I slouched in my seat, clutching the sweet drink, and tried to forget my troubles with every sip of the chocolate concoction. I remained in this state for a while, lost in my thoughts. Suddenly, the sound of Maddison's heels—*again, what kind of waitress wears heels?*—approaching our table interrupted my reverie. I hastily sat up straight, hiding the fact that I was teetering on a self-destructive precipice. I didn't want to give Maddison any more ammunition to use against me.

She dropped the plate filled with yummy goodness in front of me before turning to my mom. "Do you need anything else, Mrs. K?" she asked, a little deference in her voice; there was no hiding anything from my mom, and she knew it. I was sure she was trying not to get any more gossip spread about her than she already had.

"No, Maddison dear, I'm fine. Thank you, though."

She nodded and turned to walk away again. I rolled my eyes at my mother; she was always too polite to everyone else in public; I just wished she would be rude to someone once in a while. *Someone who wasn't me.*

As Maddison walked away, she suddenly spun around and faced me. "Oh, and Lilliann, Alec is doing great. I'll be seeing him tonight." She winked and walked off.

Bewildered, I turned to my mother, shock echoing through me, only to see my mother blushing with embarrassment as I asked her, "what did she mean by seeing Alec later on tonight?"

Alec and I both despised her in high school, although she was always trying to get his attention. I had no idea what could have changed between them. Any thought of them being together, like *together* together, had me sick to my stomach.

Mom gestured toward the food in front of me. "Eat up, dear, you don't want it to get cold."

Nausea roiled through me as I glanced down at the food, suddenly not as hungry as I had been moments before.

"He's a policeman now, hun, and you know that the diner is always a hot spot for them."

My stomach dropped to the floor. *Why would he join the force?*

As I left the Violet Bite, I couldn't help but wonder why my mother hadn't mentioned Alec's latest career move to me before today. Despite how he was raised, Alec chose to stay and join the police force instead of leaving after we graduated. I had always assumed he would have left town at the first opportunity, but clearly, he had other plans.

I couldn't help wondering why. We had discussed leaving the town together before, but I didn't blame him for not wanting to leave without me after what I had done to him.

I had hurled hurtful words at him, reminding him of his traumas at home, and then I just ghosted him. He had trusted me with something that he would have never told anyone else, and despite having that power and knowing what it would mean to him if I used it against him, I did it anyway. Back then, I'd just found out that I was adopted, and being a rebellious teenager hadn't helped the situation.

It was something that I deeply regretted, and maybe, in a tiny way, I had been holding onto that with my relationship with Jack. I thought I didn't deserve such an amazing guy after destroying the first amazing guy who had done everything for me growing up. *Just maybe.*

I waved goodbye to my mom from the doorway as I headed to my car. It was a struggle; the door fought me every step of the way before finally opening up.

I fastened my seat belt and started the engine. The apartment I rented wasn't too far from here. Since I decided not to move back in with my parents, as we still had unresolved issues to work on, I thought it prudent to get my own place.

Besides, I like living on my own, I thought, and it would be better to have some personal space before facing them in a small, enclosed setting where I would never have my privacy.

Not to mention, what new teacher wants to live with their parents and teach high schoolers? It was a disaster in the making. Luckily, Ms. Abbott had an apartment above her store that she wanted to rent out. Knowing my situation, she told me that there would be some basic furniture in the place, so I wouldn't have to worry about that as soon as I got in. That had been a relief, knowing that I didn't need to drive a huge U-Haul along with my car here, and had made it a lot easier to escape the sorry story of my life back in the city.

I backed out of my parking spot and drove around towards the front of the Violet Bite before seeing my mom enter her car about three down from the entrance.

Hmmm, how come I hadn't seen her car there when I'd pulled in? I waved as I passed her and made my way onto the main street; the thought quickly vanished from my mind.

Fortunately, the town wasn't one of those that named its main street *Main Street*. Otherwise, we'd just be another cliché community fixated on tourists. After driving through several intersections, I finally spotted Ms. Abbott's cozy little cafe, which she had been running for as long as anyone could remember, at least those from my generation.

It was a charming place, but I couldn't help but wonder if it could measure up to Starbucks or Dutch Bros, now that I had tried something different. This made me pause and consider the possibility of working there during the summer instead of waitressing. Living above the shop would be ideal, and I decided to stop by in the morning and ask if she needed any extra help.

I drove around to the back of the shop; she told me that there was a parking spot back there if I wanted to park there instead of out on the busy front street. Slowing down, I tried to determine which of the buildings was hers from the back before seeing the stairs leading up to a back door. *Ahh, that had to be it.* Darkness had fallen over the town, and I was anxious to get upstairs and see what I would be living in for the foreseeable future.

I parked near the stairs and shut off the engine. It was creepy back here. There were barely any lights, and no one was around; if this had been in the city, I never would have agreed to live there. I could only hope that my intuition about the apartment being the best place for me was right, because I was severely doubting it at this moment. I nervously looked around the empty alleyway before determining that no one was going to jump me.

Opening the door cautiously, my nerves getting the best of me, the hinges creaked as it widened. I jerked skittishly as the sound erupted in the silence of the falling night. I glanced around the empty alley, double-checking that there was no one out there. I'd lived in New York for too long. Forcing myself out of the car, I tried to close the door silently, but no, my car was as stubborn as a mule. Sighing, I grabbed a few boxes from the back and stacked them on the trunk until I was sure that there was enough there that I wouldn't need to come back out before morning for more clothes.

The car locked automatically as the back door swung shut, much quieter than its compatriot, the front door. I grabbed the boxes off the top of the trunk and walked towards the stairs. Ms. Abbott had told me that she would put a key under the mat at the door so I could get in the last time that we had spoken, so I hoped that she hadn't forgotten that today was my arrival day.

The stairs were silent as I went up them, counting each one as I went, and as I landed on the little patio walkway to the apartment, I sighed with relief. I hated walking up any stairs, which was part of the reason I counted each step. However, I would need to get used to it if I were going to live here for a while. Ms. Abbott hadn't required a year-long lease, but I had paid her several months in advance to ensure that I had time to get everything settled before school started. This was also to avoid running out of money before school began and being unable to pay rent.

I dropped the boxes gently on the ground next to the door, narrowly missing the doormat. Pushing them a little further away, I reached down to lift the mat when I heard a car stop.

Whirling around, I looked off the balcony to look down in the alley. A car sat behind mine in the middle of the alley, a spotlight resting on the tail of my car.

Oh, crap, it was a police car...

I wasn't ready to interact with Alec yet. I leaned down again, rummaging around under the doormat to find the key, hoping to find it before...

The slam of a door shutting echoed around me, and I knew I was screwed.

Sighing, I stood up and turned around as I watched a figure start walking up the stairs toward me. Leaning back against the doorway, I waited for the figure to make it to the top.

There was no point in trying to find the key now; it would be a pointless endeavor and only make me look like a complete idiot to whoever, *please don't be Alec*, was coming up the stairs.

As the figure stepped onto the patio, I was happy to see that it wasn't Alec at all but Josefina, or Jo for short, which caught me off guard. I didn't think she was one of those people to work for the police force either.

"Jo," I inquired, just to make sure. "Is that you?"

"Lillie, Lilliann King," her tone had a bit of that southern drawl to it still, "Ay, Dios mío, are you home?" she asked as she came closer. I hopped away from the door, jumped over, and grabbed her around the shoulder, embracing her in a huge hug.

"Jo, oh my," the words flew from my mouth. "What in the world made you decide to join the police force?" I stepped back and gestured toward her uniform. "You used to say that you hated any type of uniform!" I reminded her of her typical complaint any time we had to dress out for gym class.

She laughed; a pearl of joy escaped her lips as she leaned back against the railing and looked at me.

Jo had moved to town during our sophomore year to live with her grandparents when her mom passed away unexpectedly. We became joined at the hip and had been inseparable for those three years of high school before I became such a self-destructive brat.

As her laughter trailed away, I could see the anguish that still lingered in her eyes as high school memories flooded both of us.

"Sí, well, you know mi abuelo," she said as she looked at the boxes sitting next to the door. "So, you moved back to town, huh?" Her eyes were questioning.

We hadn't spoken at all during college; I'd been too ashamed to contact her once I'd started therapy, but now that she was standing in front of me, I wished that I had.

"Yeah," I scratched my head, "your abuelo," I said, my Spanish only slightly rusty, "was the sheriff, wasn't he?" I asked as I leaned back against the door again. We were somewhat awkward, but it wasn't as bad as it could have been.

She nodded. "Yeah, well, it turns out I'm a lot more like him and mamá than I wanted to be." She laughed. "But once you had taken off from town, I was at loose ends. There was really nothing for me here, but I wasn't ready to go off and live some big adventure in the city. Mamá's death still kind of holds a lot of power over me..." She trailed off at the mention of her mom.

Her mom had died in a car stop gone wrong. Her dad had never been in her life, so coming here had been the only option for her. The closest city was about a two-hour car ride, and we'd only gone there once during high school. She'd had such a bad panic attack when we got to the city limits that we had ended up turning around and coming right back home.

"Yeah," I interjected. "About that, I'm sorry about what I said… Well, what I did." It was half-assed, but I apologized. She deserved better, I knew that, but I didn't know if I had it in me just yet. Let's just say that when I left, it hadn't been a pretty sight between the two of us. I knew that I should give her a better apology than what I did, and my anxiety began to grow as I waited for her to respond. It was silent for a few moments before it seemed like the world stopped. My heart plummeted, but as she smiled at me, I could finally breathe again.

Her smile was small and a little bit sad. "No se preocupe, Lillie. I get it. You had a lot going on, and it was hard to deal with." She didn't even know half of what I had gone through but had known that I'd found out something horrible. "You remember how bad I was when I got here?"

I nodded.

"It takes time to get through things."

"Yeah, well, I shouldn't have taken it out on you…" *and Alec,* the words were left unsaid but were clearly in the air. "Anyway, what made you decide to join your abuelo?"

She brushed off my apology, as though it didn't matter to her that I'd punched her as a way to get her to hate me in that moment. She gestured towards the boxes. "How about I help get you in, and I'll fill you in on the way?"

I smiled, glad to know that at least someone wouldn't hold my snarky and dark teenage drama against me.

"That would be awesome," I replied. "But first, I have to find the key." I laughed; I'd been driving for way too long for not having a key to be funny.

I pushed away from the door and back off of the mat again. This time, using the flashlight from my phone, I was able to find the key and pick it up. Holding it up, I showed it to Jo before putting it in the door. She grabbed the boxes from the floor, and together we walked into the apartment.

I felt along the wall until a switch came into view. Flipping it, I was amazed to see the kitchen staring back at me. It was beautiful, almost magazine-worthy, and completely shocked me. "Wow!" *The place had charm and pizzazz!* I turned around and held the door open for Jo to come through. Her eyes widened as she came into the room.

"Oooh! ¡Qué preciosa! Who knew Ms. A had such a nice place up here?" she said, dropping the boxes on the table.

"Right—" my eyes narrowed. "Does she, like, rent this place out like an Airbnb? Because this is glamorous!"

She laughed at my expression. "I think she does; I know that I've come by the place a couple of times to see cars out back."

I nodded as she explained it, walking around the room to see exactly what she considered furnished. There was a full kitchen in here.

I opened the refrigerator to find that she had even stuck some basics in there for me. My heart swelled; Ms. Abbott could be such a sweetie.

I turned around to face Jo again. "Okay, so spill, why did you join?" I demanded, pulling a chair out from the table and gesturing toward the other one for her to sit down.

"Well, it was pretty quiet when you left… For like 20 minutes," she said, laughing again. "Alec had been pretty down in it. There was even a moment when he was close to being arrested himself for fighting back against his dad, but I'd stopped Abuelo from doing it. He didn't need to be stopped, apparently; he convinced Alec to join through means I still don't know. Which just left me, so he had to work hard to convince me that I should join the force. But, you know, since he helped Alec… I did it. Well, I did it because I wanted to keep an eye on Alec. I mean, someone had to…" The words she didn't say floated around us… *because you weren't there to make sure that he didn't do something stupid.*

I nodded absentmindedly as I realized that there was more to make up for than I'd originally thought. I knew my therapist would encourage me to do it, part of the whole justice and healing that I needed to get through. It didn't make it easier, though, and in many ways, I didn't want to even attempt it, but I knew better. But then, the idea of making everything better with those that I'd hurt during my self-destruction sequence made the acid in my stomach rise, and I had to take some deep breaths to calm my anxiety before it exploded. But that was the rational side of me that always got me through the hard situations at work, even when my anxiety was at play.

"Anyway, he got Alec to come in for some classes on self-defense since he was attempting to fight his dad, anyway. Well, Alec took to it without any problems, and before we knew it, both Alec and I graduated from the program and were working on the force. It gave mi abuelo great pleasure to have not just one but two of us on the force."

I smiled, glad that things had been working out for the both of them, but at the same time, I regretted some of the things that I'd done. Not that I regretted going out and getting my degree to teach, but that I hadn't kept in contact with either of them. We sat there for a while and talked about mundane things, avoiding the topic of Alec even though I was dying to verify that Maddison and he hadn't dated while I'd been gone until she looked down at her smartwatch. "Oi vaya, I better get going. I've got to do my check-in for the next shift soon." We both stood, and she reached over and hugged me again. "Promise me you'll stay for a while this time."

I smiled warily, knowing that I wanted to promise that, but at the same time, I wasn't quite ready to be back here yet, and the idea of making a promise that I wasn't sure I could keep raised my level of anxiety.

"I promise that I'll do my best." I compromised.

She smiled and hugged me again as we both headed towards the back door, the only door, really. As I walked her out the door and down to the squad car, I realized that I had truly missed being her friend and just spending time with her.

"Let's get together soon," I told her as we exchanged numbers at the car door.

She smiled again and hopped into the seat before starting the engine and driving off, leaving me alone in the alley. I walked back over to my car and grabbed the next set of boxes; might as well, since I was already down there. As I headed up the stairs, I thanked my lucky stars that it had been Jo who came tonight instead of Alec. However, a small part of me wondered if he was out with Maddison or if he was just eating at the diner, as Mom had said he was prone to do.

Three

The next morning, I rose with the sun, following the call of Mother Earth as I started a new day. As I lay in the fluffy, cloud-like bed, absorbing the soft sunlight shifting through the window shades, I reveled in the silky cobalt blue sheets. The large blue and green plaid quilt was lined with fleece and trailed lower on the bed, as the small emerald blanket underneath it covered me. In all actuality, the bed was a dream, and I was surprised to think that this was something that Ms. Abbott had picked out for the apartment. However, it was something I could get used to.

Unfortunately, there were things to do today, and I couldn't just waste the day away in my bed. I'd done enough of that while in the city, mourning the loss of my marriage or almost marriage, and now, as my therapist had told me, it was time to start fresh.

Besides, it wasn't like getting up early was something new to me. I laughed at the thought; in fact, it was something I'd been doing for years to get to school in the mornings, even during college. You know that teachers have to get there almost an hour or so before students…

Well, I just happened to be one of those teachers who were there early, because I wanted to leave as soon as possible when the day was done. And yes, by the time I'd gotten all of the boxes in last night, I had fallen into bed exhausted. I know that was totally gross, and I probably should throw all of the blankets and sheets into the washer, but it could wait. *I hadn't stunk that badly;* I had taken a quick sniff last night before falling into bed.

Yup, I needed a shower, but I hadn't needed it at that moment.

That's what I was doing this morning.

I grabbed everything that I needed to get a quick shower done, making sure that all of the toiletry things had been put into the bathroom before I even thought about getting into the shower.

Speaking of making sure that I had everything ready before getting into the shower...

I ran out into the kitchen to see if there was any cereal or oatmeal that I could set to start in the microwave while I showered quickly, but apparently that wasn't one of the many things that she provided for me yesterday. I contemplated making coffee up here, since there were some coffee beans in the kitchen, but decided against it since I wanted to ask Ms. Abbott about a position in the coffee shop.

Considering that there was no breakfast food I'd want, however, there was plenty of sandwich meat and bread. *No, no sandwiches for breakfast,* I reminded myself. I rushed back to the bathroom and ran the water, making it steamy in the room, before hopping into the shower so I could head down to the café.

Ms. Abbott had always had the café open before the sun even rose so that she could catch all of the workers for the local fields before they had to get to work. I could only imagine that she had kept up with this routine since I'd left. She'd only been a little older than Mom, that I could remember, so I wasn't completely worried that she would change the hours due to old age or something like that…

There were enough people in town that would change the hours of their businesses as they got older or until their kids would take over, but I didn't think that Ms. Abbott had ever had any children, even though she and her wife had wanted children, or so I thought I had heard Mom say once.

Using the hand towel, I cleaned a circle in the mirror as I finished getting dressed. The hot water and cleanliness of the apartment had been so relaxing that I was excited for the upcoming months of living here. Soon after I was dressed, and as I started to brush my hair, I was glad I'd made the hole in the steamy mirror to see myself. The ends were curling up as I brought the brush down through the strands, and I debated whether I should put it into a braid before deciding against it, but still put a hair tie around my wrist, just in case. I walked back into the bathroom and grabbed my wallet and phone off the charger. Checking to make sure that I didn't forget anything else, I headed to the door and walked out and down to my car.

Instead of entering the shop from the back, I opted to drive around and park in the front. The streets were still relatively quiet, although several other cars were parked outside of the coffee shop as well when I pulled into a parking spot. I scanned the area to see if I recognized anyone before turning off the engine. I sat in the car for a moment as I looked at the different cars that sat out front. Interestingly, several vehicles had out-of-state license plates, just like mine.

I observed two women, one fairly tall and slender, entering the shop with another woman who had to be her sibling. The shorter one had a pixie haircut, a classic bomber jacket, and a pair of boyfriend jeans that accentuated her shapely figure, which I admired. The clothing choice was unique, a type of strength and honesty that was not often seen in the small town of Clearwater.

Back in the city, there were always people in outfits that were classy and unique, and I admired the fact that everyone could be who they wanted to be, wherever they were. I sat there for a few more minutes, gathering my courage and fighting through my anxiety, before I opened my door. It was now loudly protesting my motion with a sharp creak that I was pretty sure my parents could hear at their house, almost a mile away. I stepped away quickly from the car and headed towards the door of the shop.

As I grasped the door handle and gave it a gentle tug, I was unaware of the two people who were just about to emerge. Due to my lack of attention, I collided with them, causing one of the cups of coffee they were carrying to spill out, making a resonant splat on the floor. I felt terrible and apologized profusely for my mistake, hoping to make amends for the accident.

"I'm so sorry! I should have looked before entering."

Glancing around, the place was empty, except for the three of us. Looking at the face of the tall blonde, I would have sworn that I was looking into a mirror. They say that you have a twin out there somewhere in the world, so maybe that was it. *Her facial features were remarkably similar yet distinct.* She smiled as though she didn't have a care in the world. Her beautiful two-piece business suit had bright colors that made her seem exuberant. She looked like she was ready to go into a meeting. The air about her, though, was that she was just out for a morning stroll.

"Please let me replace your coffee for you," I offered.

"Oh, no," she said, a light tilt to her voice, as the other presence in the incident, definitely her sibling, based on the similarities between their faces, even though their skin tones were slightly different from one another, walked past us and over to their car. The eye color was the same between the both of them as well, although the other woman's eyes were harder, as though the life that had led had been filled with significant trauma and pain.

"It's quite okay; Sirona had wanted coffee this morning, but I had just gotten it so that they wouldn't complain that I'd wasted my time coming here." Her eyes shifted between blue and green in a way that I wished my eyes could do; instead, I had the eyes that everyone always did a double-take to make sure that they had seen correctly.

It was quite beautiful.

I smiled in understanding. There had been times during college that Cade and I would go to the café on campus, and I'd get one only because he hadn't wanted to walk to the café alone. Jack had never done that with me, though.

I almost got lost in my awkward thoughts, which had derailed me from the current conversation, when Sirona, the other person, suddenly interrupted us.

"Come on, Hope, we've got things to do today."

It seemed like somebody was eager to start the day's activities, and I had to wonder if they were tourists on a visit to Clearwater or what their business was in town.

"Again, I'm sorry," I said, as I stepped aside for Hope to come through. "Will you please let her know I would love to get the two of you coffee sometime?"

"It's they/them actually, but I will be sure that Sirona knows that. We're staying in town for a while, looking for a place to start up a new business, so perhaps we'll run into each other again soon," Hope replied, smiling warmly as she walked past me.

But I nodded in understanding and waved goodbye as she reached the car. Sirona was already pulling open the door, impatient to get in. I laughed at their impatience before heading into the shop.

I waved to Ms. Abbott, who stood behind the counter, filling up a cup of steaming latte for another customer. It was pretty busy in the shop, so I took my time looking around. She had made the shop into something quite extraordinary. It was quaint, as expected for a small town, but also beautiful. The scent of freshly brewed coffee wafted through the air, and the sound of the espresso machine working diligently filled the air.

Ms. Abbott had added some large, comfortable chairs and turned one corner into a little free library, where customers could borrow a book to read while enjoying their coffee.

It was better than any Starbucks that I'd been to.

I traced my hands over the wooden tables as I walked around the shop, waiting for more people to leave. I wanted to speak with Ms. Abbott without a large audience present.

I could picture the first time that I'd come here with Alec. We'd sat in a corner, a small, dingy little table with two mismatched chairs, and talked for hours. It was the first time that he'd opened up to me about what was going on with his dad at home. I think in many ways, it was the first time that I realized that I loved him.

I pulled myself back from memory lane as I took in the charm of the shop, noticing that the table and chairs that I'd just been reminiscing about were gone. Oh well, it still didn't distract from the overall atmosphere of the shop. It was genuinely charming, and I was hopeful that Ms. Abbott would be interested in having me join her team, allowing me to spend more time in that atmosphere.

As the last person received their cup from Ms. Abbott, I approached the counter and smiled warmly at her.

"Morning, Ms. Abbott!" I said as I looked up at the chalkboard menu above her head to see if anything had changed since I'd last been in. There were a few new additions that I was eager to try, but I was distracted from deciding which one when Ms. Abbott stepped out from behind the counter and walked over to give me a warm hug. She was a lot shorter than me, but she had always been a smaller woman; her strength came from her arms. They were strong and thick as they encircled me, surprising me with the gentleness that the feeling invoked inside of me.

"Lilliann! I am so happy to see your young and vibrant face." She pulled back, her hands resting on my shoulders, and looked me in the eyes, her own brown eyes twinkling with laughter. "Ah, even with the shadows clouding your eyes, you are still so very much the happy young woman I remember from before." She squeezed my shoulders, a smile playing on both of our lips, as she stepped away.

"Did you make it in okay last night? I noticed your car, or I'm assuming it is your car, was parked in the alley this morning," she said as she walked back behind the counter, grabbed a cloth from a bucket of cleaning solution, and started to wipe down the counters. "Was everything to your satisfaction in the apartment?" she inquired, peeking up at me from where she was currently wiping.

Her brown cardigan was rolled up to her elbows, and I smiled at her enthusiasm, noticing the little details about her as she worked. Her corkscrew black hair was starting to gray, the curls framing her face, and there were fine laughter lines etched into her face around her eyes and mouth, her large nose crinkled as she spoke. She was heavier set than I remembered from my childhood, but she was still the same joyful and kind person that had made the coffee shop a hot spot during high school.

"Yes, Ms. Abbott," I responded, the reverence of respect evident in my tone, "everything was beautiful, in fact, more than beautiful. Everything is so charming around here; what have you done to the place?" I leaned on my elbows, resting my head on top of my hands, as I watched her move around.

"Ah, well, I've been watching some of those Home and Garden TV shows... I got some of the local boys to help me remodel some of the place, and well, as they say, the rest is history," she said laughing.

"Well, I wish I could be in such a charming place every day," I said, leading my way into my request, "In fact, this morning you looked so busy… Do you need any help?"

She laughed, and my hopes fell. *That didn't sound good.*

"Ah, Lilliann. Already back in town and looking for something to keep you occupied, I remember how you always needed to keep busy as a child; I see that hasn't changed much. While I would love to have you help me out, I actually am fully staffed at this time. Besides, it is summer vacation; don't you want to enjoy the sun?"

Everyone in town knew that I had always wanted to be a teacher, so it wasn't a surprise that she had guessed what I had been doing while in the city.

"Yeah, well…" I hedged. "I still like to do something; I always get up with the sun anyway."

She smiled sadly at my insistence and nodded.

"I understand, and I wish I could help you out, child, but I just don't have any availability," she said sympathetically.

I sighed. *Now what am I going to do?*

She looked at me, clearly seeing the distress on my face, before she pulled back and leaned against the counter.

"Can't you work summer school in the district?" she asked, and I shook my head.

"No," I said, the weariness and swift descent into depression echoing in my voice. "They told me that I'd have to wait until next summer because I have to go through the new teacher training first."

She hummed as she looked out into the patrons of the café before smiling again and looking at me. "I know!" she exclaimed, grabbing my hand and pulling me towards the bulletin board that she had in front of the shop.

"Why don't you offer summer tutoring?" she said, pointing to the board. "There are plenty of kids around here that need additional support during the summer, and it would keep you busy enough but wouldn't take up your whole summer."

My hand dropped from hers as I turned and stared at her in shock. *Why didn't I think of that?* I smiled crookedly as I looked between her and the bulletin board.

"That's a great idea, Ms. Abbott—" I started to say, but she interrupted me.

"Call me Linda, dear; I'm your landlord, not your teacher," she said with a little laugh as she walked back towards the counter.

I followed her at a slower pace, thinking about how I could get my tutoring services off the ground and what I could charge per hour. "I know that it is a lot to take in, dear," she continued as she walked behind the counter, "But don't make any decisions right now. Take the first week to get reoriented to the town before making any big decisions."

I nodded, smiling as I took in what she said, pushing it to the back burner, and ordered an iced Rainbow Delight tea. The board read that it was a mixture of coconut, blue raspberry, and strawberry with a green tea base. I probably should have gone with coffee, but the drink had been calling my name.

After she finished off my drink and I'd paid, she mentioned that the bookstore that had always been my haven would be opening up soon if I wanted to get there before any of the tourists stopped in. I thanked her for letting me know and took my cup to go. Walking towards the door, I made sure this time that no one was nearby, either inside or outside. Walking out the door, a cool breeze drifted past me, and I looked up and down the road before deciding that the bookstore wasn't that far away.

Walking up the main street of town sent me back to my last year in high school, and the bookstore caught my eye.

It had been my haven, my safe space for as long as I could remember. I loved going in and just getting lost in a good book. Mr. McGregor never required that I buy a book, but he did ask me to write up book reviews that he could put in the front window to try to entice tourists to come in and get a good book.

The gold calligraphy lettering on the window read *Twice Read Tales*, and the remnants of my reviews were still taped to the bottom of the large window as you walked up to the door. I smiled as I pulled on the golden door handle; the loud jingling of the bell echoed in the empty room as I walked in.

Mr. McGregor walked into the room from his office, a smile splitting his face open as he caught sight of me, his gray eyes twinkling behind a thin rimmed pair of glasses. "Lilliann King, oh my god, it's been ages since I saw your face!" he exclaimed. I giggled at his exuberant display and walked over to give him a hug. He had been the only person that I hadn't said or done anything to before leaving, mostly because I hadn't wanted him to kick me out of the bookstore when I needed somewhere to hide.

"Hello, Mr. McGregor, how are you doing?" I asked, looking around at the bookstore. Nothing had changed in here; not even one page had been moved from the last time I saw it. I swore and laughed. "You didn't feel the need to remodel, too?" I asked.

"Ah, I see, you've already been to Linda's place." He nodded towards my cup. "She was always one to try to meet the times."

His voice was gravelly, and although familiar, it sent a shiver down my spine.

There was something wrong here. I pulled away from him and looked him over, looking for the little details that I missed when he first came out. He was an old man, had been an old man when I lived here, but now, he just seemed ancient.

How old was he?

I noticed a little scar on the corner of his neck, and I wondered what happened there and why I'd never seen it before. He still wore a tweed jacket with patches on the elbows, and I asked if he had been a professor before moving to Clearwater. The wrinkles in his face were more pronounced now, like a map of skin, than I remembered, and he had a stoop to his shoulders that I'd missed when I first came in. He was the same person that he'd been, but at the same time, he wasn't. I smiled again and gave him another quick hug.

"Yeah, well, I'm renting the apartment above her store, really," I said, as I stepped away and wandered over to a nearby shelf. "You really haven't changed anything," I noted as I wiped some dust off the books before me.

"Well, except the fact that you have to be almost ninety," I exclaimed, my mouth getting the better of me before I turned around and stared at him in complete shock.

I could feel the sweat collecting in the small of my back as my heart began to pound. *Oh no, I shouldn't have said that.* Dread filled me as I prayed that he wouldn't kick me out of his store.

Instead, he laughed and walked back over to the counter, his steps slow and uneven, as though he was attempting to hold himself up without a walker or cane. I went to help him, even though he would surely tell me to leave, and in a way he did, but not in the way I expected. He waved me away as he reached the counter's edge.

"Yes, well, I didn't have my favorite little librarian to help me organize things," he said with a small laugh, deciding to ignore my loose lips and brushing off my careless comment. "You were always the one to help me find the books that were the most interesting to the tourists."

"Well, that's because you have too many books," I said, a smile playing on my lips as my anxiety dropped. I closed my eyes and let out a breath as I collected myself.

As I opened them, he said, "Too many books!" He looked mockingly outraged. "How could you even suggest such a thing? The bookstore is charming with every book that I have in here."

I laughed, and he waved me away. "Go and see if you can find the book that you need. I know you're dying to do it."

I waved thankfully to him as I walked away and headed into the back of the store, where I had always gone before.

I spent the next several hours browsing the shelves, names of books and authors catching my eye as I searched. Nothing that made me stop and say, *That's the one,* but enough to keep me busy. I heard him talking to guests as the bell rang, each one done quicker than the last. Then the bell rang, and the door slammed as it shut, and I reached out to grab another book from the shelf. At one point, I thought I heard a familiar voice, but then it disappeared. The next voice, however, that I heard didn't sound happy to be there; in fact, it sounded angry. As I went to walk toward the front to check on Mr. McGregor, a light caught my eye.

Now, there shouldn't be light back here; there were no windows, but a bright flash caught my eye, almost blue in its luminescence. As I stepped closer, the book nudged its way from the shelf toward me. I stopped and stared. *Things like that didn't happen in real life, did they?*

I grabbed the book, a powerful jolt of electricity running through me, as a flash of something went through my mind. As quickly as I tried to recall it, it was gone. I looked down at the book in my hands; the cover was blank, but it felt like something should have been on there. Opening it up, I was shocked to see that it was completely blank. The door slammed again, pulling me out of my daydreaming, and I rushed to the front of the store.

"Are you okay, Mr. McGregor?" I called out.

"Yes, dear, I'm fine," he said, wiping his forehead with a handkerchief as I stopped in front of him. "Everything is fine. Ah, something's caught your eye, has it?" he asked, gesturing towards the book in my hand.

"I guess you could say that?" There was no way that I was going to tell him what happened back there. "But it's blank."

He hummed, as though trying to solve a great mystery. "Perhaps—" pausing for a dramatic effect. "It is blank because you need it." Then he leaned in as though he was about to tell me a great secret. "Perhaps it needs you more than you need it."

His words had me rolling my eyes, but I smiled and offered to pay him for it.

He waved my wallet away as I pulled it out. "Consider it a welcome home and late birthday gift."

I thanked him for it, asking again if he was okay, and with his reassurance, I walked out of the bookstore and headed towards the Violet Bite for lunch.

Four

I had a pleasant and uneventful lunch at the Violet Bite. Despite a
lingering sense of curiosity about the unusual book I stumbled upon
earlier, unable to shake off the feeling of peculiarity, it didn't seem out
of the ordinary. Thankfully, Maddison was not present to engage in any
unnecessary disagreements, so I savored my meal in peace. Even with the
everyday townspeople coming in, no one really came to bother me while I
ate, but I was blissfully aware this would only last for so long.

After finishing my meal, I decided to take a stroll around the town to get
reacquainted with the place. I noticed a few new businesses that hadn't been
there nine years ago, but most of the establishments remained unchanged.

After walking around town for a while, with occasional stops to catch my
breath since I hadn't re-acclimated to the altitude, I made my way down to
the river. As I ventured down to the river to explore the hot springs that
lined the town's outskirts, I observed a multitude of tourists, a common
sight during the early summer months.

*Huh, I wonder if I even own a swimsuit? When was the last time I was at the
pool?*

As my thoughts spun on swimsuits, I was reminded of the small clothing shops along the main drag. I'd have to check them out when I got back to see if any of them had a suit for sale. Relaxing in the hot springs sounded like a perfect way to kill some time this summer, if I could find some kids to tutor, that is. I hugged the book to my chest for most of the walk, as if I was scared to lose it or something. It didn't make sense.

The thought of writing in the book, using it as a journal, made my stomach churn, and I contemplated returning it to Mr. McGregor before my mind drifted to another topic, and the idea fell away.

The light was beginning to fade around me, and I looked down at my phone to confirm the time. The phone had dinged occasionally throughout the day, but nothing was important enough that I had to stop my explorations. I was surprised to see that it was nearing seven o'clock already. As I walked back to my car, still at the *Riverfront Coffee and Cream*, Ms. Abbott's café, I decided it was time to go get the groceries I needed before heading up to my apartment.

It wasn't like I'd starve; there was lunch stuff in there, but I wanted some of the things I liked to eat as well.

It was a beautiful Saturday, and I was excited to get some actual food so I could cook. Not that I didn't love eating at the Violet Bite, but there was something so gratifying about eating something that you made with your own hands. Especially after such a long week of driving and the roller coaster of emotions that I'd been riding, it'd be nice to do something as grounding as cooking for myself.

I started the engine after only a mild fight with my car door to get it open, and then closed it again. The engine roared to life, not that it had ever been something for me to worry about; it was a strong car with an occasional temper tantrum. Driving away from the main road, I followed along the river for a while until the marketplace loomed in front of me. It was more rustic and artistic than it had been before, but it was still the same old *Susanna's Market and Meat Palace*.

There weren't a lot of cars in the parking lot, but enough that I had to search for a good spot to park. It was several lanes away from the main entrance, and although my legs protested the idea of having to walk anymore, I got out of the car with fewer issues than I had to get into it. The book was still held tightly in my hand as I walked up to the entrance, the sliding doors moving apart as I came near. The whizzing noise of the doors opening brought up nostalgic feelings as I thought of the many times that I'd come shopping with my mom or dad as a child.

Even though they had withheld critical information about me as a child, I had to admit that they had done a fantastic job of being parents to me.

I grabbed one of the smaller wheeled carts as I walked through the doors and headed over toward produce. There was a specific methodology to my shopping routine, starting with produce and ending with frozen goods, so that nothing I bought would begin to spoil by the time I checked out. As I wandered through the fruits and vegetables, the bright yellows and oranges of citrusy fruits blinked at me as I reached for a Fiji apple. The book rested on the kids' seat in the shopping cart, within easy reach, as I piled fruits and vegetables on top of it, as though offering the book vitality through the produce I placed down.

I walked away from the produce section, heading over towards the dry cabinet goods, my mind wandering through the store thinking of where I would stop next, when I suddenly bumped into someone. *No, not just anyone; it had to be Alec.* Our eyes met as the carts collided together, electricity shooting through both of us as if the last nine years had never happened.

He had grown his hair out to a shagginess that was rugged and appealing. I wanted to run my fingers through it just to see if it was as soft as I remembered. His eyes, those deep blue pools of never-ending adoration, were shadowed with pain and tiredness even though happiness seemed to overlap them. His uniform was wrinkled as though he had been through the wringer, and a wave of emotions hit me like a tidal wave.

Alec smiled, that little half smile that showed his dimple, although not so much with the beard he was growing, dark against his light brown skin.

"Lillie," his voice was husky and dark, shivers running down my spine, "you're back."

I smiled, nerves running wild as I thought about that voice speaking against my skin as it had years ago.

I laughed nervously, "Yeah, I got in yesterday."

I thought about mentioning Jo coming by last night, but decided against it. That was something that she could tell him if she wanted to.

"How are you doing, Alec?" I pulled the cart away from his and turned it towards the aisle.

"I'm okay," his voice didn't match his words; there was a darkness there that had nothing to do with snuggles and cuddles, and I felt the pangs of regret hit me harder.

"I just got off work and needed to get something to eat," he said, gesturing towards his cart.

I laughed nervously again. We talked for a few moments, exchanging pleasantries and discussing very lighthearted subjects, catching up on some things we'd missed over the last nine years, although we avoided the heavier topics. Alec stopped at one point, as we'd been walking around as we talked, picking up very similar items as we went.

"So, can we meet up for coffee or lunch sometime?" The words were light, but something was aching behind them.

Something that I just wasn't ready for yet.

I politely declined, saying that I had a lot of things to do before I could think about such pleasantries and enjoyable things. I had to get my apartment ready for one. He nodded and said that he had to go grab some produce to make his escape. I sighed, angry with myself for letting him go without apologizing for all that I'd done, but this was hardly the place. I'd grabbed the rest of the things I needed before heading to the cashier to check out. It was a young kid, probably one of my future students who would be in school at the start of the new year, and he rang me up quickly asking if I had any bags. I sighed; I'd forgotten that Colorado had gone to that "bring your own bags" thing and told him no. I ended up paying extra to get some that I could reuse, but at least I'd have them for the next time. After paying what seemed to be an extraordinary amount, I left the store, pushing the cart toward my vehicle. Popping the trunk, I started to put everything into the car when I noticed that Alec had followed me outside empty-handed.

"Lillie, can we please talk?" he begged, the shadows in his eyes more prominent in the last rays of sunlight, as though he couldn't bear the idea of me leaving without trying one more time. "Just one time, please. I need to know."

I forced myself to keep putting the groceries in my car as he stopped on the other side of my cart.

"Please," he murmured.

"Alec," I whispered. "I'm sorry, I want to talk, but…" My words trailed off; I didn't know what to tell him or how to tell him what had happened.

"Not here, okay?" I still needed more time to process my feelings about Jack and how I'd left Alec all those years ago. My therapist had told me I would need to face those feelings sooner or later; well, I'd hoped for the latter.

Alec sighed, watching me as I continued to put the bags in. "Okay. Bye, Lillie," he headed back to his cart inside the store, leaving me alone with my thoughts. I knew things were going to be awkward between us, but this was downright painful.

Had he really held onto his love for me for this long? I wondered, and yet, at the same time, I knew I wasn't ready for another relationship again. Not with him, not with anyone; I needed to take things slow and make sure that I was ready. That I could be my own person, owning my history, without having to rely on someone else to make me into a better person.

* * *

As I drove back toward the apartment, a sense of relief washed over me. I had faced my past by seeing Alec, and I was almost ready to start moving forward.

There was still healing work to do surrounding everything to do with Jack and my adoption before I could think about being happy with Alec. Well, I'd have to fix things with him first. But we could be happy in a way that I'd never been happy with anyone, even Jack. There would be challenges ahead, but I was determined to face them head-on, one step at a time.

I made a mental list of things I wanted to talk with my therapist, Ally, about on Monday for our second-to-last session. She wanted me to get settled here first before transitioning me to someone closer. I was grateful for her help vetting therapists in the area, ensuring we'd be able to continue making progress on my therapy goals.

I drove around to the alley, parking in the same spot that I'd parked the night before, before opening up my door. This time it was easy, as though my car was trying to give me a wish for a good night after such an emotional encounter with Alec. I smiled at the temperamental mood of my car before walking around to the trunk and popping it open. I grabbed a couple of bags, leaving the trunk open, before walking up the stairs. Counting all twelve steps before stepping onto the landing. I placed the bags next to the door before walking back down to my car. There was no point in opening the door, taking the groceries in, and then coming back out to do it all over again. *No, it was much easier if I just put all the bags by the door first and then took them in.* As I neared my tailgate, I noticed movement in the back where the rest of my grocery bags still lay. I slowed as I came closer, trying to pinpoint what the movement was until I stepped closer and saw that it was a kitten. It wasn't just any kitten, but a cute and cuddly black kitten, almost hidden by the darkness of my trunk and the oncoming night.

"Ahhh," the word slipped out of my mouth, "Aren't you just a cutie?" I cooed.

The kitten responded with an adorable meow and placed its two little front paws on the edge of the trunk. Knowing better than just to pick the kitten up, I held a hand out for it to sniff. After a single sniff, the little fluff ball rubbed its black head against my palm, demanding attention. Obviously, my heart melted, and I gingerly lifted the kitten from the trunk.

"How did you get in there, buddy?" I asked, cuddling the kitten with one hand while using my other to grab the remaining grocery bags. It took some creative maneuvering to continue the kitten snuggles, close the trunk, and get up the stairs, but I succeeded. Counting the stairs as I went.

I dropped the bags slowly next to the others as I reached into my pocket for the key to the door. The kitten clawed its way up my shirt to my shoulders as I struggled to get into the door. I was so afraid that the kitten would take off before I could get it inside the house, but as I opened the door, the kitten nimbly jumped off my shoulder and right into the apartment as though it had been waiting for me to let it in. I laughed at the audacity of the kitten before shaking my head and grabbing the bags, dropping them on the counter in the kitchen before grabbing the rest and shutting the door behind me with a kick.

The kitten was waiting for me on the kitchen counter by the time I'd dropped off all the bags and turned the lights on. It was a beautiful black kitten with a white patch of fur that I hadn't noticed right under its chin. I went to pet its head again, which it willingly allowed me to do, purring as it moved closer to my hand.

"Well, cutie, are you a boy or a girl?" I asked, knowing in my heart that there was no way I was going to let this kitten leave. I'd have to talk to Ms. Abbott about adding a pet rent, but I was already in love and knew it was exactly what I needed to help me through my blues. As the kitten's tail neared my hand, the fur soft and silky against my fingers, I saw a clear sign that this was a boy.

"Ah," I tsked, "a boy you are… Well, we must give you a name that fits." I thought about all the names that a boy kitten could be called as I moved away from him, putting the groceries away. The book rested beside him on the counter, his head lying down on top of it, as I began listing off random names.

"Adams, Jacob, George, Kennedy, Franklin, Teddy," I went for some of the more well-known names, but the kitten ignored me as I continued.

"Hmmm, not a president sort of kitten, are you? Well, let's try writers. Hemingway, Fitzgerald, Charles, Henry…"

The kitten continued to act as though I had said nothing,

"Poe."

I stopped as the kitten meowed, his eyes narrowing at me as I came closer to him.

"Ah, Poe is your name, hmm?" I said as I scratched him behind the ear.

"Well, Poe, let's go look at this book again, shall we?" I asked as I grabbed the book out from under him. He meowed as he hopped down from the counter, and with his head and tail held high, he walked out of the kitchen into the living room. I laughed as I followed him in.

Five

With the book in my grasp, I strolled across the spacious living room, enjoying the playful company of Poe. He scampered amidst the chairs, his agile movements reminiscent of a dancer's graceful pirouettes. Eventually, he made his way to what I was sure would become his preferred spot—a chair nestled beside the window. The chair's white suede cushions beckoned me, their velvety softness an irresistible temptation. It was my favorite spot as well, and I lowered myself onto the seat, unable to suppress a chuckle as Poe sprang onto my lap, settling in for a comfortable nap. As I relaxed into the chair's embrace, I became more and more entranced by the book in my hands, the engrossing idea that there was something to it I didn't know about that was holding me captive. The book became hot in my hands, almost to the point of burning.

I stopped laughing, almost dropping the book in surprise; *there was no way that a book could heat up... could it?*

This was definitely weird, but the part of me that loved ghost stories and the paranormal was so freaking curious! As I shifted the book in front of me, turning it around and looking at the thick leather binding, it started to change in front of me. This time, I did drop the book, knocking poor Poe in the head as it fell. As it landed, it fell open to the first page, words appearing out of thin air on the page as I read it.

My dearest child, it is with a heavy heart that I write this to you... The curly writing appeared on the page, letter by letter, as they formed the words. Poe looked at me, his yellow eyes questioning, as I stared down at the book.

What sorcery was this?

I went a little medieval there… but I was completely caught off-guard by what was happening. The words continued to appear, and I quickly tried to catch up.

It is the tragedy of our line of witches that mothers never get to know their children, separated by nature or force, and thus we must make it so that the magick finds you. My dearest Lilliann…

I stopped. That was my name, in this magick book, that had been empty mere minutes before. I was utterly taken aback by what I had just read. My reaction was so sudden that I jolted upright, causing both Poe and the book to tumble to the ground. Feeling shaken, I quickly made my exit while still trying to process what I had just experienced.

This wasn't happening. I swore to myself as I walked into the bathroom, turning on the faucet and letting the cold water run as I stared at myself in the mirror. I splashed some of the water onto my face, the color pale and bleak in the mirror, hoping that it would revive me from whatever dream I was in because there was no way that a book just had writing appear with my name in it. Poe meowed at me from the doorway, his tail swishing from side to side, as he regarded me.

"I can't believe it," I muttered to Poe. I turned off the running faucet and walked into my bedroom, feeling a sense of disbelief wash over me.

"Nope," I continued. "Not happening. Not at all," I reiterated as I tore through the boxes of clothes that I still had not unpacked yet. Finding the pajamas that I desired, the comfiest ones I had, I quickly changed out of my clothes, hoping that doing so would somehow make this all disappear like a bad dream.

As I crawled under my covers, I couldn't help but wish that this was all just a figment of my imagination. My mind was racing with thoughts and emotions, making it difficult to find peace.

Poe jumped up onto the bed, rubbing his head against me through the blankets as he sought to offer me comfort before finding his own place to lie down. As he curled up on the pillow next to me, I reached over and gently scratched him behind the ears. His purring erupted around me, loud and demanding, as he nuzzled into my hand.

In the end, it was only the comforting presence of my kitten that helped me quiet my panic and drift off to sleep. Even though I had no idea what the next day would bring, which made my stomach acid rumble along with my anxiety, making it hard to go to sleep, I forced my mind to quit and eventually fell asleep.

* * *

The next morning, as I gradually became conscious, I felt the blinding sunlight streaming through the window, threatening to engulf me.

I groaned; there was no way I wanted to get up today.

Yet, despite the brightness of the sunlight, I couldn't shake off the icy chill that ran through my body, confounding me as to why I was feeling so uncomfortable. I stretched out my hand to pull the blanket closer. Confused, I scoured the area for the missing blanket, but to no avail. It was then that I realized I was not even on the bed, but rather hovering several feet above it. Suddenly, the realization hit me like a ton of bricks—*I was floating in mid-air!*

Disoriented, I tried to sit up but ended up tumbling down onto the soft mattress. At least I had something to cushion my fall. I could faintly hear laughter coming from around me. However, as I was still trying to understand how I had been floating in midair, I couldn't determine if what I heard was actually there or a part of my mind that was slowly deteriorating.

* * *

When I was finally able to compartmentalize the very weird awakening, I looked around to see that Poe was still there. Although he sat on the top of the dresser, next to a set of clothes that I didn't remember putting out last night.

Curious, I went over. It looked soft and summery, something that would be breezy, and based on how I'd felt yesterday after my walk around town, it was probably the best thing to wear. As I went to grab the clothes from the dresser, my hand brushed against something that the clothes had been lying over.

The book! The cover was now adorned with golden engravings; the word "grimoire" stood out in the most beautiful calligraphy, golden and bright, as it filled the cover. I didn't remember it being there.

Had I put it there without remembering it?

It was the word of the spell book that witches in television shows and movies usually had, my mind flashing to *Charmed* and *Sabrina the Teenage Witch*.

I backed away from it, as the evening came rushing back to me.

It hadn't been a dream, and somehow, some way, I was a witch?

The thought threw me for a loop as I walked away from the book and headed into the bathroom to take a quick shower and get dressed.

* * *

Returning to the bedroom, I threw my pajamas on the bed before looking back at the dresser where Poe lay curled up with the book. I stepped towards it, anticipation and dread filling my veins; there was something there, and I just had to know what was going on. I rubbed Poe's head gently as I took the book out from under him; it glowed white for a moment, heating my hands before the glow disappeared. Okay, so not something I dreamt up last night. The book creaked as I opened it to the front page again. This time, I re-read the entire message before looking up.

If what this said was true, I was a witch who was doomed never to see my own children grow up.

The thought was depressing, but at the same time, it sparked something within me, something that resonated with the truth of it.

I was a witch, but how?

I looked back down at the book and thumbed through it; incantations, spells, and potions were littered throughout the book. I could feel power emanating from the book, and I strolled through the open doorway into the hallway before walking to the kitchen.

My entire focus was on the words I was reading within the book, and as Poe meowed somewhere behind me, I absentmindedly pulled out a can of tuna that I'd bought. *Who doesn't love a good tuna fish sandwich with a bowl of tomato soup?* And popped the top of it before dumping half of it into a bowl.

Placing the lid back onto it, I walked over to the fridge and put it away, still reading about an incantation for clarity of thought and healing. Hip-bumping the door closed, I grabbed the bowl from the counter and bent down to give it to Poe.

He rubbed incessantly against my legs, weaving between the two, before chowing down on the bowl of tuna I'd placed down for him, his thumper going before he even took a bite. I smiled and placed the book down on the counter before looking down to see him eating from the bowl delicately, as though he was trying to impress me with his manners.

I laughed at the silliness of that thought before starting up the coffee machine. I couldn't afford to get a coffee from Ms. Abbott every day, so I'd better get used to making it for myself in the mornings.

The book whispered sweet nothings to me, tempting me to go back and look at it as I went about my morning routine, preparing my cereal and adding creamer to a cup before walking back over to it. I picked it up, glancing through the pages as I waited for the coffee to finish. The coffee machine was almost done, so I dropped the book back onto the corner, closed it, and went back to the machine to fix myself a cup of coffee. Still, when I glanced back at the book, it sat upon its bindings, showing me another incantation, this one for charm, one that I was pretty sure I hadn't been looking at before.

If you want to present yourself to those around you charmingly, close your eyes and focus your magic within. Feel the light gathering around you; channel it through your veins. Once the magick is contained, whisper your word of empowerment, so mote it be.

I was aching to see if I actually had any powers; the thought of how I'd woken up this morning was already a distant memory, and this sounded like something that would help me since I'd be seeing my parents today.

I walked back over to the book, resting my hands against the counter, as I closed my eyes and felt around me through my mind, something that wasn't that hard, to be honest. Finding it around me, I gathered it like a glove covering me from head to foot, thinking of how I'd like to be sweet and endearing to those around me today, and whispered "Endearing," as I felt the magick snap against me like a rubber band.

"Ouch," I complained, rubbing my arms; that little bit of magic had hurt.

Sighing, I filled up my coffee cup and walked over to the table to eat.

Poe jumped up onto the table as I sat down, and I waved him away. "Tables are not for cats' behinds, mister; they are for people eating… Don't be sitting up here." I chastised him, and I almost could swear that Poe rolled his eyes before jumping down again.

I continued to look through the book as I finished off my breakfast. I was about to head into the living room to continue reading before I remembered that Mr. McGregor had told me that the book needed me more than I needed it. *How had he known?* Shock laced through me, and I raced to scoop up my purse and keys, dropping the book into it, before racing toward the door, desperate to know what exactly he had known.

Poe followed alongside me as I popped the door open, and out he ran. "Poe," I yelled, my voice thick with worry, "come back."

"I will," I swore I heard before he disappeared completely at the end of the steps.

I decided against taking my car today; my dress was light and airy, so there shouldn't be many issues with becoming overheated. I walked along the walls of the alley before coming to the end. The town was silent as I peered out to the street, noticing that there were barely any cars out this morning.

Well, besides the ones at the *Riverfront Coffee and Cream.*

I stepped out onto the street, my purse clenched tightly under my arm as I walked towards *Twice Read Tales.* Mr. McGregor should be there already; he opened up soon after Ms. Abbott did on a Sunday morning, or he used to.

He would want everything to be done at the shop before heading to church.

Oh, church, I realized belatedly, *would Mom want me to go to church?*

I hadn't gone to a service in years, finding that I felt more at peace within myself at a quiet park rather than suffering through a monotonous sermon, boisterous people singing in off-key voices, and pretending that it all didn't bother me. It had been a sensory overload as a child, and I dreaded the thought of going back into it.

I quickened my step as I neared *Twice Read Tales*, already seeing that Mr. McGregor had the door propped open. I approached the door, hurrying within.

"Mr. McGregor, are you there?" I said, my voice echoing loudly in the empty bookstore, although I had not spoken that loudly, "I needed to talk to you about the book I got yesterday."

The front of the store was empty, something that rarely happened, so I walked towards the back of the store where I'd found the book yesterday. I was looking through the shelves as I walked to see if I could notice him before he noticed me, so I wasn't paying attention when I stumbled across something lying on the floor. I stopped short. A foot jutted out into the middle of the aisle. My gaze followed the pant leg along until I reached a familiar face.

Mr. McGregor.

I froze, my body stuck in place as I realized that Mr. McGregor was dead. Then I let loose an ear-piercing scream as I regained my faculties and backed away from the body. My scream tore out before I even knew it was coming, raw and high-pitched, like it didn't belong to me. I ran toward the front of the store.

As I got closer to the front door, a shadow appeared in front of me, and I yelled again. My adrenaline surged. I couldn't help but see Mr. McGregor at every birthday party I had as a child, bringing me a book or letting me take one home. Now his glasses were askew, his face so still...

"Woah, Lillie, calm down," Alec said as he grabbed me by the arms. "What's going on?"

I pointed towards the back of the store, my voice lost to the emotions running high within me. He took one look at my face before cautiously heading to where I was pointing. He unclipped the lock around his gun as he stepped through the first bookcases before I lost sight of him. I plopped down into one of the chairs in the front, worried about Alec getting hurt, but couldn't help but keep seeing Mr. McGregor's lifeless face in front of me. I brushed imaginary lint off my sweater for the third time. It didn't need cleaning, but my fingers needed something to do. Something normal.

It was minutes later before Alec returned, his face grim. "How long have you been here, Lillie?" he asked as he approached me.

I blinked, trying to focus on Alec's voice, but all I could see was the way McGregor's glasses had slipped down his nose, crooked even in death.

No. Don't go there. Not now.

I stared at him in shock. "What do you mean, how long have I been here?" I demanded, "I just got here, Alec. I came to talk to him about the book I got yesterday." I was holding it together. *For now.* The real breakdown was on a delay, like thunder after lightning. I just had to keep busy until then.

Alec nodded, pulling out a notepad to take down what I was saying. "Alec, what are you doing?"

"I'm just doing my job, Lillie; I have to take down whatever details I can," he replied as he finished writing what I'd just said. Grabbing his phone from his front shirt pocket, he dialed a number before speaking into it. "Yeah, I need someone from the coroner's office to come to *Twice Read Tales.* Yeah, there's a body." His words echoed around me as the truth came crashing down.

Mr. McGregor was dead. And I was the one to open that door and find the truth waiting for me.

Six

It took forever for the coroner to show up. In the meantime, Alec asked me questions about Mr. McGregor.

I learned his first name was Damien.

Alec asked about the last time I saw him. I told him everything about the day before, how I'd come in and browsed for hours. When he asked if anything weird happened, my heart jumped. I thought he somehow knew about the book, about the way it had glowed.

I froze, just for a second. But Alec didn't push. He looked at me, really looked, and let it go.

"I'll need to speak with you again, Lillie," he said quietly. "I know this is a lot."

His voice was low, rough in a way that felt unfamiliar. Or maybe it always had been, and I'd just forgotten. I nodded without really meaning to, my eyes drifting across his face: the beard, the eyes. The space between us used to feel smaller.

But I couldn't stay there. I forced myself to look away. The bookstore felt both too big and too small at the same time.

My legs were jittery, bouncing, ready to bolt. I couldn't sit still. Couldn't breathe right.

When the coroner finally arrived, Alec said I could go. I almost laughed from relief. I needed to move. Needed to get out.

Just as I started to stand, the bell above the door jingled.

Jo stepped through the door. I was ready to bounce out of my chair with nervousness and joy at the sight of her face. As she glanced over at me, I could tell that she saw that I was all keyed up.

"Alec, ¿no ves que necesita moverse?" She rebuked him as she walked straight over to me. Alec looked at her in confusion before she clarified. "Lillie needs to move; she's all jittery. Dios mío, don't you pay any attention? ¿Estás bien?"

I nodded, thankful that someone had noticed my anxiety, something that Jo had always been good at.

Yes, Alec had noticed my nervous habits, but that was over the conversation; this was distress due to my inability to stop thinking when I really needed to.

I took her hand and stood up. "I assumed they'd need a statement or fingerprints or something, right? But can I please walk around up here until then?"

Alec looked at me uncomfortably, but Jo nodded, and I let a sigh of relief out as I stretched my legs.

I smiled over at Jo, and she blushed at my smile, something that had never happened before. *Okay,* I thought to myself, *that's weird but okay.* I half-wondered if my best friend from high school was holding out on a secret from me, but now wasn't the time to ask her. I'd probably forget it later, but eventually, it would come back around.

I walked over to the window, noticing a hole where one of my reviews had been just yesterday morning. That was odd. I wondered if I should mention it to them, but decided that it probably had nothing to do with Mr. McGregor being dead, so I didn't say anything as I looked around more intently at the front of the store.

I noticed little things out of place from what I'd seen yesterday, and again wondered if I should say anything. There were several piles of books that had not been there when I'd left, and some were scattered over one of the little tables in a corner, as though someone had been rifling through them. Jo glanced over at me one more time, although I couldn't tell if it was because I was being nosy and looking at stuff or if it was something different, before following Alec. They walked to the back of the store to see Mr. McGregor, and I told myself that there was no way I was going to call him Damien after calling him Mr. McGregor for all my life, but I had a feeling that might change.

I did my best not to touch anything, just in case. Grabbing my phone out of my purse, I started taking pictures of the oddities that I had noticed.

Surely that wasn't a crime, right?

I quickly shoved my phone back into my purse as I heard the shuffling of their feet as they headed back toward the front of the building.

"I tell you, Alec, it looks like he had a heart attack," Jo said as they stepped out from between the bookshelves. "He was old."

"Maybe," Alec argued, "but it just doesn't seem right. Damien was always very spry, and he hardly ever closed the bookshop down even when he was sick."

I nodded my head in agreement with Alec; Mr. McGregor had loved this bookstore, and I swore that in my lifetime the bookstore had only been closed a total of ten days that I could remember. Alec glanced over at me, seeing me standing there at the table where the books were scattered. "Wouldn't you agree, Lillie Bell?"

"Yeah," I coughed, all of a sudden very conscious of the fact that he had called me by my nickname. The nickname had never been said in front of anyone before. Jo winked at me from behind his back, and I was the one to blush that time as Alec turned around to look at her as my face inflamed; I could feel the heat of the blush rising.

"Anyway," he said, turning back toward me. "I'm sure that if the coroner needs anything from you, he'll contact you. You know we have to share our coroner with Durango and Cortez because of how small we are."

I nodded again; the news was nothing new to me.

"Are you sure that I'm okay to go?" I asked, just to make sure.

He nodded. "I got down everything you said, so I'll contact you if I need to." He paused. "Oh, actually, no, I can't contact you; I don't know where you are staying or your phone number." Color rose up his neck, as though he was taking it more personally than he ought to when asking me for my information for a police investigation. I laughed at his adorableness.

Smiling, I held out my hand, gesturing for him to hand me the notebook that he was still carrying in his hand. He glanced down at it, as though realizing that he had never put it away, handing it over to me after turning the page to a blank one.

I was tempted to see what he had written on the previous page, but I resisted the temptation as I wrote down my number and where I was staying. *It was all for a police matter,* I told myself, although wings of butterflies erupted in my stomach. As I'm about to reach it back out to him, Maddison comes flying in the door.

"Where's Unc Damien?" she demanded, even though by the tears on her face, I knew she was asking pointlessly. She rushed at Alec, jumping into his arms. "Alec, where's my uncle?" The words sounded muffled against his chest, and I ached with jealousy, even though I knew that Mr. McGregor had been her great-uncle.

I watched as Alec gently pat her on her shoulders. "I'm sorry, Maddi, I didn't realize that someone—"he threw a look over Maddison's shoulder at Jo"—had called you already. I thought the message would have gone to your dad."

He called her Maddi. I screamed internally; *he would have never called her that before!* She started bawling full force, her arms wrapped around Alec as he continued to pat her on the shoulders, not forcing her away like I thought he would. *He used to do it all the time in the past.* I guess she wasn't lying when she said that she would see him later. It ate at me, and Jo gently pried her away from Alec and led her towards the counter in the front of the store. Alec looked at me sheepishly as he rubbed the back of his neck.

"I'm sorry about that, Lillie Bell," he began.

I brushed him off; it's not like I wanted to get back together with him. I shook my head.

"It's fine," I stated. "You don't have to explain anything. Besides, you can date whoever you want."

"Now, Lillie," he tried to reason with me, but I shook him off as I handed him back the notebook. Our fingers whispered against each other, electricity arching between us again, and I took in a deep breath as I looked him in the eyes.

I watched the shock reach his eyes, knowing that at that exact moment, my eyes were a reflection of his. I scrambled away, desperate to get away before I did something impulsive. *Like, kiss him or hit Maddison for hitting on him during a time of sorrow.* There was no telling what I would do, although both of those options sounded like my normal Lillie shenanigans. I was scared that it would be some new weird Lillie craziness from this witchy power that I'd inherited.

I walked out the door as fast as I could without making it seem like I was running away from him. I waved goodbye to Jo, ignoring Maddison completely, as I stepped outside and walked towards the coffee shop.

Coffee. That's what I needed. Not to hover like a weirdo waiting for Maddison to storm off again. Just coffee.

Walking into the *Riverfront Coffee and Cream*, I waved to Ms. Abbott before getting in line behind the two figures I had run into yesterday. I should have felt more excited to see them… instead, everything felt muted.

The taller one was dressed in a striped, dolman-sleeve, pocket-shirred, flutter wrap dress, her hands resting in the pockets. It accentuated her figure and showcased the angular cheekbones and her amazing smile. While the shorter person had golden skin, their rainbow plaid skirt was accented by an asymmetrical hem and a buttoned-up white shirt that was left open for several buttons. The outfit was great, and I thought about how I wished that I could pull something like that off… I was too curvy for some of the clothes out there and wasn't comfortable showing off my skin too often.

"Hey," I said, forcing brightness into my tone. "Fancy seeing you here today." I laughed, although it sounded thin even to my own ears. "Can I replace your coffee for you today, considering how I destroyed it yesterday?"

Hope laughed, and I clung to the normalcy like a lifeline.

I tried to focus on their names, on Sirona's rainbow-tipped pixie cut, on anything other than the image of Mr. McGregor on the floor. I kept thinking about how his glasses were crooked. How he never let the shop get messy.

And how none of it mattered now.

I wasn't ready to talk about it. I wasn't sure I could.

"That would be great," Hope replied as Sirona took off towards the end of the counter.

"My name's Lilliann, well, legally, but I go by Lillie," I said, to fill space, to sound like myself.

Hope and I chatted, but I kept forgetting what I was saying halfway through sentences. My coffee helped. Warm. Solid. Real.

My phone dinged, pulling me out of the conversation. I reached into my purse, careful not to jostle the book tucked inside, but as I laid the bag down, it slipped partway out.

Of course it did.

I glanced at my phone. A message from my mom, politely "requesting" my presence at church this afternoon. Just like I'd expected. I wasn't in a church mood—unless they had a sermon on grief, magic, and what-the-hell-is-my-life—but saying no wasn't an option.

I sent her a quick reply and looked up, only to find both Hope and Sirona staring at the book.

Crap.

I shoved it back into the bag and dropped my phone on top of it, as if that would somehow erase what they had seen.

"Well," I said nervously, "my parents, actually, are my adoptive parents." I didn't know why I felt the need to clarify. "Have been going to the same church for my entire life. You could come with me to the church as my presence was just 'requested.'" I made the air quotes as I finished my sentence, and both sets of eyes looked at me questioningly. The joke felt hollow. "I mean, it is an okay church. The minister is kind of out of touch, but the church itself is beautiful, and the hymns are played beautifully, even if they are a bit too loud."

They looked at each other, something unspoken passing between them before they turned and nodded. "What time does the service begin?" Sirona asked, surprising me, as they didn't seem like they liked me very much before.

I looked down at my watch. "Well, you've got a couple of hours before it begins if there is something else that you need to do."

I sipped my drink and let the warmth pool behind my ribs. It didn't chase away the cold entirely, but it gave me something to hold onto.

Ms. Abbott waved to me, calling me over to the counter, and I looked at both of the people in front of me. "Do you mind if I go see what she needs real quick?"

They nodded, and I walked over to Ms. Abbott, the line down to just the old man who had come in during my order.

"How was your evening? Did you think about tutoring?" she asked, gesturing towards the bulletin board. "I was thinking of some of the kids in my neighborhood that would benefit from some tutoring but didn't want to put you out there without asking you first," she ended, biting her lip.

She probably already put me out there, I realized and sighed.

I nodded, "Of course, I do think that I'll do it. I just need to hit the library to put up some fliers."

"Okay, well then, I'll have those parents stop by to talk with you at the end of church services today, okay?" she said, automatically assuming that I would be going to church, and waved me away so that she could take the old man's order.

They were in deep conversation when I came back, and as I came back, they were at the tail end of it. I swore that I heard something, but I didn't exactly catch what it was. I coughed to let them know I was back, and they both went silent.

"So, anyway, I'd be happy to show you around town if you'd like?" I offered, thinking that this would be a great way to get to know some future residents as well as distract myself from thinking about Mr. McGregor too much. They both nodded their approval, talking at once about some of the things that they would like to see and asking me questions about the town since I was a native compared to them.

We talked for a while longer, sipping our coffees until the cups were empty. I offered to take their cups with me when I went to place mine in the bucket that Ms. Abbott had out above a trashcan to collect the dishes she used.

They both thanked me as they handed me their cups, a slight shock jumping from their hands to mine as they brushed slightly. *Why was I electrocuting everyone lately?* I wondered as I walked over to the bucket. It was so weird; I'd never been shocked by touching someone else's skin as much as I had the last couple of days.

They were standing up when I returned, and we walked out of the coffee shop, walking right past the older man I'd noticed before. There was something about the guy that just called him out to me whenever I saw him. He was staring at the three of us when we walked through the door into the bright sunshine.

It wasn't noon quite yet, which was still a couple of hours away, but it was already starting to be a blistering day, and I was thankful for my light sundress as I led the two people away. We walked towards the elementary school and neighborhoods that I'd grown up in. It was a little way away from the café, but Hope and Sirona didn't complain as we walked through the town, and I pointed out all the interesting things that I remembered from my childhood.

Some things had changed, and when I'd seen signs of businesses that were for sale, I pointed them out to Hope and Sirona.Especially the ones that I knew had always been busy during tourist times.

Seven

The tour around town went well, and by the time I'd brought them to the church for service, they were truly exhausted. However, this didn't seem to bother them at all as they paid attention to the sermon and were very polite towards my parents when I introduced them afterward.

While Hope and Sirona made polite conversation with other townspeople, I pulled Mom and Dad to the side to break the news about Mr. McGregor's death. For the first time I could remember, Mom was speechless. Dad stared blankly in shock. They needed time to process, so they numbly made their way out of the church as I went further into the crowd to find Ms. Abbott.

* * *

When I finally found her—dressed in her finest, her wife by her side—I pulled her aside and quietly told her I'd found Mr. McGregor that morning.

Dead.

Her face froze. She looked shocked, but managed to hold it in after I mentioned that the police were already involved.

The silence that followed was unbearable. I couldn't sit in it. His face was still etched in my brain, and I needed something—*anything*—to focus on.

So I told her I'd thought more about tutoring. That I'd be available at the coffee shop twice a week, and at the library any other time. It was a boundary I'd been mulling over while walking Hope and Sirona around town.

She smiled faintly and agreed, though she clearly wasn't all there. I didn't blame her. I wasn't either.

Still, she pulled me away from her wife and started introducing me to families—bright faces, eager voices. They seemed excited to hear tutoring would be available beyond summer school. I nodded, smiled, and took their numbers. Said I'd follow up next week.

It was easier than thinking about Mr. McGregor.

I was smiling a little too widely when I returned to where Hope and Sirona were waiting by the door. The walk back was filled with surface-level chatter, mainly about the sermon and the crowd. It was easier than saying anything real.

We walked back to the coffee shop where they had left their car, to my shock, I saw Alec driving by in a police cruiser. Quickly turning the other way, attempting to avoid him, Hope and Sirona caught on to it quickly. There was some lighthearted teasing involved that soon fell away as we reached their car. Promising to meet up with them again soon, as I felt a kindred spirit sort of feeling around them, and they agreed. We'd exchanged phone numbers, and when we separated, I felt better than I had in a long time…

Like pre-wedding planning. Walking around aimlessly for a while in the area, not yet ready to go home, but not ready to engage with Alec should he show up again.

I half wondered if I would see Poe again as I walked down to the river, just wanting to feel the fresh breeze. It was always cooler near the river, and the heat of the day was slowly dissipating. I'd walked along the path of the river for a while before stopping, seeing some rocks gathered as though forming an area for reading a book or a presentation of some kind. I walked over and sat down on the flattest rock I could find; the smooth surface, only slightly gravely, rubbed against my legs as I sat down on it. Scooping my legs up under me to avoid having my dress fly freely for the whole world to see, I pulled my purse off of my shoulder and placed it next to me. I sighed and closed my eyes as I took in a deep breath of air. Opening my eyes, I pulled out the book from my purse, and as I flipped it open, it was like it automatically knew exactly what I needed to see.

How to communicate with the newly deceased.

The words popped off the page, shocking me as I began to read through it. There were some herbs and things within it that I had no knowledge of and I began to wonder if I would ever know where to find them. A light meowing pulled me out of my reverie as Poe pulled my attention to him.

"Well, how did you find me here?" I asked him, laughing, as I scratched him behind his ear; he started purring, nuzzling into my hand. I smiled as I let the book fall into my lap, grabbing Poe in my arms to give him a proper loving. "Aren't you the sweetest kitten ever? I was worried that I'd lost you."

"Not going to happen, lady." I heard the words and looked around quickly, but there was no one else around. I had to be losing it because there was no way that I'd actually heard anything.

"I think I'm losing it," I whispered to myself, and Poe snuggled into my lap, falling from my arms as I gave myself a loose hug.

"No, you're not; you've just gotten started." The voice came from my lap, and I looked down to see Poe staring up at me. "Oh, now you're going to see me, huh?" he said, smart-alecky, "I was wondering how long it would take for you to realize that I was here to help you." I nearly pushed him off my lap as I realized he was talking and that wasn't possible; I tried to back up some on the rock, but Poe wasn't having it. "Come on now, I was just getting comfortable."

I looked down at him, the book beside him, and realized I must've completely lost my mind. A talking cat? A magical book? This couldn't be real. I closed my eyes and rubbed my forehead, already feeling the headache coming on. Poe nudged against me in quiet solidarity.

"It's okay, Lilliann, your family often has a familiar come to them in the beginning."

Tears began to fall as I realized that this kitten knew more about my family, my biological family, than I did, and that hurt.

I opened my eyes to see Poe looking at me, sorrow lining his face. "How is this possible?" I hiccuped as more tears fell.

"There are so many things that I could say, but then again, it would be too much... I'm here to help," he said, rubbing his head against my face. "You'll get through this."

I took some deep breaths as I tried to pull myself together. Poe purred as he head-butted me; his sure-footed movements as I went to move the book back into my bag reminded me that he was a capable animal that had been taking care of himself for a while before coming to me.

* * *

After I had dried my eyes and regained my composure, I lifted my purse and stretched out my arms to Poe. I whispered, "Let's head back home, Poe," while my mind was already racing with thoughts of how to handle the situation once we arrived. While standing upright, I caught a couple walking by. They looked at me in amazement as they saw a kitten sitting on my shoulders. Nevertheless, Poe behaved himself, tightly holding on to me as we made our way down the sidewalk. It was a peculiar feeling to be walking with a kitten on my shoulders. However, at the same time, it felt strangely natural.

Strolling down the riverside, I attempted to enjoy the cool breeze and the sweet scent of flowers, the beginning hints of summer. I was lost in my thoughts; today had been a full day of surprises, and despite the ordeals that I'd been through, I was fairly secure with everything that had happened. However, when my phone pinged, jolting me out of my reverie, I nearly jumped in shock. I fished it out of my pocket and saw that Jo had sent a message, informing me she was waiting for me at the apartment.

As I approached the café, I peeked inside and noticed the same elderly man from earlier was sipping his coffee, lost in thought. It struck me as odd because I thought that the coffee shop was closed.

It used to always close down during church services, but then I remembered that Linda had stopped closing down entirely because of the influx of tourists. That's probably why she hired people, I belatedly realized, so that she could go to church and still have people come in for drinks that weren't locals.

I continued down the alley and up the stairs to my apartment, eager to meet Jo and catch up on old times, although I was curious if the visit was to continue our chat from the other night or if it was more of an "official business" visit. Poe kneaded my shoulder as his purring increased; I half wondered if he had fallen asleep on my shoulders as I started up the stairs.

The winds shifted around me as I came to the top of the stairs to see Jo leaning against the door frame. I waved a little to her as I came closer, "Nice to see you again, Jo. Haven't had enough of my pretty face today?" I said sarcastically as I opened the door to let her in; Poe jumped down from my shoulder as soon as the door opened, and I couldn't help but wonder if he had been awake the whole time. *Had he been playing me?* Jo watched him enter, then turned and looked at me quizzically.

"¿Desde cuándo tienes un gato?" she asked, completely ignoring my comment about missing my pretty face, and entering the kitchen before walking over to the coffeepot, which still had some leftover coffee in it from this morning. Grabbing a mug from the counter next to it, she filled it up as I placed my purse down on the back of one of the chairs. I sighed as I opened up the refrigerator and pulled out the coffee creamer and placed it down next to her. She'd already stuck it in the microwave to heat it up; looking around the apartment, it was easy to see that I hadn't completely unpacked yet, but it was better than the first time she'd been here.

As the microwave went off, I walked out of the kitchen and into the living room, gesturing for Jo to follow me when she was done. Plopping down into my favorite chair, I sighed with relief at finally being home.

Now that I was comfortable, I hollered at Jo through the open doorway, "It hasn't been long… In all honesty, he was a stray I picked up yesterday." …and I still hadn't told Linda about him. *Crap.*

Jo laughed as she came in and sat down in one of the chairs. Kicking her feet up on the coffee table, she took a sip of her coffee before exhaling contentedly.

"Ah, esto es exactamente lo que necesitaba," she said and gestured towards my curled-up feet in the chair. "I see you're finally relaxed, me alegro; that had to be horrible today to see Damien McGregor dead in his store."

I nodded, the image of him lying on the floor floating through my mind, and turned to look out the window at the river.

"Yeah," I whispered, "it definitely wasn't very pleasant." I agreed.

The slow sips of Jo drinking her coffee echoed as I stared out the window. Each sip was delicate and light, as though Jo was taking her time to enjoy the simple pleasure of a cup of coffee. It wasn't like I hadn't seen a dead body before, but it was still very heavy in my mind.

"Have they determined the cause yet?" I asked, thinking of Mr. McGregor and wondering what could have possibly happened.

I tried to think of the details from when I'd walked upon him. He had been lying in between two bookcases as though he had fallen on his way to the back of the store. But what was curious to me was that he had been facing upward, as though someone had turned him... *If he had fallen with a heart attack on the way back, wouldn't his face have been facing the floor?*

"No official word yet," Jo said, breaking through my thoughts, "but it seems like Alec and the coroner are leaning towards it being biological. Damien McGregor había sido muy viejo."

I nodded along to what she was saying as Poe came into the room and hopped up into my lap, as natural as rain, and settled in. Jo laughed at the sight before taking another sip.

"I get that," I told her. "But what I don't get is why he was facing upward if he had a heart attack or something... Would he have fallen face-first?" I asked, unable to stop thinking about it. "It just doesn't make sense to me."

Jo stopped, the cup halfway to her lips as she stared at me.

"Es verdad," she said, dropping the cup down into her lap. "He would have fallen face-first. I wonder if Alec had even noticed that." She went to grab her phone to ask him, but I held out a hand to stop her.

"Don't do that yet, please?" I begged, suddenly remembering the voice I had heard yesterday that had been arguing with him. I couldn't hear it distinctly enough to tell if it had been male or female, but I could tell that there had been an accent to it. "I just remembered something... There had been someone in the store yesterday when I had been in the back looking at the books. They had been arguing, although I couldn't tell you what about; I just heard the tones. The other person sounded angry at Mr. McGregor, and when I finally got up to the front of the store, the person was gone."

Jo stared at me, daggers in her eyes, and I shrugged helplessly.

"What, I forgot, okay?" I said defensively.

"Really, Lillie, *you forgot?*" She air-quoted me, and I laughed at her expression. "Lo digo en serio, Lilliann." Oh, no, that's never good; she never calls me by my full name. "Why didn't you mention this to Alec earlier?" she demanded as she scooted forward in her chair, elbows resting on her knees. "This could mean that Damien could have been killed. I'm going to have to tell Alec; he is technically my supervisor." She said.

I groaned. "Please, I don't want him to think that I was playing stupid with him on purpose or something like that," I said, thinking of how he had wanted to meet up and talk the night before. "He'll think that I didn't tell him because I'm trying to avoid talking to him or something," I said, and Jo nodded.

"Well, ¿Eres tú?" she asked.

I hesitated in my response. It wasn't that I didn't want to talk to Alec; it was that I didn't know how to talk to Alec. She sighed in response. "Usted es. Is there anything else that you're not telling him?" she asked as though she already knew.

I shrugged. I didn't know how to answer. "Maybe, just talk to the coroner and see if they could do a toxicology report or something? Say that you got an anonymous report or something… Just don't say it was me, please?" I begged.

She got up, walked into the kitchen, and put her cup away before returning and sitting on the couch closer to me. "You've got to talk to him, Lillie. He's hurting, and you're hurting… Es lo mejor que se puede hacer."

I nodded, although inside I had a million different things that I wanted to tell Jo. Anywhere from 'Well, my pain and his pain are not exactly the same' to 'I left him here for his own good; I wasn't exactly 'healthy' when I left,' but I didn't say anything as I turned and stared back out the window. Poe head-butted me, pulling me back to the present as Jo wrote out a quick text to Alec.

"I didn't tell him you told me about the person arguing with him yesterday, but I did mention that maybe we should see about a toxicology report just to be on the safe side of things."

I smiled at her gratefully. "I truly appreciate you. I heart your face," I said as I leaned over and gave her a hug, forcing Poe to jump ship as I grabbed my childhood bestie. "You know exactly what to do every time."

She laughed at me as she swatted me away. "Oh, stop it. Now, let's binge something and eat some ice cream," she suggested, knowing that it was exactly what I needed to getout of my head. While I was desperate to know exactly what Poe knew and thought about the spell for speaking with the recently deceased, I wanted this time with Jo more.

I went and changed into my favorite pajamas and came back out as Jo walked back into the living room with two bowls of ice cream that I'd picked up yesterday. "You always wanted el demasiado dulce…" she complained as she plopped down next to me on the couch, handing me a bowl.

"Yes, but I also got the vanilla for when you were over here," I said as I gestured toward her bowl. "Which obviously, you knew. So stop complaining and help me figure out how to get this television to work since Linda has it set up for guests in the apartment. I mean, this has to be the newest television out there! It's a Smart TV, right?" I asked jokingly. "Nah, seriously, how do I get this to work?"

She laughed, and together we worked on getting a show on and spent the next several hours relaxing while we watched mind-numbing television.

Eight

The next morning, I woke up from a very vivid dream.

Inside my dream, there were bright colors of the bookends surrounding me as I pulled on one of the recessed bookcases inside a room I'd never been in before. Truly, it was like I'd been inside the bookstore but hadn't been. Eventually, the case pulled away from the wall to reveal a secret room. The imagery haunted me as I walked from the bedroom to freshen up for the day.

I was supposed to go to the library today and print out a flier for tutoring, something to occupy my mind because I didn't want to think about what I would do if I didn't have something to do for the next month and a half or so before professional development started.

Jo had gone home last night, even though I offered her the spare room to sleep in, and I didn't know whether or not I liked the fact that she didn't stay here. But then again, I could understand her reluctance to spend the night after such a long time. It's not like we're teenagers anymore, going for a sleepover.

I came back into the room to look through my clothes for something that didn't scream, 'I'm bored out of my mind,' but wasn't the complete opposite either. However, when I stepped back into the room, there was already a pair of pants and a very classy but plain shirt on my dresser.

I called out to Poe, "Are you picking out my clothes?" Suddenly very weirded out by the idea.

He came into the room, sauntering in as though he owned the place. "No, but your magic has a way of knowing what you want or need, so expect the unexpected," was his reply as he jumped up onto the bed. I was so confused when I saw clothes in my room, but I quickly kicked my chatty kitten out and made sure the coast was clear before changing. *I mean, who wants to get undressed in front of a talking animal? It just feels creepy.* He walked out of the room, and I quickly changed before entering the living room.

There were pillows on the ground from where Jo and I had laid on the floor last night watching reruns of *The Walking Dead*. It felt nice to connect with my best friend in a way that I hadn't been able to in quite some time; even with Cade, there had always been something missing.

I scratched Poe's head as I walked out of the living room and into the kitchen.

I needed to get something quick into my stomach because I wasn't sure what time the library opened up, and I wanted to be the first one in and out of there.

Poe popped onto the counter as I made a quick bowl of cereal. "So, tell me about this whole 'familiar' thing," I said, although I had a general idea from all the shows I watched and the books I read. "Are you, like, from another dimension or something?" I asked sarcastically, thinking of the kitten from *Sabrina*.

He laughed; it was so strange to see a kitten laugh. I never thought it was possible to see a kitten's cheeks crunch backward or for their eyes to wrinkle like a human's, but it so totally happened. "No, I'm not from another dimension. As I said earlier, your magick knows what you need to be successful, so it does everything that it can, within limitations, to ensure that your needs are met."

I frowned, brow furrowing, and quickly shook my head. "If the magic is supposed to make sure my needs are met, then why was I adopted? Why are my real parents not here? Why can't I find them?" I asked. The thing that bothered me the most about this whole "magic is supposed to help you do better" was that it had left me an orphan. Technically ,I'd been adopted, but still.

Poe looked at me, the shock and uneasiness filling his kitten face.

"I don't know. There has to be some explanation for it," he said. I rolled my eyes and leaned against the counter as I ate my cereal. Poe rubbed against me in a comforting manner as I ate.

"Besides, I didn't discover this magick thing until I was twenty-seven. Don't most people discover magick when they are a teen ?" I asked.

"Well, that's what Hollywood wants you to believe; however, magick comes to you when you need it the most."

I sighed; *yes, I needed magic the most when I returned home after the fiasco of my almost wedding, instead of right afterward.* "If that's true, then why didn't I discover it right after Jack left me?"

Poe stopped his movement and tilted his head at me. "What do you mean? Who's Jack?"

I explained it all to Poe, the whole meeting, Jack, falling in love, getting engaged, and then, surprise, his leaving me at the altar, although his father had approved of me as a future daughter-in-law. I did this in as condensed a version as possible, eating while keeping an eye on the clock. Poe stayed by me the entire time and sighed when I finished. "Perhaps it was that you needed the conduit of magick, which this town is running over with. It's on magick ley lines."

I nodded as if that made sense and then dropped my dish into the sink. "Welp, I've got to get down to the library; I'm supposed to get some fliers done to put up around town."

I wasn't really looking forward to sharing the information everywhere; it wasn't like I wanted my personal phone number to be public before I even met any students at the high school. *Hmmm, that's something I'll need to figure out when I get to the library.* I determined as Poe ran between my feet, swishing his tail wildly as I walked out the door.

Poe ran down the stairs and disappeared. I sighed; I might as well get used to that because it seemed that Poe was an outdoor kitten. That might work better anyway; maybe Linda wouldn't charge me too much if she knew that Poe was in and out of the apartment.

I walked down the stairs and around to the front of the coffee shop. The cereal had been filling, but if I wanted to keep my energy up today, I was going to need some espresso shots. I sighed with relief as I entered the coffee shop, the overwhelming scents of different coffees and baked goods and the innate chattering of patrons as they sat around the shop filling the air.

As I listened, I automatically closed my eyes as I was pulled back into that back room of the bookshop or library or whatever it had been. I could pick out some of the happier tones that Mr. McGregor had helped while I'd been browsing, and I wondered how many people here had a book that they got from him that they were reading this morning. I knew that the knowledge of his death had to be out by now, and I dreaded anyone asking me if I knew anything about it.

A moment later, I heard a throat being cleared behind me, and I opened my eyes. I turned around to see that it was the same old man that had caught my attention yesterday. I took a moment to look him over, my mind still not completely awake.

He had brown eyes with cheeks that were sharp like a Greek soldier with high cheekbones; in many ways, he was exactly what I thought a retired model would look like, well, except for his ears, but that was another story. His hair was a deeper shade of pepper gray, and he wore a well-tailored suit. He cleared his throat again as my look took a moment too long.

I blinked and blushed. "Sorry, I spaced out there. How can I help you?"

"Yeah," he said, his voice deep and wrathful. "You could move out of my way. I'd like to get my coffee sometime today."

I frowned as I moved backward, automatically. The coffee shop was crowded, and I bumped into someone as I moved.

"I'm sorry," I said, disquieted. "I wasn't intentionally trying to block you from the best coffee in the world. Besides, it's not like I'm the only person blocking you."

His glare could have melted ice, and I took some deep breaths as he walked around me. He stepped to the counter and ordered his drink from Linda while I turned back around and headed to the bulletin board to really look at it. I paid partial attention to what the man was telling Linda as I looked through the many different fliers on the bulletin board. There was a Fourth of July event in the city park scheduled for next month, and they were looking for volunteers to help with preparations. Maybe I could do something for that too, if I don't get very many students to tutor, that is. There weren't any other postings on the board for tutoring, and I breathed out the breath that I'd been holding.

Without encroaching on anyone's territory, I double-checked the board to be safe. That would be the worst way to start the school year at a new district. Generally, teachers went out of town for summer vacation or did something fun. But, you know, sometimes, people stayed and worked other jobs. I know I thought about going somewhere fun next summer if I was able to save up some extra money over the year. Rifling through the papers on the board, I waited, giving Mr. Grumpy Pants time to get his coffee and disappear before heading up to the register myself.

"Good morning, Linda," I said as I saddled up to the register. "How's the coffee world this morning?"

She laughed at my expression as she came to stand behind the register. "It's been a busy morning this morning; I've already seen three parents in here that were looking for you to ask about tutoring."

I groaned inwardly; I hadn't even gotten the fliers done yet, and Linda had managed to get me three or more students. I didn't know whether to hug her or strangle her.

"Thanks, Linda," I said graciously and ordered a Sludge and Mud. It was a frozen drink, so I could hopefully make it last longer, and it had a ton of mocha, both white and dark chocolate, and was topped with cookie crumbles. It just sounded delicious from the description, even if the name was a bit of a turnoff. Linda took down my order but paused me before I could pay.

"The man, a couple of drinks before yours, gave me extra, telling me that he wanted to buy your drink," she said in a loud whisper. "Something about feeling bad and wanting to make it up to you."

Frowning, I glanced over at him before shaking my head and thanking Linda for telling me. I walked to the end of the counter and waited for my drink. I leaned against the wall near the end and gazed out into the crowd of people. The old man was sitting by the little library, but had nothing out in front of him. He had his back turned toward the books and seemed to be doing the same thing I was: people-watching.

I watched him for a while, noticing how he seemed to be watching the women in the building. But only the ones under forty seemed to be his focus. *Hmmm, either he's a weirdo or he's looking for someone,* the thought crossed my mind, but I ignored it as Linda came to the counter with my drink.

"Thanks, Linda," I said as I took the plastic cup from her. "It looks delicious!" I noted as I held the cup in my hands. "How did you come up with the names for some of these drinks?" I asked, pulling a straw out of the holder and removing the wrapper before sticking it into the drink.

"Oh, well, Damien and I would…" she trailed off, her brown eyes filling up with tears. "Excuse me a moment, dear," she said before taking off into the back room, allowing someone else to come up and begin serving the other patrons who were lining up at the register.

Sighing, my heart heavy, I watched her walk away. *I wish I could tell you something that would make this easier.* The thought crossed my mind. The need to take care of others, even when I didn't know how to take care of myself, was always present in the front of my mind. Shaking my head, I walked towards a table by the front window, deciding to watch the people outside. Waiting another fifteen minutes before leaving, seeing the tourists as they went from shop to shop, should keep my mind from drifting too far into revisiting the way McGregor's face looked when I found him. Then I can

As I took my first sip, closing my eyes in appreciation, I felt the table move as someone sat down across from me. Cracking an eye open, I was surprised to see Jo sitting there.

I lowered the cup. "Surprised to see you here," I told her honestly, "thought you were going in late today."

She nodded, then brushed it aside. She lowered her tone and gestured for me to come closer. "Tenías razón, Lillie, Damien had been killed."

I nearly dropped the cup in shock and quickly placed it on the table between us.

"What do you mean?" I hadn't really thought that my wild idea had any merit to it, but apparently, I was wiser than I thought I was.

"The coroner contacted the department this morning; that's why I went in early, because while examining the body this morning, they found a bruised spot on his back. When he looked closer, pudo ver un pinchazo. A pinprick. Damien had been injected with something before his death."

My hands shook around the cup, and I pulled them back, rubbing them together to warm them; the warmth in my body suddenly fled, icy cold dread settling into my bones.

"Alec told me he wanted to talk to my 'source' about the voice arguing with Damien yesterday. I tried to tell him that the person wanted to remain anonymous, but he said that if I didn't bring the person in, he was going to have to assume that the person committed the crime and is trying to cover up for it." She lowered her hands to the table as she leaned back in the chair. "¿Qué quieres hacer, Lillie?"

I sighed, knowing that I'd have to talk to Alec about it now. "Can you give me some time?" I trailed off, reminding Jo of our conversation last night. She nodded and leaned in again.

"Sí, pero you have to come down to the station before five," she demanded, looking me dead in the eyes. "If you don't, then I have no idea what Alec will do to find out who it is."

I nodded as I picked up the cup and took another sip, giving myself time to think. My brain was like a swarm of bees in a honey hive as image after image from the last two days bombarded me; I sighed, anticipation making me jumpy. I agreed, although reluctantly, and Jo pushed away from the table.

"Okay, tengo que volver al trabajo. I expect to see you after you're done here," she said as she stood.

Her long black hair was plaited and wrapped around her head like a crown. Her green eyes were lined with worry, and I took in her full police uniform. It wasn't the typical small-town brown police uniform you often see on television, but rather a state trooper uniform with a deep, greenish-black color. The gun on her waist showed that she meant business, and for the first time, I looked at my friend in a new light. She was a complete badass compared to the little ball of fury that had no filter I remembered from high school. I nodded again, more seriously this time, and she stepped away.

"Don't let me down, Lillie." Her parting words echoed in my head as I sat there staring out at the streets slowly filling up with tourists. This return home was turning out to be more interesting and intense than I had anticipated when I first considered moving back.

Nine

I debated going over to the man to tell him thank you for buying my drink, but when I finally gathered the courage to do it, he was already gone. *I'll have to tell him thank you if I ever see him again,* I said to myself as I took a couple of swallows of the chilled drink.

Minutes later, I left the coffee shop and started walking down the street toward the library. My drink in hand, the chill of the cup was a nice contrast to the heat that I could already feel building.

I walked along in silence, taking in the towns bustling streets. There were a lot of little kitschy shops to draw tourists in, like the candy shop about a block away from the coffee shop with a taffy machine making the taffy in the window to draw tourists' eyes to the display. I laughed as I walked by it, already seeing some of the smaller kids that had to be locals walking around on the inside trying to figure out what candies they were going to buy today. As I continued my walk, I couldn't help but notice the beautiful architecture of the buildings around me. The brick buildings with intricate details and the colorful storefronts made the town feel cozy and welcoming. People bustled around me, some with shopping bags in hand, while others were just enjoying a leisurely stroll. The sound of chatter and laughter filled the air, adding to the lively atmosphere.

Shops were just opening up, and the tourists milled around as they waited for stores to open. I took my time walking to the library, listening to the people around me, taking in the newer shops, and breathing in the fresh mountain air.

This is exactly what I needed, I thought to myself as I rounded the corner to the library. It was an older-looking building, a couple of stories high, that had a lot of character. Upon approaching the library, a wave of wistful sentiment washed over me as I drew nearer to it. There was something evocative about the brick facade of the building, accompanied by towering windows, that served as a poignant reminder of my elementary school days. Without hesitation, I ventured inside to peruse the literary offerings. There was a deep-seated urge to explore the boundless possibilities that lay within the shelves of the library amidst the musty scent of aged paper and ink that wafted through the air. I wandered through the different floors, looking at the books and falling into childhood memories. Almost completely forgetting the reason behind my visit when I happened upon the computer room.

To my surprise, the old man was sitting down at one of the computers, his hand under his chin as he read something on the screen. I approached him wearily, not wanting to have a confrontation in the quiet of the building, but also the desire to thank him for my drink, overriding the fact that we did not meet under the best circumstances. I approached him, walking on tiptoes, before pulling out the chair next to him. It was silent, and he didn't move when I went to sit down. He was deeply engrossed in whatever he was reading, and I had to clear my throat to get his attention.

He jerked as though he'd been shot at and glanced over at me, the steely gaze freezing me to my seat. "What do you want?"

I cleared my throat again, suddenly thrown off balance by his reaction.

"Umm," I started to stammer, "I—I wanted to thank you for purchasing my drink earlier," I said it very quickly, the words rushing out of my mouth as though a torpedo was erupting.

He glanced down at my hands to see that the drink was still there before glancing back up at my face.

"You're welcome," he said, the grittiness in his voice raking against my skin. "I shouldn't have yelled at you earlier."

It sounded like he was dragging the words out from underneath him, clearly not wanting to admit any fault.

I wasn't sure if that was his apology, but I thanked him anyway before sitting down at the computer. I went to get on it before realizing that the library had it set up so that you needed a card to get on, and I sighed.

"Can't get on?" he said as he pushed back from the desk he was at. I nodded grimly; he gestured toward the computer he had just vacated.

"Go ahead and use this one; I've got a meeting that I need to get to," he said as he stood up.

He was an imposing figure from where I sat, and I shivered, not liking the fact that someone I didn't know could have that type of effect on me.

I stood up as well, trying to reassure myself that I was capable of taking care of myself should the situation turn sour, but when I went to turn towards him to express my gratitude again, he was gone. I rolled my eyes; I didn't know what his issue was, but I was thankful for the computer and sat down at it, pulling up the word processor to start writing out my tutoring flier. I focused on it, trying to add everything that I thought was necessary to gain the right type of student to tutor.

I didn't want to get kids whose parents just forced them to get tutoring because the parents didn't want to come up with a childcare plan. Yes, I know that not every parent was like that, but still, I wanted students who were interested in expanding their minds and becoming better readers, writers, and mathematicians.

By the time I was finished, the flier looked amazing, if I did say so myself, and I hit print to send it to the printer. I stood up from the desk, stretched out, and looked around the room. A couple of other people had stepped into the room while I'd been lost in making a detailed and eye-catching flier. There were a couple of teenagers up in the front of the room, crowding around one computer, and I had to guess that they were involved in some game or another, if I was to guess by the way they were jostling each other around. I pushed the chair in and walked towards the front desk of the library to ask about the papers I had just printed, when I recognized the person standing behind the desk.

"Mrs. Klusmeyer!" I exclaimed, excited to see that she was still working at the library. "Oh my goodness, you are a sight for sore eyes!"

Whenever I hadn't been in the bookstore, I'd been in the library during middle school. It had been my escape from Maddison after the fight we'd had.

She lowered her glasses, looking at me with a dazed look of bewilderment, before her nose crinkled up as she smiled. "Lilliann King, is that you, child?" She said as she pushed her glasses up and started to move towards the end of the counter.

I followed her, allowing her to get out from behind the desk before I engulfed her in a hug.

"Yes, it's me," I said, as I pulled away from her, "I'm so happy to see you. I didn't think you would still be working here." I laughed at her look of shock.

"Of course, I would be working here," she said, pushing away from me gently so that she could go back around the desk, "I've been with the library for over thirty-five years; where else would I go?"

My eyes widened as she said that. I never realized that she'd been with the library for so long. Again, I followed her as she went back to the computer to check out the desk before saying anything else. I took that time to process how long it had been since I last saw her. I remember in middle school, she had the most beautiful brown hair that was beginning to gray at the temples, and her brown eyes were relaxing and calm for a child who often struggled to stay in one spot during a trip to the library. Now, she was older, much older, and the wrinkles on her face were becoming very pronounced as her white-gray hair glistened under the harsh fluorescent lights. She had glasses now, too, something that she hadn't had a long time ago.

"How can I help you, dear?" she said as she finally sat down in the chair behind the desk.

The fliers, I reminded myself, pulling my thoughts away from have-beens to do-nows. "Oh, yeah, I printed up some fliers that I needed to put up; can I get them from you, please?" It used to be that when you printed at the library, you had to get the papers from the librarian, who you would pay for each sheet. I pulled out my wallet from my purse, intending to pull out money to pay her for the sheets, when she stopped me.

"We made it so that printing up to a certain number of pages a day was free, dear, so no need for money right now." She pulled several papers from the printer under the desk and handed them to me.

I smiled my thanks at her,

"How have you been?" I said, leaning on the counter gently.

She smiled warmly, "I'm doing well, thank you. Much better than old McGregor, that's for sure!"

I frowned, unsure of why she sounded almost gleeful that he had passed away.

"Whatever do you mean?" I asked, standing up straight and tapping the papers on the desk to straighten them out, trying to keep myself busy as I questioned her.

"Well, with him gone, now I might see more people in the library instead of going to his store for books," she said, a hint of a smile playing at her lips. "We'll finally be the first one to have a new book on the shelf!"

I frowned but quickly covered it as I saw her looking closely at me. "I can understand how frustrating that must have been," I eased, "but surely, you aren't happy that he's dead?"

She shrugged, and I took a step back.

"Well, I have to go sign off of my computer; I'll see you later."

I walked back towards the computer room, wanting to make sure that I had deleted the file from the computer. I don't want anyone printing misleading information, and I want to confirm that the number I signed up for on my email account matches the one on the hard copy of the flier. I sat down at the computer, noticing that the kids were still crowded around it, but another one had joined them, and I deleted the file after double-checking the phone number.

I sat there for a minute before realizing that I could look at the history on the web browser to see what the old man had been looking at so intently when I'd come in. Considering how he had been looking at all the women in the coffee shop, I wouldn't be surprised if he wasn't trying to look at naughty stuff. The thought crossed my mind, and I cringed. I prayed that I wouldn't find websites like that as I opened up the history tab. I could see all the websites I had visited as part of my research on pricing for tutoring and setting up a voice account for parents or students to call me for tutoring services, but there were more beyond that. It looked like he had been looking up different women in the city, all women under the age of forty, Jo among them, and I wondered why he was doing that.

Maybe he's trying to find a long-lost child, I thought, trying to think of positive intentions. *Or perhaps he's supposed to meet someone here, and he isn't sure if she's being truthful about who she is.* Either way, I hoped that I hadn't crossed his radar.

There was this vibe around him that I couldn't tell whether it was malicious or just one of those weird vibes that you sometimes get from people.

I continued to look through his history, seeing that he had been looking at Burke Enterprising, one of the city's premier economic companies, and some of the people employed there.

Maybe he's a headhunter, I thought, and finally shut the web browser down before exiting from the user screen. The computer reset itself as I sat there, thinking about all the things that had happened that day.

I pushed away from the computer for the last time, taking one last glance over at the kids, only to see one of them watching me as I stood up. I waved a little wave at her, a smile spreading over her face before she turned back towards the kid who was sitting at the computer. She could have only been around twelve or thirteen years old, but her face held the marks of being a beauty one day.

I took the papers and walked back towards the front of the library, waving at Mrs. Klusmeyer as I went by her. She smiled and waved back before getting back to whatever she had been working on. I stopped by the bulletin board in the front of the library and looked for a pushpin to put my flier up. It took a minute, but after finding one that wasn't in use, I grabbed one of the papers and held it flush against the board as I pushed the pin into it. The words, "SUMMER TUTORING SESSIONS AVAILABLE," were big and bold compared to the other fliers on the board, and I prayed that I'd get some responses by the end of the week.

I put the rest of the papers into my purse as I walked out the door; the heat was now oppressive, enveloping me in a hot hug.

Damn, I thought as I headed away from the library and back towards the coffee shop to put up one of the other fliers that I'd made. The last one was going on the bulletin board at the market when I went there next.

* * *

My eyes focused on the sidewalk this time around as I walked away. I got lost in a daydream of working with some students on a challenging math problem before I noticed something sparkling on the ground. I furrowed my brow as I looked at it. *There's nothing there*, I swore, but it still sparkled as bright as if the sun was coming from the ground instead of the sky. I knelt, rubbing my hand over the cement, but there was nothing there, and the light flickered off my hand as I swept the ground. I looked left, but there was nothing there, and then I looked right and saw that the light was floating a few inches above the ground, several steps away. I stood up. There was another light a couple of steps away from it, and I walked towards it. Each time I came closer to the light, it would move a little further away until it stopped in front of a glass door. I stopped several feet away and looked at the glass door.

Madam Colman, psychic at large, the words read on the door, a crystal ball in the middle that the words circled. *Why am I here?* I stepped back when the door opened, and a woman stuck her head out. "You coming in or not?" she said, a smile playing on her lips, "I've been waiting for you."

She looked vaguely familiar, and I took a step towards her. "Do I know you?" I said, a sense of awe in my voice, "You look really familiar to me."

She smiled wider. "I get that a lot," she said, opening the door wider. "Come in, it's time for us to chat."

She gestured for me to enter, and I followed, a sense of adventure and curiosity filling me.

Long, curly hair flowed past her waist, a curtain of ivory that pulled me into the blackness. She wore a flowing emerald green dress that accentuated her curvy but defined figure, and the ensemble was completed with a shiny and eye-catching tiara in her hair. Her entire presence put me at ease as well as the scent that wafted through the air. Everything was so calming. A hint of peppermint and tea tree oils hit my nose as I walked further into the room.

"Come on, child," she said as she walked further into the room, and that's when I realized that it was a house and not an actual store that I'd wandered into.

"Umm, is this your house?" I asked nervously as I gestured towards the stairs on the right. She smiled and nodded.

"Yes, but that's because this house is the perfect spot for the ley lines to give me answers," she said, "but that's a talk for another time. Come into my reading room." She gestured towards a door with a long, flowing beaded curtain over it. She waited until I was closer to it before she stepped up and pulled the curtain to one side, welcoming me into the space.

I slowly walked into the room, lights dimmed but an odd assortment of items around the room. But that's not what stood out, *oh no*, it was the giant crystal ball that rested on a table in the center of the room. I took a step back as she came up behind me and put a hand on the small of my back.

"We won't be using that one today," she said evenly and pushed me toward another table in the room. "We've got something else that is calling out to me that says you need to hear it."

I let her push me toward the table, my heart picking up in speed as she gently pushed me to sit down in a chair, and she walked around the table and sat in another one.

"Ah, the air around you is rife with so many conflicting emotions," she said, as she pulled a deck of cards from a cloth on the table. "What's your name?"

"Ummm, someone," I said, a hitch in my voice, "but the question is, who are you?"

"I am Madam Colman, psychic at large," she said with ease as she started to shuffle the cards, "however, you may call me Rosalind." She ignored the fact that I hadn't given her my name as she continued to shuffle the cards.

She held the cards out to me; I looked down at them in confusion before she bumped them toward me again. "Pick some," she said. "You need a reading done."

"But," I started to argue. "I didn't come for a reading."

"Oh, I know, but you're getting one."

I sighed and closed my eyes as I rolled them so she wouldn't see, and picked out a card from the deck. She smiled as she took it from me, placed it down on the table, and gestured for me to grab another one. We did this four more times before she put the pile back down on the cloth and covered it, the five cards sitting in between us, looking like the side of a die for the number five.

Sitting across from the psychic, I couldn't help but feel a sense of intrigue and curiosity. As she carefully shuffled the deck of tarot cards, I observed her every move with a keen eye. Finally, she laid out the cards on the cloth she had initially taken them from, and with a deep breath, she gazed at the middle card as she flipped it around.

With a sudden intensity in her eyes, she pointed at the card and spoke in a hushed tone, asking if I had recently lost someone close to me. Her accuracy took me aback, but I tried to remain composed as I nodded in response.

As she flipped over the next card, "The Hanged Man," I noticed that it was upside down and facing me. The psychic explained that this meant I was holding onto something from my past that was preventing me from moving forward. I realized that she was right—there was something that had been weighing on my mind for a while now. But I couldn't understand how it related to my relationship with McGregor since she had started with his passing.

Next, she revealed the card of the two pentacles. It was a fascinating card, indicating both good fortune and tragedy, as well as secrecy. As she flipped over to "The Magician," I felt a sudden chill run down my spine. The psychic suggested that someone I knew had been manipulating me for a long time, and I couldn't help but feel a sense of unease.

Despite this revelation, the psychic assured me that I would soon gain a complete understanding of what was happening. She asked me to draw one more card, and I handed it to her with trembling fingers. It was "The Two of

Wands," indicating that I needed to take control of my fear in order to gain clarity on what I was seeking. She paused, looking over the cards before glancing at me again. "You must have gone through some major changes in your life recently; see how you have all the major arcane cards here?" She pointed out the cards in particular, "They indicate that you have gone through great change."

I sat there, processing everything that she said, feeling an overwhelming sense of confusion.

Why do I need to know this?

I looked down at my clenched hands in my lap, contemplating how to ask her, since apparently, she had some knowledge of what was going on. I glanced up to see her staring intently at me.

"What does all of this mean?" I said, breaking the silence that had settled over us.

She shrugged, seemingly at a loss as well, before she spoke again. "Perhaps the person who passed away is trying to tell you something important for you to know. I would suggest thinking about it for a while before going on your next step." I nodded wearily and stood up from my chair.

"How much do I owe you?" I asked, aware that this was her business that I had wandered into.

"Not a dime," she replied, a smile on her face as she stood as well. "This was a call from the beyond that had to be answered; I am simply the receiver."

I gave her a tiny smile before I turned and walked back through the beaded curtain to the front hallway. She followed at a leisurely pace behind me, and as I opened the door, she put a hand on my arm, halting me from leaving the room.

"The manipulation is not just coming from the past," she intoned as though she weren't really there, "it is coming from all around you. Beware."

Her eyes glazed over, and I jerked my arm from her grasp. She blinked and then smiled again.

"Thank you for coming, and I hope to see you again soon, Lilliann." She gently pushed me out the door, and I halted on the other side. *How did she know my name?*

Ten

I was putting up the flier in the coffee shop when Hope and Sirona walked in, waved to me, and headed over to get their drink from the barista that was working the counter. It was already afternoon, and I wasn't surprised when I heard they both ordered a cold tea from the menu.

"What are you doing?" Hope asked, coming back over to me, as Sirona took their cup and headed into the lobby. She glanced at the paper I just pinned to the bulletin board and smiled. "Isn't it time for summer?" she said, and I rolled my eyes at her.

"Summer is the most important time for kids to be learning something, even if it is through a one-hour tutoring session or through the summer school program. Have you ever heard of the summer slide?" I retorted as I walked to the counter and ordered an iced tea. Glancing at Hope, I had to laugh at her expression.

Today Hope's eyes were more blue than green, and I noticed the wrinkles building in the corners of her mouth. She had to be in her thirties, just a little older than me, but she seemed so much older. There was an edge to her that seemed wiser. Something that just resonated with her experience, although I couldn't say what that experience was.

"But—but—but—" she struggled to find the words before they came rushing out, "kids are supposed to go out and have fun during the summer. They shouldn't be learning."

"As a teacher, it is my thorough obligation to ruin kids' summers." I couldn't keep a straight face. I started laughing. "Seriously, some kids need some extra help. Don't worry, I promise to make it as painless as possible. Besides, you know, sometimes money can be tight."

Maintaining eye contact could be hard, so I shifted between looking at Hope and a spot on the wall across from me. Hope looked effortlessly cool, casually leaning against the counter, sipping her drink.

"I get it," she said finally. "I don't really agree with it, but I get it. Besides, it took me and Sirona the last five years to save up the money to come back here and buy a place… although, we still haven't found the right place yet…" she trailed off, and I couldn't help but wonder if they were paying for a hotel this entire time, but before I could ask, she continued. "We'll find something; it always happens. I mean, I didn't even know Sirona was my sibling until I was twenty-eight, and, well, we found each other."

I paused, turning my head towards her, but she wasn't looking at me but at Sirona.

She had this look of hopelessness and sadness that seemed to shroud her in darkness.

"Oh," I said, trying to think of how to ask her more information, "I thought you guys were raised together. Did you have a bad childhood or something?" I asked, my ADHD making the question in my head come out bluntly instead of crafted the way I had wanted it to be.

She turned back towards me, her blonde hair flipping over her shoulder, "You could say that… It wasn't easy on either of us. Anyway, we need to finish talking about the latest house we toured, so I'll talk with you later." She pushed away from the counter, her words were pointed and hard. Like she was avoiding a subject, and it made me think back to the reading I'd just had. She had been acting as though she was trying to stop the conversation from delving too deeply. I nodded, and she smiled, trying to ease the awkwardness that had settled between us before she walked towards Sirona, who was sitting in the cozy corner now.

I left Hope and Sirona talking in the corner, even though I was tempted to go and talk with them for a while, but the atmosphere by them seemed almost intense with heat. They were having a very heavy discussion, or at least it looked that way.

I didn't want to get involved with that. Besides, I was supposed to go to the police station; I half waved at them before walking out the front door of the shop and headed down the street.

It was a beautiful day outside, and I was so tempted to just go and frolic the day away. And, yet, I was going to take some time… *I know, I know*, I had promised Jo that I would go straight to the police station when I left, but I needed just a few minutes to compose myself before going in.

This would be the third time I'd seen Alec since returning, and I needed to think of how I was going to interact with him because there was no avoiding him as I had originally, and secretly, hoped.

* * *

I walked down to the waterfront, heading straight for the area I'd sat down at yesterday. As it came into view, I was happy to see that it was empty again and breathed in a sigh of relief as I sat down. Leaning back, I closed my eyes, exposing my face to the sun. I let the warmth of the sun embrace me as I thought about what I needed to tell Alec when I got there and how I was going to act.

As I lost myself to the warmth of the sun, I must have fallen asleep at some point because the next thing I knew I was back in the bookshop, looking through the books in the back of the store. This time, when I heard the voices in the front, I stopped and listened to what was being said…

"Just tell me where it is, Damien. I need to know."

"Why, old friend? You know it does not belong to you."

"Give me the book!" The voice got louder, as though the speaker was doing their best not to yell. "You know what will happen if she gets it."

"Ah, I do know. That's what I was sent here to do."

"No, it wasn't. I ensured you were here for other reasons." I listened closer; this time the voice was clearer than it had been when it had all happened. It had to be a male, and yet something inside told me that it could also be a female. *Could it have been Sirona since it was a lower, raspier voice than what I was used to?* "You know she is better off without it. It killed them both."

"You need to leave, old friend. I will not be swayed from my duties here. I was sent to ensure her safety, as I could not do for her siblings, despite how it all began. You will leave now, or I will call the police to escort you away."

"You haven't heard the last from me," the voice said before the front door slammed, and I was jerked out of the memory.

Alec knelt in front of me, olive skin glistening in the sun. For being a cop, he sure had a lot of hair, just like when he was younger, only shaggier and so much longer. *Don't cops usually keep their hair short?* I wondered as I longed to touch it again, and as if in a trance, I reached out, letting the silky strands run through my fingers before he stepped back.

"Lillie Bell, you can't do that," he said, and I went ramrod straight… I had thought I was still sleeping, I guess.

"I'm sorry, Alec," I said as I sat up; he moved to stand, his blue eyes flashing. "I don't know what that was. Why are you here?" I questioned, although I had a feeling of why he was there.

"Well," he dragged the word out as he went and sat down on a nearby rock, "you see, my teammate, our friend Jo, told me that a little birdie had given her information about what happened at the *Twice Read Tales* and she wasn't willing to share who it was, so I made a guess…" He leaned back on his elbows, watching my face. He was looking for my tell… We'd been together since we were 14, before I had been so self-destructive. He knew every possible tell I had when I was withholding something.

I felt my nose twitch, *damn*, I knew I was going to give it giveaway that I knew what he was talking about.

"I thought so," he murmured before standing up. "Why didn't you tell me you had more information, Lilliann?"

I shrugged my shoulders and turned away from his inquisitive eyes. "I didn't really think about it at that moment; it was a lot to take in."

I could just imagine him nodding behind me, so I continued, "Anyway, it wasn't like I could identify a person for you and say with certainty that they were a killer… Besides, you weren't even sure about how he died."

I felt it as Alec sat nearer to me, as though a ghost of his presence was forever in my mind, and went into details of that day. "I was in the back of the store the other day, looking through books like I've always done. I just kind of fell back into the same pattern that I've always had when there; I ignored the front as much as possible. I heard a lot of people come in, some of the voices I recognized and some that I didn't. Everyone sounded fine, and I knew that Mr. McGregor would help them no matter what, so I just ignored it…"

I trailed off; *that wasn't true.* I had been paying attention in a sort of odd way, but I hadn't gone up front every time that I heard a voice. "Then, right when I found this book, I heard voices up front. I heard something about a book, and Mr. McGregor called the person an old friend, but the conversation, or what I heard of it, didn't sound like two friends talking. The other person was mad that Mr. McGregor wasn't giving him, her, I don't know, the book that they were asking for."

"So you couldn't tell it if was a man or a woman?" Alec clarified, and I could hear the pen scraping across the paper as he wrote down what I said.

"The voice was low, like deep, but to me, I couldn't tell." I paused for a second. "To be honest, it could have been anyone; besides, there are more than men or women anymore," I admitted and turned to look Alec in the eye. He nodded in understanding and looked partly ashamed of his sexist assumptions.

"It doesn't help much, though. I don't know what book or who it could be."

He gave me this little half-smile, and my heart pitter-pattered as though hit with a jolt of lightning, and I took in a deep breath to stop myself from doing something stupid.

It had been three months since the wedding fiasco and I was surely not ready to try anything with anyone, new or old, despite what my body was telling me.

"That's not true, Lilliann; any information you can provide is more than what we had. However, by not telling me, we've lost some time in discovering who it could have been. We could have been looking at Damien's body as soon as the coroner came to determine if it had been a murder if you had just told me what you had heard." His voice was condescending, and I hated it, but he was just being truthful.

I nodded, biting my tongue, and waited.

"Is there anything else that you can tell me? Truly tell me now, because if you don't tell me and Jo comes to me again saying that she has information and it came from you, I'm going to get like angry, *angry*."

"Well, there are two people here that were arguing, well, sort of arguing, at the café, and I kind of thought that maybe it had been one of them because the tone sounded familiar, but there is also this weird old man that keeps putting me on edge every time that I see him." I let it all rush out, like verbal diarrhea, taking a quick pause before continuing. "I don't know, maybe it's me being weird like I always am and thinking that I know exactly what is going on, or it is me being paranoid now and thinking that everyone could be a possible killer."

"What shows have you been watching lately, Lillie Bell?" The nickname sneaks out again, and I'm transported to a time when that name was a mantra as we made out; a blush spreads out as I think of where our making out usually landed us. "Have you been watching True Blood again?" His question jolts me out of my rapidly changing thoughts.

I turned towards him, indignation on my face, "I'll have you know that I only watched True Blood that one time in high school… It was not my show; besides, that show ended last year!" He looked merrily at me, a smile on his lips, the blue of his eyes brilliant against the darkness of his skin. I scooted back and off of the rock, desperately needing to get some space between us.

"Sure," he said, laughing, and got up. "What are the names of the ladies? What about the man?" He asked as he backed away some, giving me the space I'd asked for without me ever having said a word.

"I just know the first names of two of the three, Hope and Sirona. I don't know the man's name, but I'll see if I can get it." I paused, thinking of the pictures I took yesterday, and debated again if I should tell him. *He's just going to get madder if you keep hiding things.* I sighed as I reached for my phone. "So," I dragged out the word, "I took some pictures of things that weren't the same from the day before and didn't tell anyone." The words trailed off as he looked at me; I could feel the waves of anger coming off of him.

"Show me the pictures." Alec shook his head. "And no, don't try to find out the name, just give me a description, and I'll take care of it."

I nodded, although I knew I wasn't likely to let it go, and started to describe the old man to Alec as I handed him the phone. Alec stopped me as I began to describe the man, putting my phone up to indicate that he was going through the photos first. I paused and waited, and when he handed the phone back to me, I continued to describe the older man. When I finished, Alec closed his little notebook and put it back in his pocket.

"Anything else?" He asked me one more time. I shook my head and he nodded, turning away, "Okay, well, see you around." He said as he started to walk away.

"Wait, Alec!" I called out. "Do you still want to talk sometime?" I asked, knowing that I wasn't going to be able to live here without trying to make things right with him, even though I may have felt unready for it emotionally; I knew it was what the doctor would order. *Or my body.*

"I'd love to," Alec said, a smile twinkling in his eyes. "However, now that you're part of an investigation, I think it will need to wait." Flabbergasted, I looked at him. Here I was trying to distract him, and it hadn't worked.

Alec had never been one to follow the rules growing up, it had come from taking so much from his dad that he hated all authority figures and had done everything he could to be the bad boy. I know that his being in the law had been a shock, but I guess that I'd thought that he was still the secret bad boy underneath it all.

I found myself in a bewildered state, nodding my head silently as he turned and left. His final words lingered in my thoughts, resonating within me long after he had vanished from view. "Perhaps we can reconnect once the case has been closed," he said.

I remained rooted to the spot, gazing after him until he was no longer visible.

Coming home was turning out to be more interesting than I had originally anticipated. I looked down at my phone to see that it was close to the time that I was supposed to call my therapist for my check-in since the move.

I walked along the riverbank, heading back to the coffee shop and my apartment. I didn't have to go to the police station anymore, and I could honestly tell Jo that I'd talk to Alec without telling her that I had deliberately—well, not deliberately, but maybe unintentionally—taken more time than what was necessary so that I didn't have to go into the police station. As I walked around to the stairway leading to my apartment, I heard the meowing of Poe as he came up the stairs behind me.

"Okay, Poe, let's go in so I can call Ally and fill her in on everything."

Eleven

My appointment with Ally had gone exceedingly well. She had commended me on the progress I'd made by coming home.

"So, Lilliann," Ally asked after I'd gotten into the Zoom meeting. "How are things going?"

I sighed, thinking of everything that was going on.

There was so much to talk about, and I didn't know what to talk about.

I debated telling her about moving into the apartment. Then I thought about the café and how I would be conducting tutoring sessions there and at the library. But then the death of Mr. McGregor loomed over my head, and I thought that was the most important thing to tell her. It must have been several minutes of silence as Ally cleared her throat and brought me back to the present.

"You must have a lot going on," she commented, "you're normally not this quiet."

I laughed awkwardly. I'd been plenty quiet when we'd talked about the wedding; it had taken almost four sessions before I'd opened up to her about how I'd felt when Jack left me.

"I just don't know where to start." I opted for honesty. "I walked into a bookstore where the owner, someone I used to know, was dead. I moved into a beautiful apartment where my friend from high school, the one I'd told you about, caught me coming in the night I arrived. I've run into Alec, my high school sweetheart, several times, and not because I'm trying to, but because he's a police officer. Not to mention that my rival from high school is still here, and she was all over him because it was her great-uncle who passed away."

My words were quick, almost babbling together, as I rushed through everything in my mind.

"Not to mention that I'm already starting to find ways to make a little extra income until the school year starts."

"Wow," Ally looked at me, shell-shocked, "That is a lot of stuff going on. I can see how there is a lot on your mind; what part would you like to talk about right now?"

We spent the rest of the session talking about the more mundane things, like the apartment, Jo, and Alec, as I wasn't quite ready to deal with the death piece. It wasn't like it was something new to me to see someone dead, but it was the fact that it was someone I knew closely and had found dead that bothered me, but I wasn't at the place to process it yet. When I'd talked about Alec, I was sure that a look had crossed her face, but I wasn't sure what the look meant.

Did she think I was ready to start another relationship? I wondered, even though when we'd talked about Jack, she had brought up the fact that it takes three times as long to get over someone as the amount of time that you'd been with them.

Did that mean that I hadn't been over Alec when I met Jack?

The other random part of my brain was thrown out. I'd dated Alec for four years, and we'd been friends for almost every year before that. I thought about asking her about it when she'd told me that our time was coming to an end and there were some aspects of my treatment that she needed to go over before we ended the call, not to mention that we hadn't talked about the death.

So, we set up another appointment to talk, as she still wasn't happy with the people she'd been talking to as possible contenders for my treatment and didn't trust that I'd actually try to find a therapist if she didn't help out. We scheduled a few more appointments before I met with someone else.

It's a good thing there was Zoom and FaceTime.

The meeting reminded me that I'd been feeling better every day since I moved back home. But there were still times that I missed the city so much that I almost got in my car to leave. However, she had said before I left that I needed to find justice from my adoptive parents if I wanted to be able to move on and live a normal—*well, normal for a witch, I guess*—life.

The next couple of days blended into a week, then two, then three. I had a couple more sessions with Ally as we worked through the death of McGregor and how it impacted me. I still hadn't been quite open with her about all of the things that were going on; I mean, come on, there was no way that she'd understand that I was a witch.

I worked at the coffee shop, tutoring some students there as well as at the library. And I searched the internet for things to bring into my classroom for the next year.

As the special education teacher for math across the freshmen and sophomores, I wanted to ensure my room was accessible and could meet the needs of my students. I wouldn't start at the actual school until the end of July, which was still another month away, and I didn't know what kind of students I would have. But that didn't mean that I couldn't get the things ready to start setting up my classroom before then.

I was glad that Clearwater wasn't a complete backwater town where packages from Amazon and Temu wouldn't get to me, but I missed the big box stores for some of the little essentials that I wanted for my classroom. I ordered some beautiful rainbow print geometric borders for my bulletins and found some coping tools I could loan out to students, and set them to be delivered to me at your earliest convenience. I hated the idea of packing things up in the apartment until I went to school, but I also didn't want to go to school empty-handed.

Working with students kept my mind busy, so I didn't dwell too much on McGregor's death. I know I was avoiding, a typical behavior for me since I'd found out my history, but I was working through it. I was at the coffee shop working with a sixth grader on understanding the order of operations when I learned that I'd been right about something not being right about how he had died.

Jo came by the shop to get some coffee and saw me in the back corner working with Logen on some problems that I'd made up. We were getting through the additive inverse and how, when we add integers together, whether positive or negative, the larger number of the two will be the indicator of whether it is a positive number for the sum or a negative number. Jo paused by my table after she grabbed her coffee and asked me if she could speak with me for a minute.

I looked down at my watch and over at the kid. His dirty blonde hair hung over one of his eyes, and he seemed as bored with what I was teaching him as I felt. I glanced down at the number of problems we had left.

"I'll let you leave early today, without telling your mom, if you promise to work on these problems before we meet again on Saturday," I told him, giving him *the teacher look*; he smiled nervously.

He looked around to make sure that his mom wasn't in the room, then grabbed the paper and jetted out of the building.

I laughed; it was only five minutes, but he didn't know that.

I gestured for Jo to join me at the small table and waved toward Linda to bring me another cup of coffee. She nodded from the counter as Jo sat down across from me, exhaustion echoing through every movement; the sound of her plopping down on the chair was audible, and I smiled as Linda brought me a cup of coffee.

"What's going on?" I asked, picking up the coffee cup after Linda had walked away, and looked at her. She looked more disheveled than usual, and I wondered if she was getting enough sleep.

"Are you getting enough sleep?" I asked, thinking back to our sleepover at her house that weekend.

We'd been up for a long time watching reruns of old television classics. It was more like I was looking for clues about being a witch, as we watched *Charmed* and occasionally an episode or two of *Vampire Diaries*.

"You look like death warmed over," I stated finally, taking a drink to shut my mouth when she glared at me.

"Would you shut up?" she said with an eye roll and a quick muttering of

Spanish curse words under her breath. "No parezco la muerte calentada."

That was my cue for an eye roll.

"Sure," I dragged it out. "Whatever you need to tell yourself, sister."

She called me a not-so-nice name in Spanish, and I reached over and pinched her. "Ouch," she complained, rubbing the spot. "No lo hagas, I'm already regretting coming here to tell you."

I stopped, my head tilting to the side, an evil grin coming over my face.

"Tell me what?" I grinned, thinking that she was going to tell me about a new boyfriend or girlfriend, or whoever she was dating now.

"Oh, grow up," she said, shaking her head. "Not that kind of tell."

I sighed and relaxed against the chair.

"The toxicology report came back on McGregor," she said in an exaggerated whisper, leaning in as she told me, before sitting back and grabbing her cup of coffee.

I leaned in now, excited to know whether or not I'd been right about something not being right about how he passed away.

"Give me the deets," I demanded, placing my cup down with emphasis. "What did it say?"

She was the one to get a crap-eating grin this time.

"Well, it didn't say what the police department thought it would say."

I smiled in victory, taking it that it meant that I'd been right.

"So, he was poisoned or something," I deadpanned, leaning back again as I took another sip.

"Well," I said when she didn't respond, leaning back in again, "What was it?"

She sighed. "Tenía razón, you were right, it was some type of poison, so now we're looking into any and all altercations that he could have been involved in during the last month or so that he'd been alive."

I felt like doing a fist pump, so happy that I'd been right when I realized it wasn't something to be pleased about.

"Well," I said, taking another sip instead of my victory punch, "I wasn't here during that time, so I don't know what to tell you."

"I know that he argued with Maddison at the church a few weeks before you came home, although I'm not sure what it was about," she said, taking a sip herself as she finally relaxed against the chair. "There were also some small interactions with some of the local business owners. Apparently, they think that alguien les roba, and someone thought that he knew something about it."

She mentioned it before dropping it, knowing that I couldn't get involved in any other police investigations since Alec hadn't quite ruled me out of McGregor's death, even though Jo repeatedly told him that there was no way that I'd killed him.

I nodded, letting her talk it out. This was something that we'd done a lot as teens. Any time one of us had a problem, whether it was a problem at school or in our personal lives, we'd get together and let the other person talk it out while we had a cup of coffee. It had been very relaxing to know that we could share issues this way; well, it had been until I felt like she would never want to be my friend again once she found out that I'd been adopted. So I pushed her away, making her as angry as possible while completely ghosting Alec. But that was the past, I reminded myself, as she continued talking.

"What are you going to do about it?" I asked when she finally took a break. "And how can I help you?"

She laughed; it was bittersweet.

"Ya no sé, there's really nothing that you can do to help me. I'm just going to have to meet with Maddison and ask her some questions about the fight that she and her great-uncle had that day."

I smiled devilishly. "Can I be there to watch when you put the handcuffs on her?"

She laughed. "No, you may not…" she paused. "Bueno, at least not in the direct vicinity. You can record it on your phone from down the block or something."

I laughed along with her. Maddison had never been nice to either one of us during high school. She had hated Jo on sight, on a deep personal level.

I always thought it was because Jo was a lot prettier than her, but who knew?

Maddison's and my relationship was like watching a live wire; you never knew when we were going to snap at each other, just like a live wire getting ready to spark.

If only she had left Alec alone in middle school. I would have never hit her. I thought, thinking back to the fight that had ended our childhood friendship. She knew I liked Alec and had tried to ask him out before I did. It was fortunate that he had also wanted me and had refused her. I don't know what would have happened if he had said yes to her instead of me. Not that we got together right away; we hadn't started dating until the end of seventh grade. It was in the past, and I knew that one day I would have to face it and make amends for it. But I didn't have to do it right away, and I didn't think it was going to happen anytime soon.

"When are you going to go talk to her?" I asked, thinking of how I would have to find a spot to watch the conversation.

"Probably while you're working so that you don't get into trouble if Alec finds you watching from down the street."

I snapped my fingers.

"Dang, girl, what a way to ruin a girl's fun!" I laughed, knowing that it was probably for the best. "Do you think she did it?"

Jo shrugged, taking another sip of her drink. "I don't know, but I'm sure that I'll find out."

Twelve

The end of May came faster than I expected, and it hit me that school was already out for students in New York. It wasn't even the twenty-fifth yet, but it still felt like the month was slipping away. With the heat rolling in this past week, I was more grateful than ever for my decision to use all my leave time and resign early. Leaving at the end of April had been the right call.

I would've hated arriving in Colorado now.

The sun blazed through my bedroom window like it had something to prove. Even with the AC humming, I could feel the heat pressing in. If I'd waited to make the move, I'd be stuck sweating across the Colorado border, miserable and cranky. Being here already was a relief, but that didn't mean I was settled. I hated having nothing to do. My brain needed a task, something solid to latch onto. Stillness made it stir-crazy.

My routine had been set: either I was working with students, gathering materials for my new classroom, spending time with Jo catching up, actively avoiding Alec, or getting to know Hope and Sirona better as they continued to look for the best place for their business.

It didn't help that all I could think about was trying to figure out who the other person had been that I'd heard in the bookstore that day. I'd had another couple of appointments with Ally, and we'd talked a little about McGregor's death, but it was still too close of a wound for me to give her much on how I was feeling. Instead, I focused on the relationships that I was building or rebuilding.

Jo had explained the toxicology report to me more after we had our little 'Maddison Bash', and she'd told me that he had been injected with some fast-acting poison or something similar to it. I was surprised that they got the information when they did because it was just shy of what it normally took to find that stuff out, apparently, at least according to her.

They had gone through his clothing to see if there was anything on him that would help identify the killer, but he had nothing on him when they found his body. The town had planned on holding his funeral in the next couple of days, and I was planning on going to see if I could determine who the voice had been.

But the idea that he had nothing on him when they had searched his clothing had stuck with me for the last couple of days. I just felt like he should have had something, like his keys to the store. It worried me that they couldn't even find those. The bookstore had been caution-taped off so that no one went into it. In all honesty, I wanted to go back to the store because I was sure that there was something there. The fact that it was taped off didn't help, and I swore the weird dreams I kept having at night were related somehow. Each night I'd go to bed, and the next morning I'd wake up feeling as though I'd missed something.

I started writing the dreams down when they would wake me up in the middle of the night. The first few entries were a scrambling of letters, a reflection of my sleepiness when writing, but the one from last night had been the clearest.

There had been a secret room in the bookstore, as if I had been walking to it as Mr. McGregor; I didn't have another idea of where else I could be.

My hand reached out and pulled alongside one of the recessed bookshelves, releasing a door that had hidden the room. *But I couldn't imagine that there was a secret room at the bookstore, but where else would that leave me?*

The room had never seemed like a place to hide something, well, other than myself, but it had always just been a cozy little area in the bookstore.

As I walked into the room hidden behind the bookcase, with the door pulled out and the books on the opposite side, I saw the room was filled with odds and ends. Things that I never expected to see in real life and that I associated with the witches and warlocks on television.

That brought me back to the book that I'd gotten from him the last time I'd seen him. I'd reached a point where I'd go to bed reading it, taking in every last detail I could from it. The book was grasped in my hands as I fell asleep, even though it felt like the more pages I read, the more blank ones appeared.

I had been half-tempted to ask Mom about it, considering that it had my name in it, but at the same time, the idea of talking to her about it broached a subject that I wasn't sure we were ready to talk about… I mean, yes, she and Dad had apologized for not telling me about being adopted, but I hadn't asked her for the details about my biological parents.

Besides, there had been more pressing matters at the time, I'd been dealing with the heartbreak from Jack leaving me, so I hadn't really thought about the details of my birth parents when I had spoken with her after the disaster. Still, I was leaning more toward getting the information every day lately. I had my birth certificate, but I was pretty sure it was the one from the adoption because it had both Mom's and Dad's names on it, and I knew that it wasn't the truth.

So, on top of me being adopted, I was a natural witch who had no idea of what she was doing besides reading a book.

It made me wonder if other people in Clearwater practiced some magick, considering that we had an herb shop in town. I had been tempted to visit it and gather some of the herbs that I'd seen in the book repeatedly, to have them on hand, but in the end, had chickened out right outside of the door.

Maybe it was fate, because as I decided not to go in, Hope and Sirona just happened to walk by.

I called out to them, and they gladly accepted my company.

We went to get some lunch since they hadn't eaten yet. They had just been wandering around looking at some of the empty storefronts to determine which one was a prime Realtor spot.

I liked spending time with them, not nearly as much as spending time with

Jo, but enough. But I hadn't spent much time with them until I had been able to confirm with Jo that Alec or someone had talked to both of them. Since I gravitated toward Hope and Sirona, like there was something about them that just spoke to me, that made that comfortable ease that you usually had with someone that you'd known for years, I figured something had to be right about them.

She told me that neither of them knew about the murder at the bookshop and hadn't even been to the shop.

The conversations with Hope and Sirona were terrific, and I was filled with joy and happiness in a way that I hadn't in a very long time.

Sirona had even started to talk to me like a normal person!

When we started to hang out, I'd been able to glean from them that they'd both been raised by people who were not their biological parents and had found each other by chance when they both returned to their hometown, as listed on their birth certificates.

They'd had an automatic connection to each other and had found out that their birth mother had died about twenty-seven years ago.

I thought about the conversation we had about parents the other day as I got ready for my shower this morning.

* * *

"Really?" I asked. "She died twenty-seven years ago?" An ache settled in my chest at the thought. "That's... odd."

Hope and Sirona exchanged a glance and shrugged before we continued walking to our next stop.

"Well, I'm sorry she died. What about your dads?" I asked.

A shadow crossed both their faces, but it hit Sirona harder—something deeper, something sharp beneath the surface. We stopped outside the ice cream shop, standing there in silence for a beat before Hope finally spoke.

"Yeah," she drew the word out, "my dad died around the same time our mom did. I was about eight. He had a rare form of cancer we didn't even know about. After that, I stayed with my grandparents until middle school. They passed away, too.

Then it was foster home after foster home."

I gasped. "You were in foster homes?" The shock colored my voice. "I thought you meant other relatives, not strangers, raised you."

Sirona gave a bitter laugh. "Nope. We both ended up in foster care for a while."

I turned to them, struggling to wrap my head around it.

"My dad died when I was three. I don't remember him. His brother—the only family I had left—wanted nothing to do with raising a kid. So... off to foster care I went, too."

Their words carried a weight of old resentment, sharp and raw.

"That's horrible," Hope and I said in unison. From the look on Hope's face, this wasn't news she'd heard before either.

"Do you remember your dad?" I asked softly, thinking back to my own childhood. Could I recall anything from when I was three?

Sirona shook their head, and the ache in my chest deepened. No wonder they kept people at a distance. Their life had been full of loss and abandonment from the start.

I turned their words over in my mind—both of them losing their parents, both ending up in foster care. And then, without thinking, the words tumbled out.

"You know... it's kind of strange, isn't it? That your mom and both of your dads died around the same time? Do you think it was... I don't know, a pact or something?"

Hope gave a soft laugh. "I don't know how a rare form of cancer fits into a pact, but sure."

Her laughter faded as she caught Sirona's expression. Sirona looked at her, something hollow and heavy behind their eyes, before giving a small, tired shrug..

✳ ✳ ✳

I came out of the shower, wrapping the towel around me, as I thought about their stories and how I didn't even have any details about my parents. So that's where I was going this morning, after another magickally appropriate set of clothing had been laid out on my dresser, which was to seek out the information I desperately needed.

The fact that my clothing was picked out for me every day didn't weird me out as much as it used to in the beginning. Besides, Poe and I had also spoken at length about how magick was like a cloud of energy that surrounded a person, almost like a force field, that was designed to bring out the best in the user. It was always there, and as long as I did the right things for the right reasons, never intentionally hurting anyone, then the magick would continue to work for me. I hadn't asked him what would happen if I had intentionally hurt someone, half scared to find out, and the other half because I wasn't the type of person to want to hurt someone.

A knock resounded at the door, echoing through the apartment as I finished pulling on my outfit for the day. At first, I thought I was hearing something, but then it came again.

"That's odd," I said, looking down at Poe, who was stretched out leisurely on my bed. "I wasn't expecting anybody. Who do you think it could be?"

Poe looked up at me, as though I was the one with all the answers, his little kitty face blank and comical at the same time. I gave him a quick rub behind his ear before walking out of the bedroom. The knock came again, this time more persistent than the previous two. I quickened my step as I traversed through the living room and headed into the kitchen.

Another knock came, and I hollered out, "Coming."

Now, I was apprehensive about who could be knocking so insistently at my door.

I unlocked the door quickly, throwing it open mid-knock as they began to knock without stopping as I reached the door.

"I said," I huffed, "I was coming!"

The words erupted from my mouth, and the intensity of my frustration echoed through each word.

A man stood on the other side, his hand still hovering mid-air as if frozen mid-knock. He looked vaguely familiar, though I couldn't quite place him.

His eyes—dark, almond-shaped, and sharply alert—followed my every move with quiet precision, like he was assessing something unspoken. His features were striking, framed by neatly styled black hair and skin that caught the sun with a warm, golden undertone.

I glanced down, taking in the rest of him. He wore tailored gray slacks and a pressed blue button-up with the top button undone, the crisp collar framing his neck with intentional ease. He was dressed to be noticed—and somehow, I had a feeling he usually was.

"Uh, hello," his voice was high but not overly so, almost a tenor. He said this as his hand dropped to his side, where a leather bag rested.

"Are you Lilliann Luella King?" He inquired, eyes shifting between me and the space behind me.

I furrowed my brows, "Uh, yeah, I am," I replied, a little upset that he was using my middle name, which wasn't something that I liked.

"What business is it to you?" I asked, leaning against the door, bothered by the fact that he knew who I was, but I had no idea who he was.

"My name is Michael Huey, and I am a process server for Ms. Ida Nyit, one of the local attorneys." His words dropped like bombs. I stood up straighter as I looked between his bag and his face.

"Am I being served?" I asked, clearly not understanding why a process server was at my door.

"In a manner of speaking," Michael replied as he pulled a stack of papers out of his bag. Ms. Nyit asked me to bring these papers to you with the instructions to come visit her at her office at your earliest convenience." He handed the papers to me with a sad little smile on his face.

"I'm sorry for your loss," were his last words before he turned around and basically ran down my stairs.

I watched him, the papers fluttering in my hands, as he ran away, still not processing what he had said or why I had a stack of papers in my hand. When I could no longer see him, I finally looked down at the papers in my hands.

It looked like court documents, but not quite, as they didn't resemble anything I remembered from the box I'd found during high school.

I gave them a cursory glance before I saw the address on top. *Ms. Ida Nyit, Esq. had a place of business about three blocks from here.* I frowned.

I didn't remember there being an attorney this close to the coffee shop when I was growing up. I closed the door softly, the papers in my hands feeling like a ton of weights as I walked back to the bedroom. Poe was still lying as though the bed were entirely his as I entered, and I laughed softly, trying to ease some of the tension that was building in my muscles.

"Well, Poe," I said, flopping onto the bed next to him, the wet tendrils of my hair landing on him as I fell.

Turning, my hair pulled away from him but left little lines of wet fur as I started to pet him in earnest.

"That was probably the most interesting thing that has ever happened to me," I said, leaning into petting him, as it helped some of the tension and anxiety leave me. He began to purr, his eyes closed, as I lay there and brought my body back into regulation.

Thirteen

Once I was finally calm, I could reflect on my plans for the day and figure out how to fit this new "request" into them. I'd originally decided to visit my parents to talk about my adoption. I finally felt *ready*—ready to hear the truth, ready to work through the pieces of my past that still tied knots in my chest.

I glanced at the papers on the bed beside me. I'd only skimmed them earlier, but now, with my mind settled, curiosity crept back in.

I sat up, grabbed the papers, and began flipping through them. That's when I noticed it. *Damien McGregor.*

Why did I have papers with his name on them? He had Maddison and her dad. They'd receive any information about his estate before anyone else. I shook my head. None of this made sense.

"Well, I guess I'd better go to this lawyer's office and figure out what's going on," I muttered, glancing down at how cozy Poe looked. "I wish I had half your worries." I gave him one more stroke before standing with the papers in hand.

"You don't want the worries I have," Poe mumbled, words thick with sleep. "You wouldn't like it."

His voice drifted off as he fell fully asleep again. I shook my head. One of these days, we were going to have a conversation about who he was and what he did when he wasn't here.

At the bottom of the stairs, I paused, debating whether to drive over to the lawyer's office before visiting my parents. I decided against it—I'd want to be alone afterward. I slipped my keys into my purse and walked to the corner of the alley, glancing at the papers again to double-check the address before turning left.

It took about five minutes to reach the office. It was an old house converted into a business, with a well-manicured lawn and a porch that reminded me more of a bed-and-breakfast than a law office.

Her name, Ida Nyit, was written in elegant calligraphy on the window, just like the sign at *Twice Read Tales*: *Ida Nyit, Esquire, Attorney at Law.*

I stood there staring at the door, maybe for a full minute, before gathering enough courage to step forward. The door loomed, larger and heavier with every second I waited. I reached for the golden handle, my reflection distorted in its shine. My blood pulsed in my hand as it closed around the knob, like the building itself was alive and watching me.

I pushed the door. It didn't budge. I frowned, realizing I needed to pull it. *Classic.* I pulled it open and hesitated. *I could just let it shut and walk away.* But I thought of my conversation with Ally and knew I had to go through with this if I ever wanted peace.

I peeked inside. "Hello? Is anyone there?"

A young, vibrant voice called from somewhere inside. "I'm here! Come on in!"

I took a breath and stepped through the doorway. No going back now. "Where exactly is 'here'?"

A head popped out of a nearby office. Her hair was dark, her skin a deep olive tone, and her eyes were darker still. I wondered about her heritage; her name wasn't one I recognized, so she must have moved to Clearwater in recent years.

"Come on in," she said again, gesturing for me to come down to the room she was in. "You're Lilliann King, right?" She asked as I came nearer. I didn't trust my voice, so I nodded as I took in her appearance. She was dressed professionally, her suit looked to be tailor-made, the grays of it contrasted against her dark skin, and the maroon shirt underneath made her face seem flushed.

"Awesome, well, come on in and take a seat," She said as she walked away from the door and headed to the desk in the center of the room. It looked like a bookstore in here; the walls were filled with different types of books as I took them in. This could almost be as relaxing as the bookstore was to me as a child. I noticed the thick wing-back chairs that sat in front of the desk and headed over to one. The chair was velvet, soft, and smooth against my hand as I reached for the back.

I settled into a soft velvet wingback chair, running my fingers over the fabric. It was oddly comforting.

It almost relaxed me.

"I'm glad Mr. Huey found you and got the papers to you quickly," she said as she sat behind her desk. A thick pile of papers sat to her right, drawing my attention.

"Did you have any trouble understanding the documents he delivered?" she asked.

There was a lot to take in here, and I was having a hard time focusing. I frowned, still overwhelmed, unable to voice how surreal this all felt.

"Well, if you didn't, that's what I'm here for." She pulled a set of papers from the pile. "I'm the executor of Mr. Damien McGregor's will. You've been named the sole inheritor of his estate."

I dropped my purse and the papers in shock. "Whoo, whoo, whoo. What do you mean I'm the sole inheritor?"

"About seven years ago, Mr. McGregor came here to write his will. He made it clear that in the event of his death, I was to notify only his successor: you."

My jaw dropped. *Me? Inherit from McGregor?*

I stammered, "There—there's no way. His nephew and great-niece live here. They should inherit."

She nodded with understanding. I couldn't decide if I appreciated it or not. "I understand your confusion. But Mr. McGregor was sound of mind and adamant. You are his sole inheritor."

The sharp sound of heels clattered down the hall. A door slammed shut.

"Ida, are you there?" A voice I knew too well rang out. "I wanted to talk to you about Unc Damien's will… Daddy and I haven't heard anything, and we need to get the house cleaned out if we're going to sell."

Maddison strutted into the room, all tight dress and towering heels. She stopped when she saw me.

"What are you doing here?"

"What are you doing here?" I shot back, already bracing for the fight.

"I'm here," she said, dripping attitude, "visiting my friend. That doesn't explain why you're here." She gave me a once-over. "You don't even know Ida. She came after your exile from Clearwater."

"I wasn't exiled. And *I* was invited. So you can leave."

"Ladies," Ida said, raising her hands like a referee. "We can all be here right now. There shouldn't be any issues for the three of us to get along during the few minutes that we'll be sharing."

"Ida," Maddison said, softening her tone but still glaring, "what is she doing here?"

"You know I can't share client information," Ida replied, clearly annoyed.

"Yeah, Maddison," I said, letting my words drip with false sweetness. "Besides, you came in talking about selling my house."

Ida tried to keep things polite, but I couldn't let that one go.

Maddison had always gotten her way. *Prom Queen, Homecoming Queen, cheer captain. So many things for so many years.* She'd been perfect, and I'd let it go. The one time I'd won anything had been pure luck.

"Excuse me?" Maddison snapped. "What do you mean by your house?"

Contempt dripped from each word, and I rolled my eyes as I leaned down to grab my purse from the floor. Fire flickered in her eyes. I smiled as I stood tall.

"Yeah, my house." I turned to Ida. "At least, that's what I was just told."

"Ladies," Ida tried again. "This conversation is better had after probation is over."

Maddison turned to her, shocked. "You can't be serious." She glanced at me, her contempt sharp. "He left the house to her?"

Ida sighed. "Your uncle left his entire estate to Ms. King. It's in his will."

Maddison's eyes widened. "No way. You don't deserve anything from Unc Damien." She stormed closer. I dropped my purse, feeling my boundaries being crossed as Maddison got in my face.

"You're going to want to back up," I said, calm but firm.

I had let her treat me horribly in high school because I felt bad about our fight during middle school… I wasn't a teenager anymore. I wasn't anyone's doormat.

"Oh yeah?" Maddison sneered, inches from me. "And what are you gonna do about it?"

I could see that Ida was watching us out of the corner of my eye, her hand inching towards the phone on her desk. Maddison stepped closer.

"I'm not someone to mess with," I said. "I get that you're grieving, but that doesn't give you the right to get in my face."

"Oh, you're funny," she said, calm as a clam, and slapped me before I could react.

I closed my eyes, let the sting fade. *Did I really want to risk a fight?* I steadied my breathing.

"I told you to back off," I said, level. "Either back up or I'm going to move you."

There was no way that I could handle this situation positively if I lost my cool. As I released my breath, I opened my eyes to see Maddison looking at me, hatred eating through her.

She laughed again and went to slap me a second time. My hand wrapped around her wrist as I spun her around, pulling her arm under her armpit on the other side of her body. I know that I had egged her on somewhat, but I didn't think that she would have reacted with violence. I didn't think she'd actually hit me. Clearly, I'd been wrong.

I put her into a standing hold, using the training I'd received from the non-crisis intervention training I'd gone through, as I tried to leverage her height against my short stature. I struggled to keep Maddison contained, keeping an eye on her breathing. I heard Ida on the phone. Pretty sure she was calling the cops.

Sirens howled down the street. Maddison was still cussing me out as she struggled to get out of my grip.

"Maddison, all you have to do is calm down," I said evenly. "Hands to yourself."

Twenty seconds later, the door slammed open.

"We're in here," Ida called out, frustration clear in her voice.

An officer entered. I released Maddison, and she practically flew into their arms.

"Is everything okay here?" the officer asked as they took in the surroundings, paying attention to everyone's face as the officer moved Maddison back out of their space. I took a step back, making room between us, nodding as Ida walked around her desk to stand between me and Maddison.

"Thank you for coming, officer," Ida said, reaching out for Maddison's hand. *Hmmm.* Maddison let her take her hand, steam still blowing out from her ears, as the officer turned towards me.

"Ma'am," the officer addressed me. "What were you doing?"

Thinking that I had been the inciting party.

"Excuse me," I said, my tone cool. "I was protecting myself after Ms. McGregor decided to smack me." The officer looked to Ida for confirmation; she nodded.

"Well," the officer said, "thank you for your non-violent restraint." I nodded, exhaustion settling in.

"Can I speak with everyone separately?" the officer asked.

I nodded, exhaustion hitting me like a brick. Looking between Maddison and me, I nodded, just ready to get out of there and to get to my parents. I was overwhelmed by the current events and just wanted to escape into the past for a little while.

"Ms. Nyit, can you please take Ms. McGregor to another room for a little while?" The officer asked, noticing the handholding between the two women, to which Ida nodded and started to pull Maddison away.

"Come on, Maddi," Ida said, trying to lead her away.

"Hell no," Maddison snapped. "There is no way in hell that I'm going to leave her alone. She is the devil and should be arrested for handling me the way that she did," she complained, pulling against Ida's hand.

I rubbed my temple, worn thin.

"Maddison," I said wearily. "Just go with Ida. I won't press charges if you leave me alone."

The officer looked at me curiously before glancing back at Maddison. "Ma'am, I think she has a point. It would be better for you if you went to cool off." Maddison blew out a breath, a huff of air, as she looked between the three of us in the room with her.

Maddison huffed. "Fine. But this isn't over, Lilliann King."

This was not going to go well.

Her words rang with a finality I didn't like.

She pulled her arm away from Ida and stomped down the hallway, her heels clicking on the wooden floor, until I couldn't hear it anymore. Ida followed her at a slower pace, stopping only for a moment to ask me to come back at a different time to continue our conversation regarding his estate. I agreed readily and told her that I would give her a call later on to set up an appointment.

I agreed quickly. Anything to leave.

Once they were gone, the officer turned to me. "Name and number?"

I recited my info, slumping into the chair, purse digging into my hip.

"Thank you. Am I to understand you don't want to press charges?"

I closed my eyes. *God, I wanted to.* But I also didn't want to make her grief worse. I opened my eyes.

"No, officer. She's upset. I don't wish to press charges. Ms. McGregor was upset because she heard some upsetting news regarding her great uncle, and I happened to be the recipient of her frustration, but I do not wish to press charges."

The officer nodded. "Thank you. Anything else you'd like to add?"

I shook my head.

"You're free to go. I'll speak with Ms. McGregor."

I didn't wait, I didn't want to hear Maddison's voice anymore, and if I stayed any longer, I didn't know if I wouldn't change my mind. I walked away from the room, my purse and the papers clutched in my hand as I went through the front door. I walked with purpose, quick-stepped, almost running, back to my car that was waiting outside my apartment.

As my car came into focus, I sighed with relief. I pulled my keys out and unlocked the car from the end of the alley so that when I reached it, I opened the door with minimal fight, before sliding into the seat. I dropped everything in the seat next to me, resting my head on the steering wheel.

Resting my head on the steering wheel, I thought. *Well, this day just keeps getting more and more interesting* as I thought back to the comment I'd made to Poe. Things were going on that were more interesting than just having a process server at my door first thing in the morning.

Fourteen

❦

My brain buzzed with thoughts, another hive of bees swarming in and out of my head, as I leaned back and started the engine. Easing from my parking spot, I watched the street corners, peeking out from behind the coffee shop as I headed toward my parents' house. It was only about a mile away, but after the day I'd had, I wanted easy access to escape if I needed to.

As I pulled up in front of my parents' house, a wave of nostalgia hit me. The house was still brown.

I'd joked as a kid that it looked like poop, and my parents had always insisted it was "chocolate chip brown," since I loved chocolate chips so much. The yellow trim was a bright contrast to the fading paint, and I wondered if Dad had recently updated it—the last time I'd been home, it had been the brightest blue I'd ever seen, bluer than the clearest sky.

The apple trees outside looked full, some of the fruit nearly ready to drop. I'd have to remind Dad to pick them before the squirrels got to them. I sat there a moment longer, watching the trees, before finally turning off the engine.

When I couldn't put it off any longer, I unlocked the door and climbed out. Slamming it shut, I headed up the stairs to the porch. The flower pots out front were carefully tended, every inch of the house practically screaming 'perfect.'

I knocked before opening the door, knowing they always left the wooden one open so the dogs could see out. I could hear my parents talking in the background as the dogs came bounding up. Their high-pitched barking and slobbering were a welcome sight.

"Hey there, boys!" I called, dropping to the ground for kisses from the dogs I'd grown up with.

I hadn't expected them to still be around when I finally got the courage to come home.

"What are you up to, Mackie?" I asked, giving the black lab and blue heeler a big kiss on the snout as he pushed against me.

"I missed you, too," I said sweetly, hugging him until the other dog shoved his way in, demanding equal attention.

"Hello, Ottie, my little Otis boy. I missed you too," I cooed to the German Shepherd mix, his long fur already shedding as I petted him.

I sat there, basking in the dogs' love, as my parents came out from the kitchen.

"Well, it's about time you came home," my mother said as she stepped into the living room. Her short auburn hair swayed as she walked. My dad stood tall behind her, his black hair now peppered with more gray than hers, his smile easy as he watched me with the dogs.

"Leave her alone, Janine. She's saying hi to the pups—they haven't seen her either."

"Well, neither have you… Besides, she's been home almost a month, and this is the first time she's come to her actual home. Ridiculous, I tell you," she snapped. I stood up, gently pushing the dogs aside.

"Hello, Mother," I said, rolling my eyes at her attitude. I wasn't ready to talk about the meeting I'd just had with Ida.

"Hi, Daddy." I stepped around the dogs to pull him into a bear hug. He had always been the one who understood me.

Mom was always on my case about everything, while Dad was the one who listened when things didn't work out the way I wanted.

I could practically hear her eyes roll at my display before she tugged me away from Dad to hug me herself. She meant it to be gentle, but I could feel the tension in her arms as she held me.

We moved into the kitchen and sat down at the table while Mom busied herself boiling water for tea. Dad draped his arm around my shoulders and pulled me in, and I soaked up the little things about my childhood home that once made me feel safe, most of all, just being with my dad.

When Mom was done, she sat across from me with the tea kettle in the center of the table.

"Well, are you going to tell us why you've finally decided to grace us with your presence?" she asked, stirring her tea.

I poured water into my cup, the scent of midnight jasmine rising as it soaked the tea bag. I added sugar and milk, stirring slowly as I debated how to tell them the real reason I'd come.

Their eyes weighed on me as I stared down at my cup, memories of discovering I was adopted rushing back.

* * *

I'd been cleaning out the attic, looking for boxes to pack for my trip to the university, when I came across a box of things. Inside was a baby blanket and a bunch of random papers.

Mom and Dad had never mentioned miscarriages, and I was an only child, so it caught me off guard. I set aside what I'd been holding and pulled the box between my legs.

The blanket was soft pink, with little elephants scattered across it, fleece on the other side. I rubbed it against my cheek, as if it were calling my name, claiming it belonged to me. I dropped it onto my lap and dug through the box.

Paper after paper filled the box, and I rifled through them until my name caught my eye. It was an adoption paper, signed by a guardian ad litem, placing me with Janine and Bruce King. There was no maiden name listed—just Lilliann Luella—and tears started pouring down my face.

I'd gotten up, the blanket clenched in one hand, the adoption paper in the other, and raced down the stairs to the kitchen where Mom was making dinner.

"What's this?" I demanded, shaking the paper in her face. "What is this?"

My voice rose as I started to tremble.

Her eyes widened as she took in my disheveled appearance—grime on my face, dust on my clothes, the blanket still clutched in my hand—before she grabbed both the paper and the blanket and looked down at them.

I'd run out of the house, overwhelmed by the emotions swirling in my gut. Eventually, I just wandered. That's when everything started to fall apart, but I was hurt and didn't know how to handle it.

The bookstore had loomed in front of me before I even realized where I was, and I'd gone inside. Mr. McGregor had taken one look at me and ushered me to the back room, where I hid the rest of the day until he finally made me leave. He never asked questions—just let me stay as long as he could.

* * *

I went back and forth—*should I talk about my birth parents or the meeting with Ida?*

Finally, I decided to start with my birth parents and be honest. I could tell them about Ida afterward. I'd never really advocated for my own needs with them before, but it felt like it was time. I looked straight into my mom's eyes.

"Mom, Dad, can you tell me the story of how you adopted me?" I asked, finally ready to face what I'd been avoiding for so long. "I know we've talked about how you wished you'd told me sooner, but I think I'm ready to hear it now."

Mom and Dad exchanged a warm smile before looking back at me.

Mom smiled. "Of course, dear. It all started when we decided we wanted to become parents. We struggled to get pregnant; in fact, we had several miscarriages before we realized that having a child naturally just wasn't meant for us. Adoption became the right choice.

It wasn't easy to adopt in a small town like Clearwater, so we had to go to Denver to start the process. We filled out paperwork, attended meetings, went through interviews—all hoping to find our perfect match."

Mom's eyes sparkled with joy as she continued, "Then we saw your photo. The moment we laid eyes on you, we knew you were meant to be part of our family."

Dad added, "Meeting you in person was a bit nerve-wracking."

"What was it like when you first saw me?" I asked, curious about their first impressions.

Mom's voice softened. "It was overwhelming, Lilliann. You were this tiny little thing—smaller than we expected, but somehow bigger, too. You were already babbling, and the moment they placed you in my arms, my heart melted."

I nodded, warmth blooming in my chest. I hadn't expected to feel this kind of joy—hearing it from her, knowing how much she had wanted me.

Dad smiled, his voice warm with memory. "We spent the whole day getting to know you, just having fun. By the end of it, we knew—you were the one. We wanted to adopt you."

"I'm so glad you did," I said, my throat tightening. "I wish you'd been honest with me sooner, but I understand now. Therapy's helped. I love you guys... even if I haven't always shown it."

I thought about everything they'd done for me growing up—all the ways they'd loved me. That love had given me a happy childhood, *a real home*. Clearwater was home because of them.

My parents exchanged a soft smile. "And we're so lucky to have you, Lilliann. You're the best thing that's ever happened to us."

Dad squeezed my shoulder. "We couldn't be happier that we adopted you. You're our daughter. We love you."

"I love you too, Dad." I paused. "But... how big was I? Did you know anything about my birth parents? What can you tell me about them?" My voice thickened with emotion as unshed tears stung at the corners of my eyes.

"Oh, Lillie." Dad pulled me closer as a tear slipped free. I hid in his arms while Mom rested her hand on my back. "I'm sorry we didn't tell you sooner. We just... never thought it would be an issue."

Mom hummed softly in agreement before answering. "You were about ten months old the first time we saw you. The chubbiest baby I'd ever seen." She smiled faintly. "When they put you in my arms, it felt like you'd always been mine.

It wasn't easy to get information about your parents. We asked during the process—how you might contact them later—but… we planned to tell you at thirteen. Then they told us about your situation, and…" She trailed off, and I glanced up from Dad's shoulder.

"My situation?" I asked, though deep down I already knew.

"I don't know how to say this, love, so I'll just be blunt. Your birth parents were dead. You'd been in the system in Denver for about two months before the adoption. We were shocked, but… we were so grateful to have you that we didn't push for more answers. I think that's why we never told you sooner—we didn't want to cause you more pain."

"Undue stress?" I echoed, tears slipping down my cheeks.

Mom leaned in and wiped my tears away, her face a mix of sadness and love. I left Dad's shoulder and folded into her arms instead.

"Thank you for taking care of me. For loving me, even when I was the queen of mean. For taking me back, even after I screwed up by leaving. But… what did you mean by 'undue stress'?"

"Honey, this will always be your home. No matter what, you're our daughter. Being adopted doesn't make you any less ours." They said it together, like it was something they'd long agreed on. Dad leaned in again, pulling us into a family hug.

We sat like that for a while until my tears dried. I sighed, still a little annoyed they hadn't answered my question, but decided to move on.

"Do you know how they died?" I asked, my voice barely a whisper as I reached for my tea, something to do with my hands so I didn't fidget.

Mom stood at my question and quietly left the room. I looked at Dad, puzzled.

"Give her a minute," he said, sipping his tea.

She came back carrying a large manila envelope.

"I thought you might ask about that," Mom said as she sat back down. "Especially after the phone call about Jack and your…" She trailed off, shaking her head before continuing. "Anyway, I figured you'd want to know who they were, so I did some digging." She slid the envelope across the table.

I took it carefully, half-afraid to open it, my hands trembling as Mom went on.

"Your biological mother's name was AnnMarie Driscoll. Your biological father was Mark Burke. AnnMarie had two other children by other men before she married Mark."

I opened the envelope as the words settled over me.

I had siblings.

"What about their parents?" I asked, wondering why I'd been adopted instead of cared for by grandparents.

"Your mother was an only child. There's not much on her parents—she was a runaway for a while. I think her mother died in a car accident... or something like that." Mom shook her head. "It happened when she was young, too."

She hesitated. "Your father's parents... well, they were separated and didn't approve of the marriage. When they found out about you, they made it clear they wanted nothing to do with anything from a marriage they never supported."

She said it gently, like softening the blow would help. It didn't. I set the envelope down and leaned back.

Wow. What a way to treat your child's child.

"So there was no one else?" I asked, needing it spelled out.

They both shook their heads. I took a sip of my tea, letting it sink in.

I thought back to what Mom had said.

"What about her other kids? Do you know anything about them?"

She shook her head. I sighed. I'd come here looking for answers, and somehow I'd only found more questions.

We sat in silence, each of us sipping tea, as I tried to make sense of it all. Finally, after what felt like ages, Dad spoke.

"We don't have much, baby girl, but if you want to find your siblings... We'll help."

I didn't answer. I didn't know what to say. We finished our tea in quiet, the dogs curled at my feet. I slipped off my shoes and rubbed my toes through their fur, letting the motion ground me while my mind spun over everything

I'd just learned.

"Can I look at my old room?" I asked, finally breaking the silence, thinking of the envelope I hadn't fully opened yet.

"Or did you clean it out?"

They exchanged a glance, small smiles on both their faces.

"Why would you think we'd clean out your room? It's still yours," Mom said, though I wasn't sure if she was joking.

I snorted. "Because that's what parents do when their kid leaves home—they want the space back." I laughed, and to my surprise, she joined in. A beat later, Dad did too.

I stopped sooner than they did. I hadn't expected them to laugh with me. They seemed to notice because their laughter faded just as quickly.

"No, honey. We wanted to make sure that if you ever needed to come home, you'd feel welcome. We didn't touch a thing," Mom said, watching me carefully.

Dad added, "Well… except for the occasional dusting and fresh sheets so it doesn't smell bad."

I let out a softer laugh this time and stood, stretching with a yawn and popping my neck side to side before going still.

In the distance, I heard the faint strains of a country song drifting from one of the back rooms. I stepped away from the table.

Both Mom and Dad stood, almost like they were afraid I might run despite what I'd just said. "Looking for something in particular?" Dad asked, slipping an arm around me in a quick side hug. He felt more touchy-feely than I remembered—maybe it was just my long absence.

"No," I said, shaking my head. "Just wanted to step back in time for a little while."

They both nodded, and I slipped free of Dad's arm, grabbing the envelope from the table as I moved toward my room.

"I don't know if it means anything," Mom said behind me, "but what about that woman you brought to church your first week back? Hope, I think? She looked a lot like you, older, different hair color. Maybe you should ask her if any of those names sound familiar next time you see her."

She said it like she already knew I had plans to see them both later.

Who was I kidding? Of course she knew. I thought about mentioning the meeting with the lawyer, but stopped. *She already knew about my afternoon plans. Did she know about this morning, too?*

"Do you know something you're not telling me, Mom?" I gave her the look.

She shrugged innocently. Dad walked off, throwing his hands in the air as he headed toward the music coming from the back.

"Let me know when you two are done with your showdown," he called before disappearing down the hall.

"Honey, don't you think I'd tell you if I knew something?"

"No," I said flatly. "You like to have control. That's why you're the Queen of Gossip around here. You know everything…" I trailed off, realization dawning. "That means you know about Mr. McGregor, too!" I blurted, my mind jumping to the meeting with Ida and my newfound inheritance. She must have heard something.

She stepped back, surprised.

"Whatever do you mean, dear?"

"Who was Damien McGregor, and why would someone want to kill him, Mom?" I pressed, distracted now from asking about Hope. "Why would he leave everything to me?"

She stepped forward, pulling me into a quick hug before pulling back.

"What do you mean, he left you everything?" The words slipped out before she shook her head, circling back to her point.

"Honey, I thought you'd come home after finding his body. That's one of the reasons I've been so upset you didn't come back sooner. I've been worried about you."

But why? I wondered, the question hanging between us without needing to be said.

"Damien McGregor came to Clearwater about a year after we adopted you. He got along with just about everyone, like he'd always lived here, even though his nephew had been here for years and he'd never visited. He really hit it off with your father. If you want answers about him, talk to your dad."

She harrumphed.

"I don't know much about who would want to kill him. I know I'm worried about you. Please, be careful, especially if he left you everything." She let the topic of Hope drop.

She focused on my safety now, knowing Alec and the police still didn't have any leads on who killed Damien McGregor or why I'd inherited from him.

I nodded and gave her a quick hug before stepping away toward the hallway and my room.

She nodded and went back to gather the things off the table to clean them, and I stopped and watched her for a moment before continuing. I'd talk with Dad in a little while; there was no way I was listening to country music already. I'd lived the last nine years listening to actual music, and I refused to fall back into the music that I'd been forced to listen to growing up. I thought a little about what she'd said about Hope and filed it away to investigate it later. In the meantime, I headed to my childhood room.

I needed to sit in that space, let it all sink in—the fact that my biological parents were dead, my grandparents either gone or as good as. Nothing like family drama to remind you just how complicated your story really is.

I stopped outside my door. The bright pink calligraphy still spelled out "Lillie."

I turned the knob slowly. As the door opened, it felt like stepping back in time. Seventeen again, coming in after dinner. They hadn't lied—nothing had changed since the day I left.

I crossed to my bed, the handmade quilt from my grams still spread neatly across it. I lay down, the envelope floating in front of me.

Did I want to know the details of their deaths? Or was hearing it enough?

Fifteen

I must have fallen asleep because the next thing I knew, Dad was sitting on the edge of the bed, gently nudging me awake.

"Good morning, baby girl," he said with mock sarcasm. "Glad to see you've decided to rejoin the land of the living. You've been out for a while—we didn't want to wake you, but I thought I'd better. Your mom mentioned Damien left you everything. That's a lot to take in. How're you feeling? Got any plans for later?"

His words tumbled over each other as I blinked groggily, trying to make sense of them. I nodded. I was fine—still tired—but fine.

As my brain caught up, I took in his familiar, comforting presence. His gray hair was messier than it had been earlier, likely from running his hands through it while writing. The creases around his eyes seemed deeper than before. Still, there was comfort in his steady presence. I half longed to curl into his lap like I had as a kid.

He tucked a strand of hair behind my ear as I sat up. "Daddy," I said, resting my head briefly against his shoulder, "do you ever wish you could go back? Back to when you didn't have to deal with any of this?"

His laugh rumbled through his chest, shaking me off balance until I pulled back. "Oh, baby girl," he said when his laughter died down, "you have no idea."

I nodded, not really wanting to understand. But Mom's words about Dad and Damien McGregor floated back to me. I wanted answers, even if I wasn't sure how to ask. Finally, I just blurted it out.

"What do you know about Damien McGregor?"

"What do you want to know about Damien…" Dad began, hesitant, like he didn't want to add more weight to a day already full of it. But with a little encouragement, he eased into the story.

"Damien McGregor was a good man. He came to a lot of your birthdays when you were young."

I blinked at him, trying to process. "What do you mean, he went to my birthdays?"

I didn't remember him ever being there, not really. I remembered going to his bookstore every year for my birthday since I was six, but he never showed up at our house.

"Well, you were still pretty small," Dad said, thinking it over. "Yeah, that's right. He stopped coming around when you turned six." He chuckled. "That's about the time you started going to his shop instead."

I nodded, even though the memories were hazy. My gaze drifted to my bookshelf.

Rows of books lined my shelves, but only one held special meaning—my birthday shelf.

Every year, I'd gone into *Twice Read Tales*, and Mr. McGregor had given me a book for free. It had always felt like a secret tradition between us. I knew Maddison got birthday books too, but it felt different for me—more personal somehow, maybe because I wasn't family.

I stood, walked to the shelf, and pulled down the book from when I was six. *Stellaluna*. It had been my favorite for as long as I could remember. I'd arranged the books in order by age, a quiet little history of my growing up.

Dad stood too, resting a hand on my shoulder as I looked down at the worn cover.

I hummed, flipping it over in my hands. The memories were still fuzzy. I couldn't picture Damien at any birthday parties, but I could vaguely recall getting this book from him at the shop.

I glanced over my shoulder at Dad. "How close were you and Damien, really?"

Dad rubbed his chin as I slid the book back onto the shelf and began pacing, picking up random knick-knacks just to keep my hands busy. My nerves wouldn't let me stay still.

"I guess you could say we were friends," he said thoughtfully. "He always seemed so interested in you as a kid. I figured he was just trying to understand children better, especially with his nephew becoming a single father."

"But… wasn't that a little strange? Most people would find that… odd."

Dad nodded. "Yes, but he told me he'd lost his family years earlier. You reminded him of the child he lost." Something seemed to click for him then. "I know Gordon struggled with Damien early on. Their relationship was rocky. I think Damien attached himself to you as a way to feel connected to Gordon again."

I frowned. That wasn't something I'd ever considered.

A glance at the clock sent a jolt through me—I was going to be late meeting Hope and Sirona.

"Dad, I really want to hear more about this," I said, grabbing my phone and the envelope from the side of the bed, "but I'm running super late. I've gotta go."

"But… but… what about—" he started, but I cut him off with a quick kiss on his cheek as I bolted from the room and down the hall.

"Bye, Mom. Bye, Dad! I promise I'll be back soon!" I called over my shoulder, though I wasn't exactly sure what "soon" would mean.

I didn't wait for a response as I yanked open the door and sprinted to my car, silently praying I could get in without any more interruptions. The universe, for once, complied.

I parked outside the café, cutting the engine just as Hope and Sirona rounded the corner down the street. Relief washed over me. I stood by my car door, leaving it propped open as they walked toward me.

"Hey, guys!" I called, smiling and waving.

They both waved back.

"Hey there, girlie," Hope said, today wearing a one-piece that looked

practically painted onto her. Ivory, beachy, full of nautical details—
something out of a summer fashion magazine. Sirona, by contrast, sported
jeans shredded up and down the legs and a shirt splattered with paint. I
wondered if the hotel they were staying at knew she was painting in the
room.

Sirona gave a wave but didn't say anything, which didn't surprise me. They
were often lost in their own creative world, and I didn't mind. That's how
artists were, right? They didn't always talk about their work, but Hope had
shown me some of Sirona's pieces on her phone—absolutely stunning.

"What've you been up to today?" Hope asked as she got closer.

Should I ask them about it? I pondered as they stopped right in front of me,
but my mind was made up for me when Sirona asked, pointing toward the
envelope in the seat with their chin.

"What's with the envelope?" Their voice was a bit raspy, as though they
had been belting out heavy metal lyrics while they'd been painting. Again,
not a surprise, but almost a welcomed sound because it was something I'd
learned about them.

"Well," I dragged out the word, "That's kind of what I was just debating
about in my head," I admitted, leaning against the top of the door.

"What do you mean?" Hope asked, questions dancing in her eyes, which
were a beautiful blue today. "Why would you be debating it?"

Again, my mouth spoke before the words formed in my mind, "Well, I
went to see my adoptive parents today." They both nodded, knowing that
I'd been adopted and how hard I had been fighting that knowledge the last
time I'd been here. "They had information on my bio parents."

"That's awesome," they both replied, a smile playing on their lips as though
they knew something, "So why debate that?" Hope asked.

"Because they told me their names," I said, nodding toward Hope, "and
then my mom said something about you that made me stop."

"You know we've talked about our similarities before, right?"

Hope nodded, encouraging me to go on.

"Well… she thought maybe you and I could be related."

They exchanged a glance—one of those silent conversations people have without speaking a word.

"You already thought of that, didn't you?" I deadpanned as they turned back to me.

Sirona gave a half-hearted shrug. Hope rested her hand over mine.

"We'd talked about it," Hope admitted quietly. "But we weren't sure. We knew we had a sibling somewhere in Clearwater—that's why we came here five years ago. We talked a lot with Maddison back then…"

That caught me off guard. I pulled my hand away.

I leaned into the car to grab the envelope and my phone. They both stepped back onto the sidewalk as I shut the door behind me.

"Why would you talk with Maddison?" I asked, suspicion creeping in. Why hadn't they mentioned that before?

"Let's go in and talk," Sirona suggested, surprising me—I'd expected Hope to take the lead.

I hesitated, debating whether to push or wait. Finally, I just asked the question sitting heavy on my chest.

"Tell me one thing…" I drew it out, the name already on the tip of my tongue. "Was your mom's name AnnMarie Driscoll?"

Hope and Sirona exchanged a look before giving me the smallest of nods. *Confirmation.*

They both stepped forward to hug me. I didn't hesitate. I let them. It explained everything—the ease, the connection, the way we'd found each other like puzzle pieces falling into place.

That old, heavy feeling of being alone in the world slipped away as their arms wrapped around me. I belonged. I wasn't alone anymore.

Even as I leaned into the hug, a quiet thought nagged at me: Why hadn't they mentioned Maddison before? And how would that change things going forward?

Sixteen

W e grabbed coffee from the café and headed up to my apartment. They hadn't been here before—we usually met at the shop or somewhere neutral—but this wasn't the kind of conversation I wanted overheard.

The thought of Maddison lingered like a splinter under my skin. *What had they talked about back then? Why hadn't I asked?* The question gnawed at my confidence, but I couldn't seem to bring myself to say the words aloud.

While we chatted in the living room, I heard meowing and scratching at the door. It had to be Poe, trying to get my attention the way we'd agreed— no talking unless he was sure I was alone. Until then, it was meows or claws on wood until I let him in.

Sometimes I wished he were a Maine Coon, just so he could reach the doorknob and let himself in. I'd heard of cats that clever.

"I'll be right back," I told them, rising as Poe scratched again. They smiled and nodded, sipping their coffee while I slipped through the kitchen.

Sure enough, Poe leapt onto the counter the moment I opened the door, shaking off droplets of water across the surface. Confused, I glanced outside. It had started to rain.

"Oh, Poe, you sweet baby," I cooed. "You're soaked."

I grabbed a towel and gave him a quick rubdown, scratching behind his ears—his favorite spot. "I've got so much news to tell you," I whispered, giving him a kiss on his nose before filling his bowl with tuna.

"I've got to get back to my siblings," I almost giggled the word, "but I'll talk with you soon." I walked away as he started eating the tuna in the bowl and walked back into the living room. Hope and Sirona were gushing about some of the things that they had done since finding each other, and I was excited to listen in on their conversation as I pulled my legs up under me and sat down in my favorite chair.

I wondered if they knew. About the magic. About being witches. I itched to ask outright, but what if they thought I was crazy?

The thought lingered while we talked about their childhoods in the system. Sirona stayed mostly quiet, sipping coffee and offering the occasional word. Hope, on the other hand, was a fountain of stories—her childhood, her frustrations, everything in between.

I drifted in and out, catching pieces of the conversation but too distracted to focus fully. The book tugged at the back of my mind, along with all the questions I wasn't brave enough to ask.

At some point, Poe jumped into my lap and smacked me across the face to get my attention.

"Ouch, Poe! Don't do that."

"Oh, but he's so cute!" Hope cooed, turning to Sirona. "Doesn't he look like…"

"Yeah, he sure does," Sirona answered without finishing the thought. Their eyes settled on me. "Where'd you get your kitten, Lillie?"

I laughed nervously. I didn't know how to explain.

"Well…" I hesitated.

"She didn't find me," Poe said, speaking aloud. I gasped. We had rules. "I found her. I'm sure you both had a similar experience."

The grins they exchanged told me everything I needed to know. I nearly knocked Poe off my lap in excitement.

"How long have you known?" I asked, my words bunching together in my excitement. "What kind of animal familiar did you guys get?" I asked, thinking that maybe we each got a different kind of familiar, or whether we all had a kitten like in Sabrina.

"How long have you known?" I blurted, my words tripping over each other. "What kind of familiar did you guys get? Or... is it all cats, like in Sabrina?"

Sirona laughed. "I got the short end of the stick—a rat showed up in my apartment one night. I screamed, chased it around, and when it finally stopped, it spoke to me. Pretty sure I fainted." They grinned. "When I woke up, it was sitting on my chest like it owned the place. Told me I was a witch and I'd better get used to it."

My eyes widened. "That sounds... really mean."

"Oh yeah, Brutus has a nasty streak. Probably because he's a rat." Sirona's shrug said it wasn't just the rat's personality at play.

"What about you?" I turned to Hope. "I'm guessing you got a kitten, since you recognized Poe?"

She smiled. "Yeah, thank the goddess. I have no idea how I'd explain a rat to my friends. Sirona's always been more of a loner—no one's surprised they've got a pet rat."

There was warmth in her teasing. Sibling energy. I wondered if we'd ever fall into that rhythm ourselves.

"My kitten's named Emily. Bit of a prude, honestly."

"What?" Poe asked, staring back at me, his face unreadable. Usually, he had more... expression.

"Emily's always been a bit of a prude," he added, like it was common knowledge. I blinked. *How would he know that? Did he know the other familiars?*

"Oh, did you grow up with Emily?" Hope asked as she slid from her chair to sit beside me, her hand moving automatically to scratch behind Poe's ears. I found myself wondering—again—how Poe could look so young if he'd been around that long. Clearly, they'd had their familiars longer than I'd had mine.

"In a manner of speaking," Poe murmured, purring beneath her touch.

I thought about all the strange things that had come with learning magic and finally decided to ask. My questions were pretty basic—*how had they learned? Did they have anything that helped them figure it out?*

Both of them shrugged. They hadn't had training. By the time their familiars showed up, it felt like everything was pointing them toward waiting for… something. Or someone.

"What do you mean, waiting on something?" I asked, confused. I had the book in my room that answered my questions when Poe wouldn't, but I hesitated to bring it out.

"Well, our familiars showed up right after we found each other," Hope said, settling back into her chair now that Poe was sprawled across my lap, purring like an engine.

"That's right," Sirona added. "We'd just started really getting to know each other, and within a week, the animals appeared. It was freaky. I didn't know how to tell you back then." They grinned.

Hope smiled too. "Neither did I. If Emily hadn't shown up when I went to Sirona's place, we probably wouldn't have pieced together that the familiars were tied to us being… related."

Sirona nodded thoughtfully. "Wasn't it that day they told us we were waiting on the third?"

"A third?" I asked. "What do you mean?"

"A third witch," Poe mumbled sleepily. "In your family, every third generation has three witches born. Your grandmother was the daughter of the third witch from her generation. It's just how it works."

We all stared at him as his tail swished lazily over my lap. When he didn't elaborate, I poked him.

"What do you mean, Poe? That didn't answer anything. That gave me more questions." I prodded him again until he finally lifted his head.

"Keep poking me, and I'll bite you," he warned without heat. "The power's stronger when there are three witches. It only happens every three generations—any more often, and your bloodline would be too powerful. If you want more, look in the book."

With that, he hopped off my lap and found a quiet spot to stretch out.

"Book?" Both of them looked at me, curiosity gleaming. "What book?"

I stood and went to my bedroom, returning with it in hand. This time, I sat on the sofa and placed it in my lap so they could sit beside me.

"This one," I said. "I got it the day before Damien McGregor died. From his bookstore."

I hesitated, unsure how to explain what felt unexplainable. "He told me the book needed me more than I needed it."

Before I could say more, the book flew open on its own. Pages fluttered like caught in a sudden gust of wind, then stilled. Fancy script shimmered across the page, appearing as though written just for us.

My dearest children, it read.

I'm sorry I cannot guide you on your journey of self-discovery. The curse on our family ensures I will never see you once you've left my body.

Tears pricked at the corners of my eyes. I heard Hope and Sirona sniffle beside me. This was likely the first time either of them had heard anything from our mother.

This book will help you discover your magic as you come together with the power of three. I wish you the best in ending the curse so you may live long and happy lives. I only wish I could be there to see it. I love you, my girls.

Forever, Mom.

By the time we finished reading, we were all crying. We clung to each other, letting the grief settle between us.

When we finally quieted, I wiped my face and drew a shaky breath. There were questions I still needed to ask—about our powers, about how we would do this together.

If this curse was real… things were going to get harder before they got better.

"I've been having dreams," I said, easing into the questions crowding my mind. "Weird ones. Like I'm living someone else's life. They started the second night after I found out I was a witch, and they've only gotten more intense."

Hope and Sirona both nodded like this was completely normal.

"Is that… weird?" I asked.

"Not really," Sirona said. "What's weird is painting pictures of things that come true without knowing why you painted them." Their tone was dry, edged with frustration. I could practically feel the weight of how much they hated not understanding their powers. For a moment, I wondered if they'd ever painted something about us, but Hope spoke before I could ask.

Hope snorted, even more sarcastic. "No, weird is falling asleep in one place and waking up in a totally different part of town, wearing nothing but your pajamas."

I whipped my head around to stare at her. "Please tell me you wear something to bed."

"I do now," she said, and her laugh was so contagious I couldn't help but join in. The mental image of Hope standing naked in the middle of the street was enough to send us all into hysterics.

"Did you get a ticket for it?" I asked, breathless from laughing.

"Nope. The officer was really understanding when I told him I had no idea what happened. Figured it was some sleepwalking thing."

I nodded. "Well… was it?"

"The goddess?" I asked, wanting to be sure I understood. "I mean, on TV there are deities and pantheons and all that, but don't you have to pick a specific goddess?"

Sirona laughed. "Nah. When it comes down to it, there's one goddess we always circle back to—she's why we have seasons. She and the god are tied to the sabbaths, and the rest of the deities? They branch out from them."

I nodded, filing that away to research more later.

We swapped more stories about our abilities—what we'd figured out, what still made no sense. Eventually, I told them about the dreams I'd been having of the bookstore. Specifically, the secret room.

The moment I mentioned it, both of them jumped straight to the conclusion: someone had killed Damien McGregor trying to get to whatever was hidden there.

But now that I knew he'd been part of my life since I was a kid? I wasn't so sure.

By the time we stopped talking, it was nearly midnight. The rain still tapped against the windows, lighter now but steady. I offered for them to stay—there was a second bedroom with a bed, after all.

Hope took the bedroom, claiming oldest sibling rights. I offered my bed to Sirona, figuring it was only fair since I'd learned tonight that I was technically the youngest. But they waved me off.

"I like sleeping on the couch," they said, ushering me out of the living room. "It reminds me of the better foster homes. There were never enough beds for everyone, and somehow, the couches were always the comfiest."

I nodded, yawning around my goodnight.

In my bedroom, I changed quickly, slipping into pajamas while Poe snored in the center of the bed like he owned the place. I tossed my clothes in the hamper and paused for a moment, thinking about Hope and Sirona asleep in the other rooms.

Maybe it was fast. We barely knew each other. But they were my siblings—my connection to the past I never understood. There was comfort in knowing they were here, more comfort than I'd felt in nearly a decade.

I crawled into bed, nudging Poe out of the way so I could steal back my blanket. I closed my eyes, finally letting exhaustion pull me under. For all the changes swirling around me, one truth remained: I was better off here in Clearwater than I'd ever been in New York with Jack. Here, I had parents who loved me, siblings I never expected to find, and a friend who still showed up even when I didn't deserve it.

That thought wrapped around me like a blanket as I drifted off to sleep.

Hours later, I woke with a jolt—Hope's hand grabbing mine, dragging me toward Sirona. Her eyes were closed, locked in sleep. The last threads of my dream, something about the bookstore's secret room, unraveled as she clasped Sirona's hand.

And just like that… we vanished.

The next thing I knew we were standing in the middle of a house, in a room that looked an awful lot like the bookstore stood in front of us. I looked at Hope and Sirona, who had fallen to the floor when we had landed here.

"What the heck," they demanded as we both looked at Hope. She was still asleep, at least I thought she was. I pulled my hand from hers and pinched her cheek. She jumped, her eyes flashing as she looked at me.

"What was that for?" she demanded, rubbing her cheek.

"I don't know," I said sarcastically. "Why do you think?" I gestured to the room around us. "Why did you bring us here?"

"Huh?" she looked around wildly as Sirona got up and rubbed their side. "What do you mean? Where did we go?" She took a step and stumbled, clearly not quite awake yet. "This is ridiculous. Why would I come here?"

"Why indeed," Sirona posed as they leaned against me.

"You okay?" I inquired, watching as they continued to rub their side.

"Yeah, I didn't expect to take a spill when I first woke up," they said sarcastically, looking at Hope, clearly agitated that they had ended up on the floor while we were both still standing. "Why'd you bring us along, and how did you have us tag along?"

Hope was still a little lost, and so I explained it to her, telling her how she'd taken me out of bed and dragged me into the living room, and once she touched Sirona, we'd just popped away. The look on her face was a dead giveaway that this was not normal for her. "I've never taken anyone else with me when I've transported," she whispered, still looking around in amazement at the house. "However, this place looks amazing! Sirona, we should look into this place."

"Focus," I told her, and stepped away once Sirona stopped rubbing their side. "We need to figure out why we're here." I thought back to the fading dream I had before Hope woke me up; it was still vivid in my mind, as though I was meant to remember it and follow through.

"I think our powers have something to do with this."

"Well, why does it need me? Huh?" Sirona said sourly. "I was just getting some good sleep." Sirona was agitated by the fact that they had been dragged around, but they didn't seem agitated by where we had landed.

"I don't control it," Hope and I responded at once. We laughed as we looked at each other, and then I continued. "Does this place look familiar to either of you?" I asked as I looked around, noticing where we had landed, and took a few steps back. We walked around slowly, making sure that we didn't touch anything that could possibly set things off. There was a place within a hundred feet, I swore, that had a heavy feeling of malevolence. I took tiny steps, trying to figure out from which way it was coming before determining that it had to be somewhere outside.

There was no way that I would go there, even if the devil tried to drag me through it, I would go kicking and screaming!

I pointed this out to both Hope and Sirona, telling them not to go over there, as it would surely harm us. They didn't argue with me at all, their heads shaking in agreement, as we walked gingerly around the building. It looked like a normal home, with a minimalist style reflected in almost every room, except for the one that resembled his bookstore. I ached to go look through that room, the remnants of my dreams pushing me toward it, but there was no way that I was going into it when I didn't even know where we were.

What if someone was sleeping upstairs? I turned to see Sirona start walking up the stairs, as though they were in a trance, and I quickly followed them. I had no clue where Hope had disappeared to, but the way that Sirona was walking made them more interesting at that moment than my oldest sister, and wherever she was.

I followed a few steps back from Sirona, making sure that I was as quiet as possible. A few steps creaked as Sirona stepped on them, and I avoided those steps as I followed. When they reached the next floor landing, they paused as though reorienting themselves to the environment. *What are they doing?* I wondered as I stopped, leaning against the wall, and watched them. They continued down the hallway, as though knowing exactly where to go. I continued to follow them, Hope completely erased from my mind as I watched them walk.

They stopped in front of a door, looking right and left really quickly, before opening it and walking into the room.

I quickened my step and got to the door before it shut, praying for them not to be waiting directly on the other side. I leaned to the edge of the door, peering in between the frame and the door. Sirona was walking around, hands gliding over furniture as they walked toward the window. I sighed with relief as I opened the door more and snuck into the room behind them. As I stood inside the doorway, I noticed the pictures on the nightstand next to the bed. There was a mixture of images of Maddison as a young child, as well as pictures of me. I frowned as questions flooded my mind. *Why are there pictures of Maddison here? Why are there pictures of me here? Just exactly where were we?* I was getting more weirded out by the second, and Sirona was completely oblivious to anything as they scanned each corner of the room.

I watched Sirona touch the surfaces of everything around them for several seconds, each second like an eternity, before I cleared my throat, and they jumped as they turned around.

"What are you doing?" I said quietly, still unsure of where we were and if there was anyone else inside the house.

"Oh mi diosa," Sirona exclaimed, "¿Qué haces ahí en silencio?" I looked at them, picking out words that I understood but still not comprehend before they translated. "What are you doing there all silent-like?"

I laughed, the sound echoing in the empty room.

"What am I doing?" I said, amazed that they were so nonchalant about being in a stranger's house that they could try and turn it around on me. "You're the one that is acting all weird. How did you even know about this room?" I exclaimed in a whisper.

"I've been here before," they started to explain and I laughed again.

"Yeah, that's pretty obvious." I shook my head, not believing them. "What were you doing here?"

They shook their head, clearly agitated that I didn't let them finish their thought earlier. "As I was saying, I've been here before. This is going to be Hope's room soon, I've seen her staring out the window in one of my paintings." I thought back to the conversation we had about strange powers, Sirona painted things from the future.

"So, this is going to be the house you guys buy?" I asked, incredulously. "So, who owns it now?"

Hope cleared her throat from the doorway, watching the two of us in the room. "It's old McGregor's house apparently," she said, holding up some mail in her hands. "It's a pretty huge house for a single old man."

I stopped dead, dropping to my knees, the pictures of me and Maddison finally making sense. "This is going to be my house," I said, the words flat as the realization hit me. I turned to Hope in despair as she entered the room. "Why did you bring us here?"

"Again, I don't know how to control it just yet," Hope said with irritation. "I have no idea of why we are here, but obviously we need to do something here."

I sighed and looked over at Sirona who was still looking around the room in wonder.

"What do you mean, it's going to be your house?" Sirona asked, as they stopped in front of the bed and looked at me.

"I got notice of his last will and testament this morning." I said, nervously, "He left me everything."

"Mmmm," Hope said, walking from the door to stand next to Sirona. "That's pretty convenient, isn't it, Sirona?"

They nodded and looked harder at me. "Don't tell me you think I did it!" I exclaimed. "I didn't even know about it until this morning."

They looked at each other and then back at me, weariness lining their eyes.

"Come on," I said, knowing that there had to be a copy of his will somewhere in the house. "Let's see if we can find a copy of it here." I walked towards the door with purpose, my steps echoing in the room before I stopped and looked back at them as they stood there.

"Are you coming or not?" I said before they both took a step toward me, and I walked out the door. Walking in and out of every room on the second floor, looking for something that looked like a desk or something that he would have kept essential documents in, but there was nothing. Sighing, I walked back down the stairs, my steps making the loudest noise in the house due to my agitation. Walking back toward the room that resembled his bookstore, the way it was structured now made perfect sense. Entering the room, I saw a large desk sitting in the corner. Searching through it, I found a book that McGregor must have kept about his book sales. It made a lot of sense considering how he had been such an old-fashioned kind of man. He must have written down every book he ever sold in a log, and to whom he sold it.

It must have been his way to see if people were reading or not.

I rifled carefully through his papers, each time that a paper made a noise, it ratcheted up my anxiety until I found a file with several copies of his testament in it, dating back as far as the first year that he moved here. I grabbed the file and the book log, thinking that it might have some vital information in it, before I turned around to see that Hope and Sirona were in the room, looking at me anxiously.

I looked around the room this time, finally noticing that it was filled with the deep scent of aging paper, the musty aroma of fine books, and the nostalgia of happier times. I wonder how often he sat in this room and read to himself. I thought as I took in my surroundings. There was a large single chair next to the window, a little table, and a lamp sitting next to it. I walked over to the chair, feeling like I'd been here before, suddenly relating to Sirona and the experience they had moments before. I stopped as I stood before the chair and closed my eyes.

Turning, I walked as though in a trance, following the same steps that I'd seen in my dreams, towards the recessed bookshelves on the wall. There weren't a ton of books around us, but enough that it didn't look bare.

I opened my eyes as I stopped in front of a single one and looked down at the floor to see if there were any marks to indicate that something heavy had been dragged across them recently, but saw nothing.

Hope and Sirona looked at me as I walked, as though trying to determine if I was being ridiculous or if this was something else. I ignored them and continued to feel along the wooden sides of the bookshelf. It was smooth, the aged cedar was dark, as there were no lights around us to help.

I wish I'd known that we were going to leave and be out in the dark; I'd have grabbed a flashlight before leaving. Just as the thought entered my mind, Hope and Sirona cupped their hands together, as though holding hands, and light built within them. I watched in amazement as they let go of each other, and a thousand little magickal fireflies fluttered out from their hands and around us, lighting up the back room in a dazzling display.

"Wow," I whispered as a few of the fireflies flew lazily around me. "How did you do that?"

"We've done it before," Sirona said as they stepped closer to me. "It was something that Brutus and Emily said we could do, and we just had to try it out."

"You'll need to teach me that," I remarked and turned back to the bookshelf, now able to see exactly what was around the bookshelf so that I could see if I could find the latch.

"What are you looking for?" Hope said as she stepped closer as well. They were both still in their clothes from the day, and the wrinkles in her shirt were pronounced under the lights of the fireflies. "You look kinda funny doing that."

"I know," I growled, hating that she was pointing out the exact thought I had been thinking a little while ago. "But, this is where I went in my dream that I was telling you guys about earlier. There was a door here."

Sirona rolled their eyes. "Sure," they exaggerated the word. "There is a door there… but it sure looks like a bookcase to me."

I stopped for a moment, turned around, and smacked them in the arm before muttering, "Don't be a jerk."

They laughed as I went back to my searching, but almost immediately, I felt something as I put my hands around the bookcase again. I started to tug on it, slowly at first, not wanting to look any funnier than I already did (*thanks, Hope, for making me even more self-conscious than I already was*). Still, when I felt it slowly moving, eventually it gave way as I pulled harder.

They both must have realized that I had something because they grabbed onto my shoulders and helped pull me back as I continued to tug at the bookcase. With our joint effort, the bookcase gave way, and we stumbled backward as it arched outward towards us, not once touching the floor underneath it. We stood behind the open bookcase door, pulling our bearings together when the smell came. *Oh, that smell!* The scent from the room drifted out and overwhelmed us, as the heavy scents of herbs came fast and hard. *What in the world was that?* We looked at each other before I took the first step to peer around the bookcase.

I peered into the darkened room, wishing for it to light up a little more, and the magickal fireflies fluttered around us and answered my unspoken request as they entered the room, lighting it up from within. I stepped around, Hope and Sirona still hanging back, obviously working through everything that was happening, and walked into the room. It was a smaller room, although not horribly small. There were tons of herbs around, and I thought back to the store that I'd almost gone into within the last several weeks.

They knew Damien McGregor very well because he had jars upon jars on the shelves, each with a label on it. From anise to dried yellow carnations, and everything in between. On the other side of the room was another shelf, but this time it was filled with candles, gems, and stones, as though he had been, no, I reminded myself, he used to be a practicing witch, or are they called warlocks or wizards, like in *Harry Potter* or *Charmed*?

I heard Hope and Sirona move toward me as I walked over to the little table that he had set up in the middle of the room. There were all kinds of things on it, like several candles, specifically blue, purple, and white. Then, there was a blue candle in the middle, wrapped with a plant. I tried to name it just by looking at it, but I had no actual knowledge of plants. Hope and Sirona joined me at the table, seeing a mortar and a pestle with herbs sitting inside it.

"He was a practitioner," Sirona said in awe as they gazed around the room. "A very well-stocked and active practitioner by the looks of it," they continued.

"What is all of this, do you think?" I asked, still learning and thinking of the book, wondering if any of this was in it.

"It looks like a protection spell," Hope said as she pointed out the spell written down next to the candles, something that I had missed during my inquisitive glance around the room.

The writing on the spell looked vaguely familiar. As I bent down to look at it, I didn't want to pick anything up, fearing that something awful would happen.

Call upon Soteria, for she is the protector from unseen enemies. The paper began. It called for an item to be charmed, but I hadn't seen anything around the room except the herbs and other magickally inclined materials. As the directions went, I followed along to see that Damien had almost everything there, but the charm. Finally, it read, *In the name of SOTERIA, by the power of the Source, Protect from harm.* It repeated that last sentence six times with a circle around it, which I took as a sign that the practitioner needed to walk around the charm six times. *The Keeper of this charm* was the last words before the parchment ended.

"What do you think this all means?" I asked as I stood up to see that Sirona and Hope were both searching through the items on the shelf, with no trouble whatsoever with touching things. *Maybe I was just too cautious at times.*

"Well," Hope sighed. "It looks like your Mr. McGregor was a practitioner of the arts. How well did you know him?" She glanced over at me from the shelf with all the gems on it, a pinkish gem in her hand.

"Honestly, he was one of the people I spent a lot of time around but didn't really know. His bookstore was my hideaway during high school, especially once I found out that I'd been adopted." I stopped as I thought about the information I'd learned yesterday about him coming here soon after I'd been adopted. "Well, that and apparently he used to come to my birthday parties as a kid. My dad and he were friends. I'd always come in every year after I turned six and get a book for free from him for my birthday." I trailed off. "My mom mentioned that he moved here about a year after they adopted me. I don't think he has any other family... That's why the bookstore has been closed off still, well, that and I own it now."

We looked around the room a little more before deciding that we should head back to my apartment. We walked carefully out of the secret room, shutting the bookcase slowly behind us, and Hope and Sirona headed back toward the front of the store. I was nervous about walking out the front door of the building and opted to go out the back so that no one would see us and have to try and explain how we ended up inside. When I mentioned this to both of them, they stopped and looked at each other. "That makes sense," Hope and Sirona readily agreed, and we walked back towards the back of the house, but this time heading slightly to the right inside. As we neared the back door, I remembered all of the little fireflies that were floating around us.

"Hey, guys, what about these firefly things around us?" I asked, quickly stopping in front of them to turn around. "Are they just going to keep going with us or what?"

Hope and Sirona exchanged a glance, and then Hope clapped her hands, and the fireflies disappeared, leaving us alone in the dark. We walked the rest of the way, gently touching the walls around us to help us get to the door that was now darker than night. As we reached the door, I felt around it to see if there was anything on it that could possibly go off when we opened it. Not feeling anything, I gently open the door, only for it to be opened wide as it was yanked out of my hands. I shrieked back into Hope and Sirona, hoping to the goddess that we would all be safe with whoever was on the other side of the door. I could feel something evil lurking nearby.

Eighteen

"Who's there?" A female voice demanded as we exited the house. A female voice that I easily recognized, and I groaned out loud. "Lillie, es que?" the voice continued, and I knew there was no point in trying to hide myself because only Jo would recognize me from my groan.

"Yeah, it's me, Jo. But I got Hope and Sirona with me. Don't arrest us, please?" I begged as I came closer to the open door and stood in the dim light of the patio where she could see me. I could distantly see a guest house in the backyard, *that's where the evil felt like it was coming from,* but I couldn't focus on it as Jo grabbed me by the arm.

"What are you doing at McGregor's house?" she demanded as she pulled me out into the alleyway. I quickly stuck the book log into my pants at the back so she couldn't see it. Hope and Sirona followed at a snail's pace behind me.

"Well, about that, you see..." I trailed off, trying to think of how I was going to get myself out of trouble on this one.

If it was Alec, I could smile and flirt my way around it, or at least I was pretty sure that I could have, but with Jo, I was going to have to offer her something of the truth.

That was one of the things that had always drawn us together during high school, the need for truth. "I got some interesting news today and had to investigate it." Going with the least conspicuous one was the best at the moment.

"And why couldn't that wait until the morning? Or, I don't know, maybe call me before you broke into a *house*, of a dead man. Now I'm going to have to get Alec involved and tal vez incluso mi abuelo."

I shuddered, and she could feel the shudder as she held onto my arms. "Please, don't call Alec or Abuelo, Jo. I can explain it."

"Yeah, well, you can explain why you also brought people with you that you even had doubts about at the beginning," she said, with no filter whatsoever as she exposed my worries from before.

"That's because we're her siblings," Sirona said blandly, as though speaking to a small child. "We just discovered it tonight." They stood near the guest house that McGregor had in the back, and I ached to tell them to step away from it. Hope stood a ways away from them as she took in my conversation with Jo, understanding dawning in her eyes.

"Yeah," Hope continued, and internally, I was surprised that neither of them had been offended by my initial lack of confidence in them. But by the look in Hope's eyes, I knew that this was a conversation we were going to have later, without Jo around, and my earlier elation fell. "She told us that she inherited everything from McGregor and didn't feel comfortable going to look at the house by herself." This time, the word was emphasized towards Jo, and I could feel her flinch. "And she thought that you and Alec, or Abuelo, or whoever it was, would think it suspicious if she inherited the house after finding him dead, so she wanted to see if there was anything in the house that could clear her name without trouble." Hope did not know Alec or my history with him, but obviously, she had read between the lines. I held up the file weakly, showing Jo that I had indeed found something in the house. Jo rolled her eyes and gestured for us to move toward the police cruiser that sat in the alley nearby.

* * *

Cold sweat trickled down my neck as Jo opened the back door of the police cruiser with an ominous creak. I glanced at Hope and Sirona, their faces pale and tense, before we wordlessly climbed into the cramped space. The air was thick with unease, like a fog that refused to lift. As the door slammed shut, I couldn't help but feel trapped, like an animal backed into a corner.

"Everyone okay back there?" Jo asked her tone all business as she started the engine. I tried to shift in my seat, but there was no room for movement; my knees pressed painfully against the divider between us and Jo.

"Define 'okay,'" I muttered. My heart raced as I thought about the danger that lurked in every shadow, waiting to strike again. This whole secret room, along with the voice from that day, everything seemed to be falling around me. I could feel my anxiety spike as we drove, each moment another one that led to us possibly being taken to the police station.

We needed to solve this murder quickly. I wasn't sure how much more danger I could handle. My thoughts were a whirlwind that raced through my head. *What if we didn't solve this in time? What if the real killer struck again? And why did I have the nagging feeling that something much darker was lurking beneath the surface of this whole mess?*

Cramped didn't even begin to describe our situation in the backseat of the cruiser, despite the comforting smell of worn leather and polish that lingered in the air. My siblings and I were practically sitting on each other's laps, and I could hear Hope's heavy breathing as she fought to keep her composure. Sirona leaned against the window, their expression a mix of annoyance and concern.

"Sorry, Lillie," Jo said, catching my eye in the rearview mirror. "But you know I'm just trying to keep you safe, right? I can't just leave you and," she paused. "What are your names again?" she said, although I was pretty sure that she remembered them.

"Hope Glisson and Sirona Santos," Hope responded, her breathing quickened for a moment as she said it. *That was curious.* Did the police make her more nervous than she had mentioned before?

"Right, Hope and Sirona, well, I can't leave the three of you outside of a crime scene, or a place associated with one, when I caught the three of you leaving from it. As I said, es sospechosa."

"I'm telling you that I'm not involved in his death, Jo. I just got back home two days before he died. Why would I do it?" I demanded, anger heating my blood at the thought that Jo might even think that I was part of the murder.

She sighed. "Yeah, I know, Lillie. So, we need to figure out what is going on so that I can keep you safe."

Safe felt like a foreign concept these days. But I nodded anyway, feeling a flicker of gratitude towards Jo for sticking by me during this whole ordeal. If nothing else, it was nice to have someone in my corner who wasn't related to me, even if there was the slightest thought in her head that I could be involved in it.

"Can we get out of here already?" Hope snapped, her patience wearing thin. "The sooner we figure this all out, the better."

"Agreed," Sirona chimed in, their eyes darting to the darkened streets outside.

"Alright, let's get going," Jo said, glancing in the rearview mirror. The cruiser lurched forward, and I clenched my jaw to keep from biting my tongue.

Here's hoping we can find some answers, I thought, sending a silent prayer for help to whatever cosmic force might be listening.

The car ride wasn't long, and I thought for sure that we were heading toward the police station, sure that Alec would be called, considering that he was running the case regarding Damien McGregor. Hope and Sirona sat, hands clasped together, next to me, unspeaking, and I wondered how much more horrible things could happen to me. I'd just found out that I had siblings, and now they were in the back of a police cruiser with me.

Yes, technically, it was Hope who had taken us to the house, but I had to wonder if it was the magic that had brought us there because of my dreams. *Would this have happened if I hadn't let them spend the night?*

"Alright, everyone out," Jo announced as she pulled the cruiser to a stop outside my apartment building. I was relieved to finally escape the cramped confines of the car and stretch my legs, but even more relieved when I realized that she was going to work with us instead of taking us to the police station. Yet, the thought of what lay ahead weighed heavily on me as though

I knew that things were only going to get worse.

We all climbed out of the vehicle, and I couldn't help but notice the tension in the air as we approached the entrance. Jo, ever the protector, guided us cautiously up the stairs and into the apartment. As we stepped inside, the familiar scent of lavender and vanilla filled my nostrils, offering a small sense of comfort. I'd recently added a wax warmer to give the place a sense of home, and the smell was exactly what I needed in that moment to relax.

"Alright, let's get down to business," Jo said firmly, her emerald eyes piercing through me. "We need to figure out what's going on, and we need to do it fast."

"Agreed," I said, my voice wavering slightly. "But first, can we just take a moment to process everything? Maybe grab something to drink?"

"Fine," Jo conceded, nodding towards the kitchen that we had just walked through to get to the living room. "But let's not waste too much time."

"Right," I sighed, leading the way to the kitchen and grabbing a few glasses from the cupboard.

"Look, Lillie," Jo started, her voice softening as she leaned against the counter. "I know this is all overwhelming, but lo resolveremos. We need to stick together and keep our wits about us."

That's easy for you to say.

"Thanks, Jo," I whispered, grateful for her support, although the book began to stick to my skin as it lay against my back. "I just hope we can find some answers before it's too late."

"Yo también," she agreed, giving my hand a reassuring squeeze. "Now let's get back in there and start piecing this rompecabezas together."

With a deep breath, I nodded, clutching the glasses tightly in my hand. Whatever lay ahead, I knew that at least I wasn't facing it alone. I could feel my heart pounding in my chest as we settled into the living room, our makeshift interrogation area. Jo's unwavering stare bore into me like a laser, and I had to fight the urge to squirm under her intense scrutiny. Hope and Sirona sat nearby, exhaustion playing on their faces.

"Alright, Lillie," she began her tone authoritative yet laced with concern. "I want you to tell me everything you know about this murder. Leave nothing out."

"Okay," I replied, taking a deep breath to steady my nerves. The book cut into my waist and I fought the urge to pull it out. "But there really isn't much more to tell, I've said a lot already."

"Wait," Jo interrupted, holding up a hand. "Don't even try that card with me. Before you start denying anything, I want you to think about something for a moment."

"Um, sure. What?"

"You could be next, Lillie. You were the one to discover the body and you heard a voice the day before that sounded threatening. You could be in danger, so don't hold anything back, and let's go over it all over again from the beginning. Especially now that there is even more that is involving you in this."

"Okay." I took a deep breath, mentally preparing myself to recount the scene I had stumbled upon weeks before. As I relayed the details, I could feel my heartbeat quicken, my breathing becoming shallow. It was as if I were back at the bookstore, surrounded by the chilling atmosphere and the scent of death, even though time had passed, it had remained with me.

Jo listened intently, her expression unreadable, occasionally interjecting with a question or request for clarification. She had a knack for asking just the right questions, ones that forced me to dig deeper and reveal information I hadn't even realized I'd been holding onto. She asked questions about why we were there tonight so I mentioned the will again but not in too much detail because even I wasn't quite sure about it. I even mentioned the altercation to Jo at the lawyer's office that I'd had with Maddison.

When I finally finished speaking, Jo leaned back in her chair, her gaze never leaving mine. "And you're absolutely certain that you didn't take something out of his house that could relate to the crime?" she asked pointedly.

"Positive, the only thing I had was the file I gave you," I replied, my voice shaking slightly. "I was too scared to even move, let alone think about tampering with anything else that could be considered evidence."

A nagging voice echoed in the back of my head about the book that was currently wedged in between me and the back of the seat.

"That file was everything?" she asked, eyes pinning me down.

I nodded again.

"Bueno," Jo nodded, a hint of relief flickering across her face. "Now, is there anything else you've been keeping from us? Anything at all that might help clear your name?"

I hesitated, biting my lip as I considered whether or not to mention the book log I'd found hidden in the desk. *Would it make me look guilty? Or would it provide us with the lead we so desperately needed?* It dug into my back and tempted me to tell her about it. Finally, I broke.

"Actually," I said, my voice barely more than a whisper. "I did find something else tonight." I reached behind me and pulled out the worn ledger, its pages filled with cryptic notes and names from my pajama bottoms.

Jo's eyes widened as she took the book log from me, her fingers tracing the edges of the pages. "Dammit, Lillie, this could be evidence. I just asked you if there was anything you took that could be evidence." She sighed as she looked through the pages and then back at the three of us. "But, it could also be a game-changer. Hmm," she murmured, her excitement barely contained. "Veamos qué podemos encontrar."

Together, we pored over the contents of the log and the different copies of his last will and testament, our minds racing to make sense of the clues hidden within.

My determination to solve the murder and clear my name grew with each passing moment, fueled by the knowledge that time was running out. The rain pitter-pattered against the window as it continued to drizzle outside, the early light of the day creeping up upon us.

"Look at this," Jo said suddenly, pointing to a particular entry. "Does this mean anything to you?"

I stopped and looked at the entry. Hope and Sirona were out cold on the couch, leaning into each other.

"Maybe?" I whispered, my heart pounding in my chest. I sensed that we were on the verge of a major breakthrough, and I couldn't help but feel a glimmer of hope.

"Keep talking, Lillie," Jo urged, her voice steady and strong. "We're going to figure this out together. Te lo prometo."

I thought about the voices I'd heard that day; there had been at least five voices, of which three I had known, and the entry she was pointing to had several names that had just been initialized or were single-named. They gradually got sloppy until the one that Jo was pointing at was a conjumble of letters, or so I thought. "Hmm, maybe, I don't know, Jo," I muttered, looking over at Hope and Sirona again.

"Okay, that's enough," Jo said suddenly, eyes flashing red as she slammed the log closed and rose to her feet. "I can't shake this feeling." She looked over at my siblings, and they shifted slightly in their sleep as her exclamation jostled them. "There is something there, specifically about those two, that just doesn't make sense."

I sighed, wondering if Jo was feeling left out, considering that she'd just learned that I had sisters, no *siblings*, I reminded myself, when we both used to consider ourselves sisters to each other. "Jo, what are you talking about?" I asked, my voice louder than hers with alarm at the sudden change in her demeanor.

Hope and Sirona both jumped, awoken from their sleep by my loudness, which was hard to ignore, and looked at both of us.

"Your siblings, Lillie. Hope and Sirona," she paced around the small apartment, her green eyes narrowed in suspicion at Hope and Sirona. "It's awfully convenient that they just happen to be your siblings after Alec and I had been investigating them. And neither of you thought to mention it?" she pointedly asked them.

They looked sleepily at each other. "You were investigating us?" Sirona asked sleepily.

"Like you didn't know. I know that some other officers pulled you aside. Alec wanted someone unrelated to the case to look into you, and you answered them too readily. Demasiado prolijo."

"Jo, we just discovered it yesterday, I didn't even think that it could be relevant," I tried to explain, but she held up a hand, silencing me.

"Maybe it's not, or maybe it is. But right now, no confío en ellos," she declared, her voice firm. With that, she grabbed the book and headed for the door.

"Jo, wait!" I called out, scrambling after her as she exited the apartment. My fear for my siblings and our precarious situation propelled me down the hallway and out into the cold night air. Hope and Sirona stared at me as I trailed after her. "Jo, please," I pleaded as I caught up to her at the police cruiser. "You have to listen to me."

She turned to face me, her expression guarded but not entirely unsympathetic. "What do you want, Lillie?"

"Look, I know you have your doubts about my siblings, but they're not involved in this mess," I insisted, my words tumbling out in my desperation. "And I didn't think about calling you after the meeting with Ida because I was still in shock over it, and then with the information Mom and Dad gave me, I just got lost in all the details. Besides, I don't want to tarnish your reputation in the police force, considering that we were just starting to be friends again."

Jo's stern façade softened slightly, and she sighed. "Lillie, I understand why you kept your secrets. But I need to be sure todo el mundo is on the right side here." I could tell that she wanted to do what she knew was right for her job, but she also wanted to show support to me since we had just renewed our friendship.

"Jo, please," I begged, my pleading eyes meeting her green ones in a silent plea for understanding. "I'm doing everything I can to solve this murder and not get my own name involved in it. I need you to trust me."

"Muy bien," she agreed reluctantly, her gaze never leaving mine. "But Lillie, if I find out there's something you're not telling me, nuestro trato se cancela."

"Deal," I agreed, relief flooding through me as I stared back at her, determined to prove my innocence and protect my siblings from harm. "Jo, there's something else I need to tell you," I said, my voice shaking as I glanced around the dimly lit street, nervous to admit to someone about my dreams. The shadows seemed to dance in the flickering glow of a nearby streetlamp, casting an eerie pallor over the scene.

"¿Qué es?" Jo asked, her eyes narrowing as she assessed me closely.

"Ever since this whole thing started, I've been having... these visions or dreams or whatever you want to call them. The dreams I mentioned aren't exactly just a recollection from the day before or even the day when I found Damien McGregor. It's like they are memories from the past, but they're different, somehow. Unnatural. Like I'm living the dream as someone else." My hands were trembling, and I clenched them into fists to steady myself.

"Visiones? Lillie, are you sure you're not just stressed out?" Jo's skepticism was clear, but I could see a glimmer of concern in her eyes.

"Stressed? Of course, I'm stressed, but that doesn't change the fact that these visions feel real like I'm living them as someone else. And I think they're connected to the murder, somehow, someway."

"Alright, let's say I believe you. What do these visiones have to do with el caso?" Jo crossed her arms, waiting for an explanation.

"I don't know for sure yet, but I think they're leading me to the truth. They're showing me clues, pieces of a puzzle I need to solve in order to understand what really happened with McGregor." My heart pounded in my chest as I stared at Jo, willing her to understand.

A frown creased Jo's brow as she processed my confession. I could see her weighing the trust she had in me against the strange circumstances I was presenting. For a moment, everything hung in the balance. "Okay, Lillie. I'll help you follow these… visiones. But we're doing this for the book. No more secrets, got it?" Jo's stern tone left no room for argument, and I nodded gratefully.

"Thank you," I whispered, tears pricking at the corners of my eyes.

"Júrame, Lillie," Jo said, her gaze locked onto mine. "Swear that you'll be honest with me from now on."

"I swear," I promised, my voice resolute. "I won't let you down, Jo." Out of the corner of my eye, I swore I saw movement, but when I looked toward it, there was nothing there.

"Alright, Lillie," she said finally, pulling my attention back to the unswerving glint in her piercing eyes. "I've got your back on this. But if we're going to do this -" she waved between us, "- then you need to know that I'm putting my career on the line for you, so no more hiding things from me. Understood? No more trying to 'protect my reputation.' Sé lo que hago."

I nodded. "I understand, Jo," I agreed, my voice barely louder than the sigh of relief that escaped my lips.

"Bueno." Jo nodded, her face set in an expression of undaunted truth. "Now let's finish going through that registro de libros and see if it can help us piece together what's been happening." We returned to the apartment, our resolve bolstering our steps.

Our focus was now on solving this mystery and clearing my name. I grabbed the book from the living room and told Hope and Sirona that they could go to bed if they wanted to. I walked back into the kitchen with it, placing it in the center of the table as Jo made some more coffee. As we settled down at the dining table, leaving Hope and Sirona in the living room, the book log spread out before us, an odd feeling settled over me. It was as if time itself held its breath, waiting for some crucial revelation.

"Here," I said suddenly, pointing to the conjumble of letters, finally able to read the single name scrawled across it. Richard. "This is the last entry before mine, it's just blank besides the name. See, because here is mine with the letters LLK, wait, is that what he wrote down for my birthday present?" I paused and looked at the name of the book next to the letters in my name, family, before shaking my head and continuing, "This was just before I came up. It had been a male voice." I confirmed.

Jo leaned in closer, studying the entry with a furrowed brow. "Interesante. It's not much, but it's a start. We'll look into this guy first thing this morning." She glanced at the clock above the door, noticing that it was already well after five in the morning.

"Thank you, Jo," I whispered, overwhelmed by gratitude. "You don't know how much this means to me."

"Hey," she replied, giving me a rare, genuine smile. "That's para qué sirven los amigos."

It felt like we were finally making progress. *This was it* - the first tangible lead in the case. Little did we know, however, that this single name would lead us down a path darker and more twisted than either of us could have ever imagined. And at the end of that path, something waited. Something that had been lurking in the shadows all along, its presence hidden just out of sight, patiently biding its time. But for now, all we knew was that we were one step closer to solving the murder. We had no idea of the storm that lay ahead.

Nineteen

I walked Jo out to the cruiser a while later, the sun now heading overhead as seven o'clock rolled around. Hope and Sirona had taken my advice and gone back to bed, taking both bedrooms this time, after Jo came back in. And, well, she hadn't really apologized to them, but she hadn't made it more awkward, so I gave her brownie points for that. As Jo took off down the street, I heard a car door open and close behind me, and I whirled around. I was nervous and jumpy now, knowing that there was some connection between me and McGregor's death. However, fear need not appear at this moment because it was Alec. He strode toward me, his face a mask at a distance, but as he got closer, I knew I was in for something.

Come back, I called to my fear, *I do need you. I don't want to be alone with him.*

Finally, Alec and I stood face to face, mere inches apart, as he stopped in front of me. The air between us crackled with tension as if it were charged with an electric current. No matter what, there was always some current that ran from him to me, and I shuddered as the electricity ran up my spine. My heart raced as I tried to swallow the lump in my throat. His shaggy hair framed his deep blue eyes, which were haunted by a mixture of pain and weariness.

"Talk to me, Lillie," Alec snapped, his jaw clenched. "Why are you hiding from me now? We used to tell each other everything."

"What are you talking about, Alec?" I went with the innocence card. *How long had he been out here?* I wondered if he was accusing me of hiding things from him. Could he have been the shadow that I thought I saw earlier?

"Don't play games with me, Lillie Bell. I know that Jo was here; she just drove away. Not to mention that she was here for several hours. You told me that you were going to be honest with me about what you knew or remembered from Damien McGregor's death." He deadpanned, his fingers clenched into fists as he tried to contain his anger.

"Things have changed, Alec," I replied defensively, averting my gaze to avoid the intensity of his stare. "You can't just waltz back into my life after nine years and expect everything to be the same. I've changed, and there are things about this that I don't think you need to know."

"Dammit," he swore. "Changed or not, this is my case, Lillie! You are supposed to be working with me on this case if you have anything! You can't keep important information from me. I shouldn't have to seek out Jo every time that you remember something to get answers." His frustration was palpable, and I could see the veins bulging in his neck as his anger leaked out even further.

"Fine," I spat out, finally meeting his eyes again. "You want to know what I've been hiding? I left during high school because I found out I was adopted, and I didn't want to burden you with my problems on top of your own." The words slipped out inadvertently, and I groaned internally. I hadn't meant to tell him that. Things had taken a turn here that I hadn't intended to ever talk to him about; therapy or no therapy, he was better off without me.

Alec's eyes widened, and he took a half-step back, clearly not expecting that bombshell. He ran a hand through his shaggy hair, looking completely lost for words. "What? Lillie, why the hell wouldn't you have told me about something like that?"

"Because it wasn't just about me back then!" I snapped, my chest tightening as years' worth of unspoken pain bubbled to the surface. "You were already dealing with so much crap, Alec. Your dad…I couldn't add more weight onto your shoulders."

He shook his head, disbelief etched across his face. "So instead, you sit there and tell me that I'm going to end up like him. Really, Lillie? That's going to make everything better? Lil, you don't get to decide what I can or can't handle. We were supposed to be in this together – thick and thin, remember?"

"Of course, I remember!" A bitter laugh escaped my lips. "But sometimes, Alec, life doesn't work out the way we plan. Do you think I wanted to leave town without saying goodbye, to push you away? To lose my best friend and the person I cared about most?"

"Then why, Lillie?" His voice cracked, his hands balling into fists at his sides. "Why did you push me away when all I wanted to do was to be there for you?"

"Because I couldn't stand the thought of dragging you down with me. I did it because no one here deserved to have such a wasted nothing like me around, I thought that my own parents didn't want me so why should anyone else," I whispered, tears pricking at the corners of my eyes. "And now look at us – stuck in the past, fighting over something that happened almost a decade ago."

Alec stared at me, his blue eyes swimming with a mixture of hurt and confusion. It was clear neither of us knew how to bridge the chasm that had grown between us.

"Alright, Alec." I sighed, wiping away a stray tear. "You really want to know the whole truth? Fine. I was afraid you'd hurt me. I thought that if my parents didn't want me and you had your issues, we were bound to just destroy each other." But I didn't mean it. The words ached to leave my lips but I bit down hard, not wanting to give him more than I was willing to give.

The words hung heavy in the air between us as if they'd taken on physical weight. Alec's face paled considerably, his eyes widening as he took a step back from me.

"Y-you really thought I could become like him?" he stammered, his voice barely above a whisper. His mouth hung open slightly as if he couldn't believe what he'd just heard. It wasn't difficult for me to imagine the thoughts racing through his head – or the pain my confession had caused. It was like high school all over again and my heart cracked even more. I thought the pain from Jack leaving me had destroyed it, oh no, it was nothing compared to how Alec looked right now. As though everything I said to him in high school hadn't truly hit until this moment.

I shifted my weight from one foot to the other, my gaze dropping to the ground. "I didn't want to take the chance, Alec," I admitted softly. "After everything we'd been through, after all the times we'd promised each other that we'd always be there…I couldn't bear the thought of losing you like that. Especially knowing that we both had our own traumas, I couldn't chance it."

"Jesus, Lillie." Alec ran a hand through his shaggy hair even harder, I could see the tension in his fingers as his deep blue eyes searched mine for some kind of understanding. "How could you think that about me? I mean when you said it back then, I thought you were just saying it to get rid of me. That you wanted to go out into the world without having some small-town hick boyfriend holding you back. But, really, that's what you thought?"

"Because I was scared!" The words burst out of me like a dam breaking, raw and desperate. "You have no idea how hard it was to watch you suffer, to see you fighting so hard to keep your head above water. And then there was me, drowning in my own problems, trying to stay afloat when all I wanted to do was sink. I just wanted to disappear into a hole where no one could find me."

Alec stared at me, his expression a mixture of shock and disbelief. But beneath the hurt, I could see something else flickering in his eyes – a glimmer of understanding, perhaps, or maybe even forgiveness. And at that moment, I knew that despite the pain we'd both been through, there was still a chance for us to heal and move forward. Together.

"God, Lillie," he murmured, his voice cracking with emotion. "I never wanted you to feel that way. I never wanted you to be afraid of me."

"Neither did I, Alec." I met his gaze, my heart heavy with regret. "But fear is irrational, and it makes us do things we never thought we were capable of. Besides," I said, tears welling up in my eyes. "I just didn't know how to say it." My voice trembled as I struggled to find the right words. "I had just found out that I was adopted. I… I didn't want to overload you with my own troubles."

Alec's eyes widened, and for a moment, he looked as if I had slapped him again. His fists clenched at his sides, and his jaw tightened as anger replaced the shock and hurt on his face.

"Are you kidding me, Lillie?" He spat the words out like they tasted bitter. "Did you really think that I couldn't handle that? That I was so weak, I'd crumble under the weight of your problems?"

My heart ached at his words, but it wasn't just about him. "No, Alec. That's not it at all. It's… the whole point I left was because I didn't want you to put me first. You've done that forever, even when things were going horrible for you at home, and I wanted to put you first for once when we left. I wanted you to feel as important as you had always been to me. But I couldn't – not when I learned the truth."

His anger seemed to falter for a moment, replaced by a flicker of confusion. "So you ran away? To protect me?" The disbelief in his voice stung like a slap.

"Yes," I whispered, my voice barely audible. "I thought it was the only way."

We stood there, our emotions laid bare, each of us trying to make sense of the past and the decisions we had made. It was painfully clear that neither of us had truly understood the other's actions or intentions, and now we were both left grappling with the aftermath.

"To protect me?" Alec scoffed, his voice dripping with sarcasm, his anger still hot under the surface. "From what? From knowing the truth about you? From being there for you when you needed someone the most? If that's your idea of protection, Lillie, then you should really rethink your priorities."

"Rethink my priorities?" I shot back, the hurt in his words fueling a fire inside me. "I was trying to save you from drowning in my problems while dealing with your own! How is that not putting you first?"

"Maybe," he retorted, his voice icy and distant. "But you didn't give me a choice, did you? You just decided it was best for me and left without looking back. You never even gave us a chance to see what could happen."

"Us? There is no 'us,' Alec!" I spat, tears pricking at the corners of my eyes. "There hasn't been an 'us' for nine years because I changed, I wasn't just Lilliann Luella King anymore. I wasn't even sure if that was my name!"

"Changed?" He took a step forward, his blue eyes blazing with anger. "You're still running away, Lillie! And now you're running from me, too! You're going to Jo about the case that I'm in charge of! So tell me, what exactly has changed?"

"Everything has changed, Alec!" My voice cracked with emotion as the weight of our history pressed down on me. "But you're so hung up on who I was back then that you can't see who I am now. And maybe—"I paused, swallowing hard "–maybe that's why I'm afraid to let you back in. Because I'm not sure you'll ever truly see me."

"Is that what you think?" He shook his head, disbelief written all over his face. "You think I don't see you, Lillie? I've been seeing you every day since you walked out of my life, wondering what I did wrong, what I could have done differently."

"Stop making this about you!" I cried, my voice breaking. "This isn't about your guilt or your regrets, Alec – it's about me trying to protect myself and the people I care about!"

"By pushing them away?" He took another step forward, his anger barely contained. "Do you really think that's the answer, Lillie? Do you honestly believe you can keep everyone safe by shutting them out?"

"Maybe not," I admitted, my voice barely more than a whisper. "But it's all I know how to do."

For a long moment, we stared at each other, our words hanging heavy in the air between us. And then, without another word, I turned and walked away from him, my heart pounding in my chest and my vision blurred by tears.

As I stumbled up the stairs to my apartment, my steps growing heavier with each passing moment, I knew that despite everything we had said and everything we had been through, the gulf between Alec and me was wider now than it had ever been. And as much as it hurt, I couldn't help but wonder if maybe, just maybe, it was for the best.

Twenty

I gently closed the door behind me as I entered the apartment, finding Poe standing on the counter by the door, waiting for me. I sniffled and pulled myself together.

"Are you okay?" he asked, leaning into me as he purred.

I wiped my eyes, trying to clear my face from lingering tears. "Yeah, I'm fine." *or I'm going to be, anyway.*

He continued to convey his love for me, purring and rubbing against me, until I picked him up and walked into the living room with him. I rubbed the soft fur between his ears as we sat down on my chair facing the street. It was still early in the morning, but I was thankful that I didn't need to start getting ready for my tutoring sessions. I'd barely slept.

Both Hope and Sirona were still sleeping, and I didn't want to wake them up, especially after Jo had accused them of being part of Damien's murder, even though there was no objective evidence to show that.

We'd gone through the book log, and the only evidence that I saw was the name Richard. I wanted to say that the name sounded familiar, but the only Richards that I knew were students under the age of eighteen, and I didn't want to believe that a child would kill an old and defenseless man.

I absentmindedly petted Poe as I watched the streets below me begin to fill up with traffic, never really noticing when I was no longer watching it as I fell asleep.

* * *

Sometime later, I woke up to the gentle rousing from Hope and blinked my eyes in surprise to see both of them standing in front of me. I jerked as I woke up, suddenly filled with a sense of urgency and dread as I took in their appearance, noting that their clothes were still slightly rumpled, but they didn't look as haggard in the eyes as they had when Jo left the apartment the first time this morning. I took in a couple of deep breaths, reminding myself that nothing bad was going to happen.

"Hey, sleeping beauty," Hope whispered, not wanting to startle me any further. "Sirona and I were going to go back to the hotel to change and come back, but we didn't want to leave without telling you first."

"That's a lie," Sirona grumbled. "I totally was down for leaving without telling you anything."

Hope shot them a nasty look, and Sirona snapped their mouth shut.

"Oh," I said, suddenly feeling very awkward. "That's okay. I mean, you don't have to come back if you don't want to." The words tumbled out of my mouth before I even thought them, and then I felt like slapping myself in the face. *Why would I tell them that?* It's like saying that I don't want them to be my siblings. Hope smiled, and Sirona rolled their eyes.

"I mean, I know you guys have a lot of things to do in order to find a place to start your business and get a place and whatnot."

"Yeah, well about that," Sirona said, ignoring the look that Hope shot them. "I told Hope that the bookstore would be a great spot for us, prime realtor spot and whatnot… We're going to see if we can get it, but we are going to wait a little longer for the investigation to be over since we're being investigated as well."

I could hear the anger in their tone at being investigated, and I sat up, knocking Poe off my lap in my hurry to explain.

"It's not like that," I said. "Well, maybe, kinda. I was at the bookstore and heard someone's voice the day before he died, and when asked if there was anyone that the voice could have matched, I told Alec that I wasn't sure and that I'd met several people over the last couple of days that could have possibly been it. I didn't know."

I rushed through it all, feeling as though if I didn't explain it, Sirona and Hope would surely decide that they didn't want to be related to me at all.

"It was the first day that I had a tutoring session, and I heard the two of you arguing. It sounded kinda familiar to me, and I just told Alec that maybe it could have been one of you. But I didn't know you then, so please don't hold it against me. Besides," I begged. "I may be getting the bookstore since I inherited everything from him."

A look crossed Sirona's eyes that I couldn't decipher, and I was dying to ask them about it, but decided against it. I didn't want to lose the only people that I could actually say I was related to because I hadn't known who they were in the beginning.

"It's fine," Hope said at the same time that Sirona muttered, "You could have just asked us."

They looked at each other, eyes rolling, before looking back at me. "We get it," Hope continued. "We just hope that you will continue to get to know us and know that we were not involved in the murder. We are here because we were trying to find you."

I smiled and nodded. "Oh, and please don't take Jo seriously. She gets that way whenever she feels threatened by someone taking her place in my life. She did it when we were in high school, and I kinda had hoped that she outgrew it when I moved away, but I guess that she didn't. She'll get to know you guys and we'll all get along great," I said with as much enthusiasm as I could muster.

They both nodded and looked at each other again, an awkward silence falling over all of us. I kept glancing at them and back down at Poe, who slept on peacefully despite the fact that I'd dropped him on the floor in my haste to apologize to them. I chuckled at the fact that he was still out, breaking the silence, and both of them looked at me questioningly. I pointed Poe out to them, and they both laughed as well, easing us out of the silence.

"I was going to say," I muttered hesitantly. "If you both wanted to, you could stay here in the apartment for a while to help save money while you're looking through houses. It could give us a chance to get to know each other as siblings instead of just friends," *like we'd been doing.* I let the words hang there as I gauged their reactions. "Or maybe if I do get his house as part of the will, you guys could move in with me?"

Hope's face lit up with an all-encompassing smile at the thought of getting to know each other as siblings, while Sirona's was a mixture of hope and distrust. They still didn't quite trust me after finding out that the police had investigated them, and I couldn't blame them for not believing in me. "Anyway, you could leave some clothes in the spare room if you want until you decide. That way we could have overnights and whatnot until we're more comfortable with each other," I offered as a compromise.

They nodded, and then Sirona looked at Hope with that look of come on. Hope laughed a little before turning to me and unexpectedly hugging me.

"I'm so glad that we found you, Lillie. It was like it was always meant to be," she said, the words disappearing into my hair since she was slightly taller than me. I tried not to cry again as she stepped away, and Sirona stepped forward. Sirona looked at me and then, somewhat awkwardly, gave me a quick hug before stepping back.

"I know that you're our sibling and third witch and whatnot, but I'm more of a realist than Hope. I don't think that you really trust us right now, and I'm not sure that we completely trust you, but I'm willing to give it a try. I got it from the bookstore owner." They paused. "What was his name again?" They paused as though trying to put me off of something that was on the tip of my tongue, but gone again as they shook their head. "Anyway, I want to see what all is in there." I nodded in understanding before I looked at my watch in dismay.

"Oh, crap," I exclaimed. "If you could come back as soon as possible, I can show you what I know about the book, but I'll have to get ready for tutoring at two." I paused this time, looking them over before continuing, "I really want to show you something interesting about the book, so please hurry."

They nodded, gave me a quick hug again, and headed toward the kitchen.

I followed them, intending to walk them out and start my morning routine as soon as the door closed behind them. I had about an hour and a half before I would need to leave to get to the library, and I was sure that they'd be back within the next forty-five minutes. As the door slammed shut, I heard the soft meowing of Poe as he looked up at me from the floor. His golden eyes were pleading, and before he said a word, I knew he was asking for a bowl of tuna. I sighed and quickly went through my morning routine, including grabbing his tuna before rushing off into the shower.

* * *

By the time I'd dressed and come back out into the kitchen, I could hear the heavy footsteps of Sirona as they came up the stairs to the door.

I flung the door open in my haste, excited to see them, knowing that they had chosen to come back to get to know me despite learning that I had a hand in the investigation that they had inadvertently gone through with the local police department.

"You guys came back!" I jumped up and down in my excitement as they entered the apartment, carrying a small bag in each of their hands. "I was half afraid that you would decide not to come back," I said in a quiet voice as I walked out of the kitchen, Hope and Sirona following. There was a quick, tiny chuckle from Hope before they both looked at me and pulled me into a hug.

"You're our sibling, and we want to give you a chance," Hope said as I smiled through the sweet embrace. They pulled back and said questioningly, "Where are we staying?"

"Do you mind sharing the spare room for now?" I asked, thinking of how I would need to make changes to the apartment or how we would make things work once the whole inheritance issue had been dealt with.

Hope smiled, agreeing with the room before they walked to the spare bedroom and put their clothes away. As I went to grab the grimoire from my room, Sirona hung back, a look in their eyes that said that there was something that they needed to say but weren't sure how to do it. I paused, walked over to them, and put a reassuring hand on their shoulder.

"Is everything okay?" I asked.

Sirona refused to meet my gaze.

"Sorry about the whole 'maybe they're murderers?' thing. You're my family… I really do want the opportunity to get to know you.

A hiccuped cry came from Sirona's lips, and as Hope came back from the bedroom, we both stood by them as we looked at each other in hopelessness.

"Sirree," Hope said, leaning down to look them in the eyes. "What's going on?"

Sirona shook their head, pulled in a deep breath, and wiped their eyes quickly. "It's nothing, I promise," they said as they pulled away from both of us. "I need to use the restroom. I'll be right back." They walked away, a quickness in their step that showed that there was more going on than what had been admitted.

"Do you know what that's about?" I mouthed to Hope, as she stood straighter and looked at me. She shook her head, and I sighed. I didn't have any idea of how to be a sibling, but I was willing to try. I walked into the bedroom, grabbed the grimoire from the nightstand by my bed, and came back out into the living room. Hope was sitting down on the couch, and we both waited for Sirona to come out of the restroom.

* * *

Several minutes later, Sirona exited the room and walked toward where I stood awkwardly in the middle of the living room. As they neared, I placed the book down on the coffee table in the living room before telling them I needed some fuel to keep me going and was going to grab a coffee and something small to eat. They both nodded in agreement.

I walked toward the kitchen, grabbing a cup of coffee and a bowl of oatmeal, before coming back out into the living room. It had been silent when I'd gone out into the kitchen, but when I came back, I noticed that they had both moved and were now sitting on the floor where Hope had Sirona in a hug, no words exchanged, as the grimoire sat down in front of them.

I sat on the edge of the table, placing both dishes next to me before grabbing the book from between them. "Let me show you what I mean," I said, awkwardness filling my every movement. I didn't know how to help or even what to say to them at the moment. I opened the book when both sets of eyes landed on me and proceeded to tell them about what had happened to me the first couple of days that I'd had the book.

The book still had many blank pages, but each day, more and more pages with words appeared. I'd shown them the spells that I'd learned about projecting my charm onto those around me, as well as the original letter that had scared the bejesus out of me. They took it all in stride, and as I finished, Hope held her hand out to take it, but Sirona was on point and was able to rip it out of my hands before flipping through the pages.

"So, you're telling me that our magick just does things for us?" Sirona asked doubtfully.

"Oh, don't be so doubtful, you know that random weirdness has happened to you, too." Hope brushed off their negativity and grabbed the book out of their hands. I grabbed my dishes and stepped away from the coffee table in case it turned into an all-out war. As I sipped my coffee, oatmeal already finished, Hope and Sirona finally shared the book between them. I could hear the faint ringing of my phone from the other room where I'd placed it on the charger during my shower.

I rushed into the bedroom, landing on the bed, as I grabbed the phone and quickly swiped to the right to answer the call. By the ringer, I knew that it was Jo and thought maybe she had more information for me about the name that we'd found earlier.

"Hello," I stammered, trying to catch my breath from the jaunt into the room. "Do you have something new, Jo?" The question quickly followed as I sat up in bed.

"I don't know what new things you expect from her," a voice on the other end said, and my heart sank; it wasn't Jo. "But I guess I should have expected that something was going on between the two of you since you'd avoided giving me any answers earlier," Alec continued. "But that's not why I'm calling."

"Why are you calling from her phone?" I demanded, knowing that they were partners, but I would have thought he'd call from his own phone, considering that I had to give it to him because of the investigation.

"I'm calling because Jo's been assaulted," Alec said. This time, I could hear the sadness weighing heavily in his voice. "I know you were the last one to see her, so I needed to see if there was anywhere that she had told you that she was going."

A cold shiver ran through my body, hearing that Jo had been hurt.

"What do you mean, hurt?" I demanded, and the sound of rustling clothes and stomping feet echoed around me as I looked deadly into space. "How was she hurt, Alec?" I said.

"She was beaten," Alec said, pain dripping from his voice. "They don't know if she's going to be okay. She was pretty badly hurt."

Tears started pouring down my face. Hope and Sirona rushed around me, confused looks echoing between their faces, as I took in big, gasping breaths. "When did this happen?" I asked.

"Sometime between when she left your apartment and about forty-five minutes ago," he replied, and I could hear his corresponding deep breaths as he attempted to calm down while he told me. "She was found on the riverfront trail about 30 minutes from your place if you walked there, but the cruiser was nowhere in sight."

"Where is she now, Alec?" I asked, worry echoing through the phone to him, "Where is she?" I said again when he didn't answer.

"She's at the hospital, in the ICU. I don't think they'll let you in to see her, though, Lillie. She's really bad."

The tears came freely now, and Hope and Sirona wrapped their arms around me, not knowing what was going on but feeling my pain nonetheless. "I don't know anything, Alec. We'd just looked at the book log, but she took that with her."

I started doing my breathing exercises to calm down.

"She didn't have anything like that with her when they found her," Alec mused. "I'll keep an eye out for it. Be careful, Lillie, this person could come after you next."

I nodded, as though he could hear it, and hung up the phone. Letting it drop limply from my hand, I dropped my head onto my siblings' shoulders.

"What's wrong?" Hope asked, always the first one to try to take care of me.

"Yeah, tell us," Sirona demanded, trying to make sure that everything was okay.

I shook with silent tears as I told them that Jo was in the ICU, since they had heard part of the conversation already. They both gasped in shock and hugged me tighter before I lightly pushed at both of them to let me go. They did, and I stood up from the bed, staring blankly into space.

"You should go check on her," Hope suggested as she stood up next to me. Sirona nodded in agreement, although her face said otherwise, and I nodded complacently.

I went to grab my purse from my room to head to the hospital. When I walked by the clock on the wall, it read: one forty-five, and I stopped dead in my tracks. There was no way that I could go to the hospital right now. I had a tutoring session with Jameson. Both of them looked at me in surprise at my sudden action before I explained I had to be at the library in fifteen minutes.

"You should go to the hospital," Hope said, trying to reason with me.

"There's no way I could get to the hospital, spend time with her, and be back before my next tutoring session at the café," I argued, thinking of the special request that Anahi's parents had made to fit her into my schedule today.

"Why do you need to go to work today anyway?" Sirona asked as they walked into the kitchen to make a cup of coffee for themself. "It's not like you need to do any tutoring anyway."

Hope nodded in agreement as I stood in the middle of the living room, staring at the clock. "It's the summer, for goddess' sake!"

"Yeah, well, I've got three tutoring sessions and one of them is new. I had a family come up to me at the library earlier this week asking if I could fit their daughter into my schedule and even paid me extra to make sure that I would take her on since my scheduled times were already full," I mumbled, thinking of the little girl that was going to meet me at the café. She was entering the sixth grade the following year. She had already been identified with a disability, so even though she had received summer school for the last several weeks, her family wanted to keep it going even when the program stopped. It wasn't a long tutoring session, only 30 minutes, but it would still feel like forever.

"Just beg it off," Hope said. "It's not like the parents wouldn't understand. It's a small enough town that they probably know already that someone in law enforcement had been hurt enough to be placed in the hospital."

"But that's not who I am," I said, rubbing my arms nervously. "I should go and still do the tutoring sessions that I have for today. I mean, there are only a couple of hours and three different kids." I tried to work out a compromise, a reason that would justify going in for my shift.

"Fine," Hope said with exasperation. "But then go right after work," Hope demanded, and I nodded, feeling as though this was all my fault. She took one look at my face before demanding that I stop blaming myself.

"How'd you know?" I asked, looking back at her.

"Because it's the same expression that I wear," she said with a sad smile. "Everything will be okay, I promise. Go and do the tutoring sessions, finish what you need to, then go check on her. Meanwhile, Sirona and I will look through the grimoire." She paused and looked at Sirona. "Is that what you call it," she whispered to Sirona for confirmation, who quickly confirmed it, before she continued, "to see if we can find anything out that could be helpful."

Twenty-One

s I walked on autopilot to the library, my thoughts kept spiraling to Jo. Each worse than the last, as worry and dread threatened to drown me.

I didn't really register walking into the library, or waving at Mrs. Klusmeyer reading at the check-out desk, until I slumped into my seat at the table in the room I had reserved for tutoring.

Jameson sat at the table in the room, a book and a pile of papers scattered over the top of it, as his phone lit up his face in the dimly lit room. At first glance, Jameson would seem to the casual observer to be a relatively normal fifteen-year-old. At first glance, Jameson looked like most kids his age—acne on his cheeks, a bit of softness still clinging to his features, and clothes that clearly weren't chosen to impress anyone. His dark hair was longer than most of the boys I'd worked with recently, curling a little at the ends like it hadn't seen a barber in a while. Nothing about him stood out immediately, but that in itself made me pause. He wasn't trying to be noticed. Not loud, not stylized, not rebellious. Just… quiet.

There was something familiar about the way he occupied space… like he was always waiting to be dismissed or ignored. I'd seen that posture before. On kids who flew under the radar, who weren't struggling enough to flag intervention, but weren't thriving either. I wondered what his teachers had said about him the previous year, if they had said anything at all.

He had been the only child to contact me without a parent involved, asking for help to understand algebra, as he didn't want to seem 'stupid' next year. I cleared my throat, and he glanced up from his phone. "Oh, hey, Ms. K, whatcha doing?"

I laughed nervously, trying to push away the thoughts about Jo getting worse while I did my tutoring sessions, and sat down across from him at the table. "I'm doing okay," I said quietly. "Did you work on the papers I gave you for finding the slope from a graph?" He nodded and pushed a pile toward me.

"Yeah, although, why would I need to find the slope from a graph if there are already points that I can determine from the graph?" he asked, pointing out a particular problem.

I nodded. "I can get why that might seem frustrating," I agreed. "Slope is how we describe the steepness of a line. As we look at any slope, we can see that the line remains constant; there are no changes. But it can also tell you information about the direction of the line on the coordinate plane, so the slope can be calculated either by looking at the graph of a line or by using the coordinates of any two points on a line. I wanted to see if you could understand it by looking at a graph of a line, but today we're going to actually have two points to graph and then work on determining the slope from those points." I pulled some papers out from the bag I'd brought with me, and pushed a copy toward him as I grabbed out the graph paper that was in a separate folder.

"Do you remember the equation for finding the slope?" I asked, and we worked on the problems for the next forty-f minutes. It was a nice distraction from my thoughts and gave my brain a break from the constant apprehension that filled me.

"Excellent work, Jameson, I'm glad that you are catching on quickly," I said with a smile as my timer went off. "I'm sure by the time school starts in August, you will have a better grasp on algebra than you did previously."

He smiled nervously at me before thanking me for the time spent helping him. I grinned in response. "It's no problem. I really enjoy helping people understand math and reading or writing more."

He pulled the papers together, including a copy of the next set of problems for him to work on until we met again, before pulling his wallet out and passing me his payment for the session. I thanked him as I took the money and stood up. We parted ways, and I waved to Mrs. Klusmeyer again as I walked out of the library, thoughts of Jo hitting me full force as I landed on the pavement.

I walked toward the coffee shop, where I was scheduled to meet Anahi in around an hour. As I walked into the shop, I noticed that it wasn't that busy. There were probably only three or four other people in the lobby, and one of Linda's workers was manning the counter this afternoon. I was looking at the faces of the other patrons in the lobby as I walked up to the counter, only to do a double-take when I saw the man from several weeks ago. I gave the girl behind the counter my order, including two blueberry scones, and decided to go over and talk to him. This was my opportunity to apologize for my behavior and to do things that were outside of my norms. I waited at the end of the counter until my name was called, and thanked the girl for making everything.

Grabbing everything off the counter, I walked over to his table, determined, a coffee cup in one hand and several scones on a platter in the other, before placing the platter down in front of him. I smiled as I noticed for the first time that his nose was prominent and strong, but it was his ears that struck me as odd because they didn't seem to fit with his face very much. They were not symmetrical. One ear was slightly higher than the other. He thanked me as he reached for a scone, and I noticed the bruises forming on his knuckles.

"Ouch," I said, "That must have hurt. What happened?" I inquired, trying to find out something about this guy that would ease my nervous feelings about him.

"Oh, nothing," he was quick to reply. "I just got a little too into my workout routine this morning, that's all." He smiled, trying to put me at ease, but his quick response did nothing to ease the tense feeling that I had about him.

I smiled and gestured towards the seat opposite him, ignoring the warning flags that were going off in my head. "Do you mind if I sit down?"

He gestured toward the chair congenially, and I pulled it out as I sat down.

"Thanks."

He smiled warmly at me, and I told myself that there was nothing weird about him; I needed to stop worrying. "I really wanted to apologize for how I behaved towards you the first time we ran into each other."

He laughed, and my anxiety eased a little as he smiled.

"It's fine," he said. "I wasn't in the best of moods that day either. I had come here looking for someone, but couldn't find them like I had hoped to."

Well, that explains why he was looking up women in the area on the computer that day. I thought to myself, and another piece of icy dread melted, and I relaxed a little more in my chair.

"I'm sorry that you haven't found them," I said, reaching for my scone. "Do you think you are close to finding them?" I asked, taking a delicate bite out of the scone before lifting my cup to take a sip.

He frowned, shrugging his shoulders, before answering, "Not yet," he said, "but I think I'm close."

"Oh, that's great!" I replied, after swallowing the coffee, "Who were you looking for?"

"I was looking for my granddaughter. My son died when he was young, and I'd hired a private investigator to find his widow and child, as she took off before I could do anything to help them out."

I nodded, thinking of how that must have really impacted him as a grandparent.

"I'm sorry that something like that happened to you," I said, sincerity in every word. "I'm sure that you'll find your granddaughter soon." I tried to think of anyone in town whom I knew who was raising a girl by themselves. We chatted for a while longer about the city and its people. He was an excellent conversationalist. Soon, however, I heard the bells ringing as Anahi and her family walked in through the door.

"Oh, I'm sorry," I exclaimed as I stood up and grabbed my bag from the floor before taking my cup up from the tabletop. "I have to go, I have a tutoring session." I smiled, intending to grab the platter to drop it off in the bucket of dishes on the side of the room, before he reached out and placed his hand over mine.

"It's no problem at all," he said, with a warm smile. "Thank you for keeping an old man company and providing me with such a delicious pastry. I'll put the plate up, go on and meet your student."

I thanked him and walked toward Anahi and her parents.

"Hi there!" I said with a bright smile, waving to the little Hispanic girl, whose long, brownish-black hair was plaited in two braids, and her brown eyes widened as she looked at me. "My name is Ms. King, but you can call me Ms. K if you'd like."

She smiled softly and reached out to shake my hand.

"Hi," she whispered. "It's nice to meet you."

Her mother smiled as I looked up at them. "Thank you so much for taking her on as a tutee. It means so much to us that you were willing to help her out even with your full schedule."

I smiled warmly at her. "It's my pleasure to be helping her reach her full potential! We're going to go over to that library-ish corner over there to work on some of the things that you mentioned during our interview. I'll set a timer and we'll meet up again in about forty-five minutes if that works for you?"

Both her mother and father nodded, giving Anahi a gentle nudge toward me, before walking over to the counter to place their order. I gestured toward the table in the corner, and Anahi followed me at a slow pace as I walked to the table and put my cup down. She sat down across from me, and I pulled out the folder I'd made with work for Anahi during our tutoring session. We were working on both reading and writing as well as math, so the idea was to give about fifteen minutes to each section to touch on all three aspects.

"Anahi," I began, pulling out a monitor reading passage for her to read, "I understand that you have some issues with decoding words, do you mind if we do a couple of reading passages so I know where you are?" She nodded, almost numbly, as though she was petrified to be doing the work in the coffee shop. I smiled warmly at her, trying to dispel her nervousness. "No one is going to pay any attention to us in here; they're all here for other things, I promise. This is going to be easy and go super fast for you, okay?"

She smiled this time, and I could see it reaching her eyes. "Okay, I can do that." She grabbed the passage that I held out to her.

"Great, I'm going to have you read the first time, without looking at it first, for about a minute as I follow along with you," I began. "Then, the second time, I'm going to have you reread it, for a minute, but I'll give you a little time to look it over, then, okay?"

She nodded, and we began our session.

* * *

We read aloud from a short article about weird animal facts, and she stumbled over the word *camouflage.*

"Break it down," I said, drawing a line with my finger under each syllable. "Cam… ou… flage."

She squinted at it. "Cam-uh-flaj?"

"Pretty close! The *ou* says 'uh' here, and *flage* is said like 'flahzh.' It's French."

She wrinkled her nose. "Why does English steal so many words?"

"Because it's greedy," I whispered, and she giggled.

Next was math. I slid over a laminated place value chart, and she worked through a few multi-digit subtraction problems with regrouping. When she paused, I asked, "What's your first step?"

"Line up the place values. Make sure the numbers don't wander," she said, reciting the phrase I'd drilled with her last week.

I nodded. "Exactly. Keep those decimals in their lane."

Her pencil moved faster after that, and she finished the page with only six corrections, a good baseline to start. We celebrated with a sip of her iced cocoa and a break to people-watch.

Finally, we opened her writing notebook. She'd been struggling to get past the first sentence in her paragraph assignments, according to her parents, so today we focused on using sentence stems to build momentum.

"I don't know what to write about vacations," she mumbled, fiddling with the edge of her page.

"How about starting with this: *One of the most surprising things about my last vacation was...?"*

She wrote the stem, paused, then added: *when we got lost and ate pancakes in a gas station.* Her grin spread like sunlight across the booth.

"That's amazing," I said. "Now tell me more. What made it surprising? What kind of pancakes?"

She didn't stop writing for a solid three minutes.

By the end of the forty-five minutes, her posture was taller, and she didn't shrink when I told her how proud I was.

Her parents came up to the table.

"Ready to go, Anahi?" Her father asked, and she smiled at him.

"Sí, papa," she said, and I handed her the folder I'd made for her to work on at home until our next session.

"This is the folder that you can work on with your mom and dad, and we'll go over it next week," I said, as a way to also let her parents know, even though I'd told her that she'd have a folder to work on each time in between sessions. They all thanked me, and her mother sent me the session fee via PayPal. As they walked away, I noticed that the old man was still at the same table we'd been at, sipping away at another cup of coffee.

I looked at the time to see that it was close to five and knew that the hospital's visiting hours would be closing soon. I pulled out my phone and called to check on Jo to see if she was awake yet. Talking with the nurse's station, I was able to find out that she was still out of it for the most part and that they had recently extended visiting hours, so I had time to finish my last tutoring session.

I sighed with relief as I put my phone back into my bag.

Gage was already flipping through his GED workbook when I slid into the seat across from him. "You're late," he said with a smirk, tapping his pencil against the margin of an algebra problem.

"Technically, I'm right on time," I countered, pulling out my notes. "And I brought highlighters, so I win."

He chuckled but didn't miss a beat. "You okay?"

"I'm fine," I said, glancing down at the page—but the words blurred for a second. I tried to refocus, walking him through a couple of factoring problems, but I could feel his eyes on me more than the math.

"You keep checking the door," he said after a minute. "If you need to be somewhere, just go. I've got this section. It's mostly review anyway."

I hesitated, caught between guilt and gratitude.nb

"Seriously," he added. "You're usually laser-focused. This is… not that."

I managed a small smile. "I owe you."

"You already paid me in highlighters," he said, waving me off. "Go check on whoever it is. I'll text if anything explodes."

"Please don't let anything explode."

"No promises."

Twenty-Two

I noticed that Hope and Sirona came running in through the front of the coffee shop.

"Lillie," Hope screeched as she came to a resounding stop at the table. "Lillie, we found it!" She held the book up with a triumphant grin. I shot her a look of shock at her displaying the book so openly, and she understood my look quickly as she dropped the book back down into her stomach and then stage-whispered to me, "We found it, Lillie, we found what was in that room."

Sirona rolled their eyes as they stood behind Hope and glanced around the shop. I followed their eyes as I stood up, noticing that they were looking toward the menu. The old man had a newspaper in front of him now. *Hmmm,* I thought, I swore he didn't have anything with him a little while ago. I shook it off as I motioned for Hope to hand me the book. She handed it over, as covertly as she could, before smiling at me.

"I put a ribbon in the spot where we found it," she whispered, and then looked at the board. "Oooh, can I order a coffee while I'm here?" she asked, looking around to see if I still had a kid nearby. I shook my head, letting her know that my tutoring session was over and that we could grab a drink before I headed to the hospital.

I rolled my eyes as I laughed, "Well, duh, go get one." She and Sirona had gotten the same drink every time that we came, and it was the same one that she had given me that day I'd replaced the coffee I had accidentally spilled. I nodded, still holding the book close to me. Her smile was like a light bulb going off, illuminating her face. She bounced over to Sirona, and they walked up to the counter.

I brought the book up and placed it in the middle of the table, waiting for them to return. Sirona pulled a chair up for them as they sat down at the table, and I gestured toward the book that lay between us, flipping it to the page they had marked with the ribbon. In the background, I could hear the old man get up and put his dishes in the container as he headed toward the door. That's when I realized that I had never exchanged names with him. He made sure to go around the back of Hope and Sirona so that they couldn't see him and didn't even say a word or wave goodbye as he left.

"That's so weird," I said out loud, trailing after him as he walked out of the building and down the street until I could see him no more.

"Nothing," I lied. "Let's take this to my apartment. I don't want to talk about it here—not with half the town in earshot."

* * *

Once Hope and Sirona had their drinks, we walked around the *Riverfront Coffee and Cream* to my apartment in the back. It was the closest thing around that would provide privacy, and it would give me a chance to get ready before I went to see Jo.

"Okay, so tell me what you found."

Hope started telling me about how she'd found out information about our mother and grandmother, and boy was it a doozy.

"So, apparently, the book is a family heirloom. Passed on from matriarch to the next generation. A couple of generations back, our grandmother, well, I don't know what she did, but someone cursed her and the following generations," Hope paused for a breath before continuing, "There's a page in here where she wrote a letter to our mother."

I paused at that. *Why didn't I see that before?*

"What's in the letter?" I asked, letting the slight annoyance that I didn't see the letter go in favor of understanding more about our history. Sirona shifted anxiously in their chair.

"See," Hope said. "There isn't anything specific in the letter to Mom… It just says that she made a decision out of love, something that caused someone to curse us, and that she was sorry that she didn't get to see her grow up." Hope sniffled. "It sounded like grandma blamed herself, but at the same time knew that she had done the right thing. She said that the curse would impact Mom too, that she had to keep her children safe so one day we could break the curse."

The word caught my attention…

"Children?" I asked, clearly questioning the word. "Like she knew mom would have more than one child?"

Sirona nodded this time, biting their lip as Hope turned to the page in question, pointing out the word to me. I tilted my head as I read through the note, seeing that it had the word children on it, and frowned.

"How did she know, though?" I wondered.

Hope and Sirona shrugged.

"I mean, Poe did mention I was the youngest of three sisters, so maybe it's a hereditary thing? Or maybe it is the magickal bloodline thing…" I questioned, then shrugged it off. "Is there anything else?"

Hope nodded, turning to another section of handwritten pages that, upon second look, seemed to be a diary of sorts.

"Mom used this as a diary for a while," Hope said, an emotion coloring her words that I couldn't identify.

"Okay," I dragged out the word when Hope didn't say anything for a while.

"Well," Hope said, a sigh echoed in the words she spoke. "She ran away when she got this book. It just appeared to her one day at the school library, a bright flash of light, and she took it home."

I nodded, it sounded a lot like how I'd gotten the book at the bookshop that day, not so long ago.

Hope pointed out something in the book, and I leaned down to read it. *I brought you home with me today. Something is telling me that I should take you with me. I hope I won't get into trouble at school, I couldn't stand it if Dad found out.*

I looked up, "Dad?"

Hope nodded.

"It continues," she said, flipping to another page in the book. *I went looking through the papers in Dad's study today. I don't think I should have... A* tear stain made the words expand as I continued. *I found my birth certificate, but it has a different date than the one I've been celebrating. It doesn't have either Mom's or Dad's name on it.*

"What does she mean?" I asked, looking up from the section I was reading, feeling closer to our mother than I had since I found out. Hope sighed, as though dreading the idea of explaining what she meant. Sirona looked bored as Hope and I talked about everything.

"He kidnapped her," Hope said. "At least, that's what she believed. It's in a later section. She found papers showing that he had paid a tremendous amount of money to change her birth certificate and to make it seem like her 'mom', had given birth to her in a private birthing area where there would be no questions about her."

I gasped. "No!"

She nodded, and I looked over at Sirona to see that the news didn't seem to be as shocking to them as it was to me. Maybe because they already read about it.

"Yeah, she ran away soon afterward, according to the rest of the entries she wrote. She seemed to have been writing in the book every day until my birth, and then it stopped."

"But why?" I asked, not understanding why it would stop at Hope's birth. She shrugged, and the book seemed to heat under our hands. I jerked my hand away and gazed down at the book in shock. This was developing news.

Echos of concern about Jo circled in my head, but I knew that she was safer in the hospital than I was at this moment, especially considering this news. I absolutely needed to figure out how our magick connected with McGregor's death because something just ate at me that they had to be connected.

"Do you think it disappeared when you were born?" I asked, trying to figure out how the book had ended up with McGregor.

Hope shrugged, and we began discussing various theories about what could have happened, which led to the book going blank.

Sirona remained silent for much of the conversation as Hope and I exchanged ideas back and forth. They sipped their tea silently, eyes bouncing between us before I turned and looked at them.

"You know something," I said with finality. "You've been silent, twitchy, and generally not yourself since we discovered that we were related, so what gives?"

Sirona looked at me with wide eyes as they leaned back in their chair.

"¿Qué quieres decir?" Their accent was thickening as they spoke. "I've done nothing wrong."

Hope glanced back and forth between the two of us before frowning. "She's right," Hope said after a moment. "You are acting strange."

"Ay, díos mío, you two are going to be a nuisance, aren't you?" they said, as though trying to change the subject.

"True," I said with a little nod. "I don't like feeling like I'm missing something important, and you are too silent for your own good."

Sirona paused, closing their eyes, and took a deep breath in. "I know something. Eso es verdad."

They opened their eyes, and the intensity of it jolted through me as they planted their eyes on Hope. "Remember when I told you I was going to go see a tarot reader because I wanted to understand our magick better?" Hope nodded, a little uneasily, as though the memory of this tarot reading had been bad.

"I lied when I told you that the tarot reader couldn't tell me anything," they admitted, shame coloring their words. "They told me that my grandfather was still alive and looking for us every day. I started to investigate our mother more and found her birth certificate, the true one, and was able to find out who our grandfather was."

They paused, as though this was a heavyweight they had been carrying for years. "I even took us to see him, but I didn't want to tell you. I thought you were still mad about finding out that Mom had died and left us alone." Tears welled up in the corners of their eyes.

A dawning feeling of understanding filled my stomach as clues from my conversation with my dad echoed around me.

"You came here to find our grandfather, didn't you?" I asked.

Hope swung her head around to look at me. As though she didn't know what to say. Sirona nodded, and I pulled the pieces together for Hope out loud.

"You came to meet McGregor," I said, a feeling of deep longing joining the understanding in my stomach. They nodded. "Because you knew he was our grandfather."

All those years of him giving me books for my birthday, making friends with my mom and dad, and being a solid presence in my life, even when I was a spoiled brat. It was because he knew I was his granddaughter. Anger rose out of nowhere. *How could he not tell me that?* I thought as tears began to fill my own eyes. "He had the book in his store because it came back to him after Mom died."

I pictured McGregor again…his worn boots, that gruff laugh when I misquoted a line from a classic novel. He always smelled faintly like pipe tobacco and old paper. *Grandfather.* My grandfather. How could he keep that from me?

So, whoever killed him wanted the book from Mom. Did that mean that someone else knew Mom was a witch?

Sirona nodded solemnly, and the world went silent.

The apartment felt smaller after that conversation, like the walls were listening. I mumbled something about needing a minute and slipped into the bathroom, locking the door behind me.

The silence hit me first. No humming of the coffee pot, no distant buzz from Hope's speaker, no questions hanging in the air about our mother or the grief we still hadn't named. Just the echo of my own thoughts—loud and unrelenting.

I sat on the closed toilet lid and tried to breathe past the tightness in my chest.

Magic had dragged me deeper into this world every day since I returned. *One spell, one reveal, one ancestor at a time. Empowering? Maybe. But isolating too.* Because no matter how much I wanted to lean on Hope and Sirona, I couldn't shake the feeling that I was the variable none of us fully understood.

My ADHD brain wasn't helping. Jo was in the hospital. Alec's voice still ringing in my ear. Hope seemed to be holding back more. Sirona's been twitchy all day. *And me?* I was just trying not to drown in everything new: new job, new apartment, new magic… new truths.

There was a soft scratch against the door.

"Give me a minute," I called out, voice rougher than I meant it to be.

Another scratch, then a familiar, sarcastic mrrrow.

"Poe?"

The handle jiggled slightly before his little shadow slinked in through the gap I hadn't latched properly. He headbutted my leg and stared up at me, judgmental as always.

"Traitor," I muttered, reaching to scratch behind his ears.

He blinked slowly, then turned and padded back toward the door like a feline oracle. Message received.

I stood, gave my reflection a once-over, and opened the door.

Hope and Sirona were back on the couch, the grimoire cracked open between them again. Sirona's fingers were lightly tracing a page, their brow furrowed. Poe leapt up beside them and flopped like he'd never moved at all.

"Everything okay?" Hope asked, not looking up from the book.

"Define 'okay,'" I muttered, stepping closer. "But yeah. I'm back."

I looked between the two of them; clearly, they had some words while I was trying to regulate. Sirona looked distraught but was pulling themself together while Hope was angry but making peace with it.

"Look," I said, "I know that you guys have been together a lot longer than you've known me, don't let whatever is going on with me make your situation worse." I felt horrible thinking that they were fighting over something that I caused, even inadvertently.

"No," Hope said, looking at the book, "we are supposed to be together, I know it."

Sirona nodded in agreement. "I shouldn't have kept the truth from Hope. That was my own fault."

I swallowed, looking between the two of them.

"Are you sure?"

Hope gave a slight smile. "Yes, we're sure. Now, let's figure out what's going on with this book so you can go check on Jo."

Twenty-Three

So, while we couldn't prove it yet, the one theory we all agreed on was that the book was a family heirloom—one that only responded to the magick in our bloodline. That had to be why it revealed itself to me that day in the bookstore. After the heaviness of everything we'd just uncovered about our mother and McGregor, I needed a break, something lighter, something that reminded me this wasn't all grief and secrets. So I asked Hope and Sirona to show me what else they had found in the book. They flipped through page after page, pointing out strange spells, long-forgotten hexes, and half-translated curses I'd never seen before. Eventually, they landed on a page about charm magick, and it echoed exactly what we'd seen in that hidden room.

"It was a charm that he was trying to make in there," Sirona said as they traced the words that were a repeat from the paper on the table in that room. "He was trying to make a charm of protection for someone -" they paused, trying to think of how to phrase the following sentence before continuing, "- a protection charm that we think was meant for you." They looked at me with such intensity that I scooted back in my chair.

"A protection charm for me?" I asked, clearly confused about why I needed a protection charm.

"That's what we were thinking," Hope continued, "although, like you, we haven't quite figured out why you needed a protection charm." As Hope stirred her coffee, looking at me and the book the entire time, "But there was something there that he thought someone needed protection from, and you are his granddaughter. Or at least one of his granddaughters." She finished with a tight laugh.

I opened my mouth to argue the fact and then stopped. She was right, there weren't many people that McGregor could have had a good connection with. I mean, yeah, he had his nephew and Maddison that you could say that he wanted to protect, but then why would he have given me the house if he hadn't known? So, while the logic was sound, I didn't like it. I took a deep breath and glanced at the time. *Crap, visiting hours end in less than twenty minutes.* I realized with a start.

"So, you're heading to see Jo now, right?" Hope asked, leaning against the table as I reached down for my purse. I paused and looked at her as though she was insane for insinuating that I was going to do anything else.

"Of course I am, I need to make sure she's okay after everything…" I trailed off. I didn't want to say anything about Alec at that moment. The truth of the matter was that I was still processing what had happened between us this morning, and then with his call about Jo, I didn't know where my feelings were. Hope nodded in understanding as we picked up the cups from our drinks and carried them over to the crate where the rest of the dirty dishes from patrons were stored.

Sirona followed us at a slower pace, obviously still dealing with the guilt of not having told Hope the reason they came to Clearwater in the first place. We walked to the front, and I opened it, holding it so that they could walk out in front of me. As Sirona passed, I gave them a light squeeze on the shoulder to try to convey, without saying a word, that it was okay and that Hope wasn't going to hold it against them.

The sun was starting to hit the edges of the mountains, and within a couple of hours, it would disappear entirely into the night sky. I thought about what I could do so that Hope and Sirona could get in and out of the apartment easily without creating another key that could impact my lease with Linda. Then I remembered that Hope could teleport and turned to her in the middle of the stairs as we walked up to the apartment. "Did you guys teleport out of the house to come downstairs?" I asked, "I mean, you could have just walked down too…" I trailed off and turned back around to finish our journey up to the apartment.

Hope laughed and then said, "No, I didn't teleport. We locked the bottom lock and then walked around. My teleportation is still kind of on the fritz. I never know if they will work properly or when it will happen, as you saw last night. Sometimes," she paused as we walked through the door into the apartment, "Sometimes, it happens while I'm sleeping, other times it is when I'm really emotional. I don't know if I can control them."

I nodded my head in understanding, although by the look of concentration on her face, I wondered if it was going to be on the fritz for much longer. I walked through the kitchen with a quick pat on Poe's head before gesturing towards my room, and they waved me away.

Not that I didn't love the smell of coffee after I was done tutoring, but I wanted something clean if I was going to see Jo. I dressed quickly, and another outfit was already ready for me on the dresser. *My magick was at play again.* I walked out into the front room, the question on the tip of my tongue when I saw Hope and Sirona leaning over the book again.

"Hey, does your magick ever get your clothes ready or anything weird like that?" I asked when they both looked up at the sound of my footsteps.

Hope nodded. "All the time. It weirded me out like nothing else in the beginning when I'd wake up and my clothes would be lying on my chair. I even accused Emily of doing it, but couldn't find any small holes in the clothes to confirm that suspicion."

Sirona looked at us both in confusion. "You're telling me that your magick chooses your clothes for you?" They looked back and forth between us, "Well, obviously it knows that I'm a fashion goddess because I've never had that happen."

"You guys never talked about your magick?" I asked, confused about why Sirona wouldn't know that about Hope.

"We did, but it was never anything specific. We just talked about how awesome it was to have magick," Sirona continued. "But my paints and supplies would always be ready for me when I'd get ready to paint, even before I was in the room. Like the exact colors and everything needed to make something amazing."

I frowned; magick was not as clean and cut-and-dry as television made it seem. "Maybe our magick helps us in the ways that best support how we live our daily lives?" I suggested as I walked toward them and sat down on the edge of the coffee table. "We'll need to test things out now that we're together," I said with finality.

They agreed enthusiastically, pointing to the book again.

"We'll need to look at the book together, I think, to get the best answers," Hope stated, as her hand landed on top of the protective charm spell that they had pointed out to me earlier. "But, I think that we need to finish that spell that our grandfather," she paused as though it was difficult for her to say it, "was trying to make for you." I nodded.

"He could have been making it for either one of you, too," I supplied, and she continued.

"Yeah, sure. But let's finish making the charm for you. Sirona said they had this awful feeling about something happening, and they've rarely been wrong." She gestured toward Sirona, who nodded in agreement. "I agree with them, something doesn't seem right."

"Okay," I said, "but how are you going to get all the stuff again?" I asked. "And what are you going to use for the charm?"

"Well, that's what we need from you," Sirona interjected, as they stood up to grab some coffee from the other room. We were all running on fumes at this point, but there was stuff to be done and no time to waste. "Do you have something special that you keep with you at all times?"

I sat there and pondered if there was anything special that I wore and never really took off. When I'd been in New York, it had been my engagement ring, but I didn't have that here. Then I thought of it, and I ran into the bedroom, pulling out my jewelry box. The coffee table's legs echoed hollowly on the floor as I stopped. Sitting on top of everything was my college graduation ring. I used to wear it every day until I got my engagement ring. I could go back to wearing it with no problem. I tried to ignore the other ring that sat nearby. I wasn't ready to face it just yet, even though it was a constant reminder of my childhood. I walked back to the living room, holding it up between my fingers, and Sirona jetted over to me, a cup held between their hands.

"Oh, what pretty we have!" they exclaimed. "Where did this come from and why haven't we seen it before?"

"It's my graduation ring, it was the first thing I bought with my own money when I got my job teaching. I wore it every day up until the day that Jack asked me to marry him, and then I retired it because I thought two rings looked trashy."

Hope rolled her eyes but looked at it as Sirona passed it over to her. "I'll start wearing it every day again after you put the charm on it," I promised them as I waited for them to respond.

"This will work," Hope said finally. "At least from what I understand from the reading."

I nodded, glad that there was something that they could use.

"Well, am I free to go check on Jo now?" I asked to focus on getting to the hospital before visiting hours closed. I knew that they used to be open until seven in the evening for visitors, but things could have changed in the last nine years. At least I had assumed that it might have changed. Besides, I didn't think that I needed to worry about how they were going to get the stuff for the spell. I figured that they would do their own thing, although I had a feeling that Hope was going to try to focus on her teleportation. She had just this look of concentration and determination earlier, which led me to believe that she would try to improve her power so that it was more useful to her. I couldn't imagine what it would be like to teleport away from a place randomly.

"Yeah, get out of here," Sirona told me nonchalantly, and I smiled at them. Grabbing my purse from the bedroom, I made sure that I took the key to the apartment off my set of keys. I hadn't talked to Linda about them coming into the apartment with everything else going on, so I was going to have to play this by ear until I could speak to her about it. Waving goodbye as I went out, holding out the key for them to see. I asked where they wanted me to put the key, reminding them that since I was leaving the key to the apartment with them, they should not lose it. I didn't want to try to explain that to Linda before I even talked to her about them moving in with me temporarily.

Hope gestured toward the kitchen, and I assumed that she meant by the door on the counter, so I dropped it on the counter as I opened the kitchen door. Poe followed me out of the apartment and disappeared, going wherever it was that he went whenever he left the house, skipping down the stairs and jumping every other step to get to my car faster. I was ready to see Jo and make sure that she was okay. Pulling my keys out, I unlocked my driver's side door. I hadn't driven my car since yesterday, when I'd left my parents' house, so I half expected it to argue with me when I went to shut the door behind me.

"Hallelujah!" I exclaimed as the door shut without a lick of trouble. "It's a miracle!" I put the keys into the engine, backed out of my parking spot, and headed towards the street. The hospital was towards the other end of town, and I was already halfway there in my mind.

Twenty-Four

I arrived at the hospital and parked in the parking lot. The large open windows of the hospital stared out at me as I stepped out of my car. It wasn't a huge hospital like the ones back in the city. It was a small hospital with only about twelve beds, so if anything significant happened, people would have to be airlifted to the next closest hospital. I walked up to the front entrance. The Emergency Room was located on most of the first floor; it was on the second floor that they had the ICU, ensuring that the Emergency Room beds remained empty. I waved hello to the registration person at the front as they pointed to their wrist to indicate that visiting hours were about to come to an end.

"I promise, I'll make it quick!" I said as I ran up the stairs to the second floor, stopping at the nurses' station as I came into the ICU.

"I need to know which room Jo Martinez is in," I stated as I leaned against the counter.

"Who?" the elderly lady on the other side of the counter asked as she looked at me.

"Oh, I forgot, Josephina Martinez. I was told that she was badly injured, and I just wanted to make sure she was okay."

The lady's white hair fell into her eyes as she nodded and then looked down at the computer. "Josephina is in room 211, but she's still out of it."

I exhaled in a rush; that wasn't good news.

"But remember, there are only 30 minutes left of visiting hours before you'll need to go."

I nodded, thanked her, and walked towards the room. Another nurse was coming out of it, this time it was a stocky young man with a full head of ginger hair, and I ran over to him.

"Hi," I said a little breathlessly, as I ran down the hallway toward him.

The man stopped his hand still on the doorknob and stared at me.

"Are you the nurse for Jo?" I asked. I stood in front of him, my brown hair falling around me and the small maxi summer dress, whispered against my skin as the motion stopped. He nodded, as though his tongue was stuck, and I continued.

"Could you tell me a little about how she's doing and what's going on?" I asked.

His brown eyes glazed over as though in a trance. I snapped my fingers in front of his face and he turned a bright red, almost to the color of his hair, and it traveled quickly over his face. In many ways, he was a bright tomato ready for the picking.

"Oh, yeah," his voice was a little squeaky as though he was still prepubescent before he coughed to clear his voice and continued. "Josephina was brought in this morning around eleven forty-five, unconscious." He started to tell me everything about what led Jo to be admitted before he stopped abruptly. "Wait, why should I tell you anything? Are you friend or family?" He looked me over again, and I wasn't sure if it was a look-over like he was interested or a look-over like he wanted to make sure that I was actually supposed to get the information. I mean she was part of the police department.

I felt like slapping myself in the head for not clarifying that when I first came up to him and then I felt like slapping him for not checking before he started saying anything but I stopped myself and smiled brilliantly at him, the wattage of my smile dazzling him as his eyes went out of focus for a moment. "Yeah, she's my best friend, practically family. I would have been here sooner, but I wanted to give it some time to make sure that she'd been taken care of first."

He shook his head and smiled at my explanation and then started going into what the ICU department was doing and what her prognosis was.

"What about family?" I asked bluntly, wondering if anyone would be in the room when I got there.

His smile deepened. "You just missed her grandfather, the police chief… You know him right?" he said, and I nodded encouragingly. "Well, he was here but had to leave. Something about trying to find her police cruiser."

I wondered if Alec was still trying to find it as well. That was probably where Abuelo had gone, considering that Jo had told me that they had gotten close after Alec joined the police force. I let the thought go as I turned and absentmindedly looked at the door, wondering if she would be awake, so I voiced my question. "Has she woken up at all?"

Despite the fact that the nurse at the station said that she hadn't woken up, I was hopeful that the nurse who had just been in her room would say differently.

He shook his head negatively, a pang of fear went through me at the thought that she was still out. "So the nurse meant what she said when she mentioned that she was still out of it? That Jo was just still asleep or is there a possibility of a coma?" I asked, concern oozing through my words.

He laughed at my question, as though it was extreme, before responding. "A coma really isn't a concern here." He laughed again, and I was beginning to hate the sound of it. "She was assaulted and badly injured but not to the point of a coma and everything looks, and sounds, like she will be waking up eventually."

I nodded and followed along with everything that he said, completely engrossed until something caught my eye.

That's when I noticed it. A flash of blue and peppered grey was in my peripheral vision.

It was the old man, he had on a nicely ironed blue button-up shirt, or I assumed it was button-up because I could only see the back of it as he came out of a room down the hallway, it was a different shirt than the one I had seen on him at the coffee shop earlier. I wondered why he was here, considering that he was a tourist and there hadn't been any other real accidents around that I would think called for him to go to the ICU. Unless he found his granddaughter? The thought passed my mind but it didn't feel right.

My brain could do nothing else but focus on him at that moment, everything else that the nurse was saying was lost as I took in a full head of peppered grey hair and the tall straight posture. The nurse's voice completely faded away as the man turned around and my suspicions were confirmed. *Now, this was too coincidental.* I thought to myself as he paused, seeing me standing there with a nurse before he continued on, walking right past me. I put a hand up to stop the nurse, not wanting to continue a conversation that I wasn't fully part of, as I turned around on a whim, my dress fluttering out around me, and called out, "Hey, Richard, how's it going?"

The man faltered for a second, missing a step before he shook his head quickly, almost invisibly before continuing out of the ICU. I turned back to the nurse, my mind full of thoughts like a hive swarming, and apologized to the nurse quickly for interrupting him.

"It's fine, although, I think you had the wrong guy," he said, pulling attention back to why I had stopped him.

"Yeah, I thought it was someone else I knew, but it's okay. So, do you think she'll be okay and can leave soon?" I asked, redirecting the conversation back to Jo and double-checking what I had heard previously.

He smiled and nodded. "I don't know how soon, but I would say that she should be okay from what I've seen during the last several hours." I smiled happily at him, and asked if it was okay if I went into her room, he nodded and I thanked him before stepping around him to go into the room. I stopped dead in my tracks, the door swinging shut behind me, as I saw Jo lying so helplessly against the hospital bed. Her face was black and blue and her right side was swollen over her eye. I rushed to the bed, reaching out to grab a hand before I noticed that there was a cast on her left arm and IVs ran out of her right. I stopped and dropped to my knees beside the bed, the tiled floor cold against my knees.

"Oh, Jo, I'm so sorry. I should never have involved you in this," I whispered as I brushed back the hair from her face. "I'm so sorry, I've gone and screwed everything up again."

I sat there for a few minutes just staring at her, my hand gently tracing the side of her face, trying not to touch anything too hard. It wasn't long before I realized that I had to call Hope or Sirona to tell them about Richard, as that man had to be Richard, and I was sure that he was the killer. The idea of calling the police, calling Alec, flashed through my mind briefly before it floated away. I mean I knew that I should have called Alec or the police department but there was something about this man that told me that he could evade the police if he really wanted to. Besides, I wasn't going to let Alec take care of this when I had powers at my disposal. I was angry enough about Jo getting hurt that I knew I could take care of it on my own, and screw the consequences. I had to tell my siblings about this guy though, because he had killed our grandfather and they had a right to know who it was in case he came after them next. He was shady, that was for sure.

I stood up from the floor and looked around for a visitor's chair before seeing it. I walked around to the chair, pulling it close to the bed, the soft beeping of her vitals echoed in the silence as I pulled out my phone from my purse.

I pulled up my contacts and dialed Hope's number first, I listened to it ring as I watched Jo's chest rise and fall with each breath, letting it calm my nerves even though they ran like lightning under my skin. Eventually, it stopped ringing and went to voicemail. *Well, that's odd.* I thought before hanging up and calling Sirona's phone next.

It rang and rang before it went to voicemail as well. *Well, crap.* There was no option now, I said a quick hello before I launched into the tale about Richard, making sure that they had a good description of him and what he was wearing right now so that they could stay clear of him, I mentioned calling the police station if they saw him and to ask for Alec, giving the number to them, just in case they didn't have it. I ended the message by telling them to be safe and that I would see them soon as I would be leaving in the next ten minutes or about that since visiting hours were almost over. I let the phone drop to my lap, falling into the open pouch of my purse, as I reached over and grabbed Jo's free hand in mine, needing confirmation that she was still there but careful enough not to touch the IVs coming out of it.

I held her hand, the defense marks bright against her skin, watching her breathe as rage boiled within me. I alternated between swearing to make it better and to get the person who did this to her, barely giving breath to my uttered curses. Now that I knew who it was, I was angry at myself for not going after him when I realized that it was him. My angry thoughts were interrupted by the sound of the door opening. I turned to see the night nurse sticking his head in. I took in a quick breath, trying to regulate my breathing, as he spoke.

"Hey, there, sorry visiting hours are over," he said softly, his eyes kind as he looked at us.

I nodded, dropping her hand softly to the bedside before standing up, pushing the chair back unintentionally. I heard it scrape against the floor and grimaced at the noise, my entire system on high alert.

"Thanks," I said as I walked closer to the door. "I appreciate the time that you gave me with her. Oh, by the way." My smile was genuine as I looked at him and that blush spread over his cheeks again, rising to his eyebrows. "I think that guy I called out to earlier is involved somehow, but I'm not sure. Can you keep an eye out for him? I don't want Jo to get hurt worse," I said with a small smile before telling him that I would be back tomorrow.

He nodded and opened up the door so I could walk by him. His blush was cute, in a weird sort of way, and I swore that I could feel his eyes as he watched my hips as I walked out of the room. I walked out of the ICU and downstairs. The floor was empty as the registrar had already left, and an eerie silence filled the floor, making my anger turn in the other direction, now nerves and anxiety filled me with dread. I walked quickly out the door and sped to my car, as I reached it, something caught my attention out of the corner of my eye, but it was too late. Everything went black.

* * *

I woke up with a pounding headache and closed my eyes again tightly as wave upon wave of discomfort hit me. *Why does my head hurt so badly?* I thought, trying to turn, completely uncomfortable in the chair that I was

196

sitting in, but unable to.

Where am I? I opened my eyes in tiny slits to see where I was, the last few minutes foggy in my mind.

The room was bare except for a few threadbare chairs and a couch in the middle. There wasn't even a television set in the room, and I shook my head lightly, trying to place where I was. This wasn't my apartment. I tried to think of where I'd been moments before, but everything was jumbled in my head. I moaned a little in distress as I tried to figure out what was going on.

Footsteps echoed around me, and I opened my eyes wider. The room was darker than I thought, because the next moment there was a flash of lights as they were switched on by whoever was coming into the room.

"About time you woke up, sleeping beauty," a voice said, and I tried to place it. *Why do I feel this way?* I was getting upset; nothing made sense at that moment.

"Where am I?" I groggily asked. "What's going on?"

"I guess I hit you harder than I thought I did, princess." The word, although pretty in meaning, was said with such venom that I knew that whoever it was wasn't being sweet.

A man stepped around and knelt on the floor in front of me. His brown eyes were dead inside, and I wondered why I had never realized that before, as memories and thoughts started to come back to me. "Come on, princess, wake up and remember what's going on… This isn't any fun if you don't understand."

"What do you mean?" I asked, still not quite understanding, my head pounding.

"What did I do to you, Richard?" I said, using the name that had been supplied to my slowly awakening mind. "I don't even know you."

He smiled, and despite its beauty, it was an evil and angry-looking face. "Oh, but Lilliann, you represent everything that I hate." The words were filled with ice, and I shook with the chill, a deep intensity, like a winter storm. "You're the reason that I lost everything."

I shook my head, not understanding. "Why did you kill Damien then? He didn't have anything to do with me."

"Oh, but he did!" He exclaimed, jumping to his feet with a start. "He had everything to do with you. He was here to report to me about how you were growing up. To tell me when you started to show 'signs.'"

He made air quotes in the air, and it took a moment before I realized that he knew that I was a witch. *But how?*

"Signs so that I'd know that it was time to kill you. I refuse to have another witch out there that could destroy another family."

I was awake now, eyes wide as I took in Richard's appearance. He wasn't so meticulous anymore. His hair was a wild array as though he'd repeatedly run his fingers through it. His shirt was untucked, and a few buttons were undone.

"What do you mean, another witch that could destroy another family? I'm not a witch," I tried to deny, trying to understand how much Richard knew and how this was all connected. "Why was Damien McGregor reporting on me to you? Who are you? Why did you attack Jo?"

"I thought you knew everything, girl," he sneered, the heat rising in his voice, "Don't you know who I am?" He looked at me then, his deep brown eyes, the Greek cheekbones, everything that screamed model, but it wasn't his good looks that made the situation undeniably difficult to understand; there was a pure malice that hung over him like a curtain, and I wondered why I had never recognized it before.

"Who are you?" I repeated, still unable to place how I might know him.

"I'm your grandfather, girl," the sneer came out again, "Not that I had any choice in the matter. No, your father, my heir, Mark, wanted your mother even though she was nothing but trouble. I tried to show him the private investigator reports, but he didn't care. Saying that he loved her, he offered to marry her despite her protests that she would be the death of him if he stayed. I even offered to pay for a one-way ticket out of the country for her, but no, she stayed because he wouldn't give up on her. Told me that she'd find a way to make it safe for him. Fat lot of good that did," he spat.

"She was pregnant with you before the wedding even happened," he continued as he paced around the room, occasionally throwing dagger looks my way, "I didn't understand it all until *he* came, telling me all about her being a witch and the curse on her family. I tried to tell Mark to leave her and that he would die if he stayed, just like she told him, but he didn't care. He was so excited about your birth that nothing I said meant anything. And then, he died." The pain in his voice was heartbreaking, although he hated me for something that was out of my control. "My heir, the one that was to take over the company and to lead the next generation of Burkes to victory in the business world. Dead."

"I sent Damien here to watch you. I didn't dare have you in my house, knowing that you were a death omen walking. He reported to me every year until you moved, and then I had private investigators watch you in the city. I knew that he had something, I found it in my investigations into his past, that one thing that related him to you, but never thought he knew anything of it."

He paused, stopping as he looked down at me, "I knew you were coming back, and I knew your siblings would be here. I had run into them when they were looking into your mother as well. Nothing good would come of it, I was positive. So I came down here to demand the book that he had for you. He denied me, of course."

He shook his head, "And you never deny a Burke."

I stared at him in confusion, each word an overload to my muddled brain.

"You're my grandfather?" I said, distrust dripping from my words. "Why would my grandfather attack my friend? Why would he have someone watching me?"

I was still a little concussed because nothing made sense. I thought that McGregor was my grandfather.

"Your friend?" He asked, rounding on me as the two words dropped like bombs. "You mean that little police officer woman who came sniffing around me this morning?"

I nodded, confused as to how she knew exactly where to go.

"Yeah, well," he paused dramatically, "She came sniffing around the hotel room this morning with questions on how long I'd been in town and who I was visiting. I faked an appointment to get away from her, or at least I thought I'd gotten away until I saw her trailing after me as I walked down the riverfront. It was empty, so I walked as far as I could before she caught up with me. As soon as she came near me, this look of pure intention on her face, I was so sure she thought she could arrest me, so I attacked her." He laughed diabolically.

"She never even suspected it." His laughter echoed around me, and I could feel the tears slip from my eyes as I thought about my friend lying in the hospital bed.

"But I couldn't very well leave her police vehicle by my hotel, so I had to dump it somewhere. I drove it as far as I could without leaving myself without a possible way back, and left it there. The police should be finding her car about now."

He smiled dastardly at me, "I wiped it down well enough, there should be no issues. Especially, once I get done with her as well."

"What are you going to do?" I asked, my heart tripping me as it stuck in my throat.

"Wouldn't you like to know?"

Twenty-Five

I watched Richard as he continued to pace the floors of a small house. *So this is that grandfather who wanted nothing to do with me as a baby?* I thought to myself as I slowly regained my faculties and congratulated myself on not being raised by this erratic and unhinged person.

Wiggling my hands around trying to find a way to untie them, the tears on my face slowly drying as I promised myself retribution against him for harming Jo and Damien, my mother's father, as I finally figured it out. I pulled my hands, as though trying to separate them, to find out how well he'd tied me in. A giggle almost escaped as I found out that the cord was tight but not too tight. Did he know that he had to tie my hands, or was it a fluke that he had gotten it as tight as he had?

As I sat still, my ears perked up at the faint sound of an engine in the distance. It was barely audible, but enough to make me pause and consider my options carefully. With Richard close by, I knew I had to be cautious and stay alert at all times. I took a deep breath and tried to calm myself down, knowing that getting anxious or panicking would only exacerbate the situation. I needed to formulate a plan to get out of this situation.

As I heard the engine's sound growing louder, I tried to brainstorm any possible solutions. *Maybe I could reason with Richard or find a way to distract him.* However, I knew that I couldn't rely on anything and had to be prepared for the worst. I took another deep breath and braced myself for whatever was about to happen.

"They should be arriving soon," he muttered to himself, and I couldn't help but wonder who he was referring to. "Where are they?" His words were rapid, tumbling over each other as he repeated them, occasionally glancing out the window.

"Who should be here?" I asked weakly, knowing that I was in trouble if someone else came, as if he were working with someone else. *No one knows where I am.* I thought to myself, and I began to pray that Hope and Sirona had gotten my message about Richard and had gone to get Alec like I'd told them to. *Oh, please listen to your voicemail, Sirona.* I begged the air silently.

"Your sisters," he said, his voice filled with malice, and suddenly I wondered how he knew about that.

"How do you know about my *siblings*?" I asked, emphasizing the word, trying to get him to talk as I continued to work on loosening the cords around my wrists. "It's not like they were with my mom when she met my dad."

He laughed, and it echoed around the nearly empty room and vibrated against my skull. I could hardly remember what he had said minutes ago, but I was sure that he had mentioned them.

"Oh, yes, your sisters," he countered, "I had the pleasure," he said the word as though it was mud coming out of his mouth, "of meeting them when they were looking for AnnaMarie years ago. Here she thought by having their fathers take them away before they could be impacted by the curse that she was sparing them, oh no, she sent the curse with them when she did that," he stated, and I realized that he was talking about my mom.

"What do you mean, she thought she was sparing them?" I could feel the cord around one wrist loosen enough that I could pull my hand down, and the cord went over my thumb. *Yesss!* I shouted in my head at the victory and continued to work on freeing myself.

"In your family, whenever a child is born, the mother always tries to send them away with the father to keep them from losing both parents. AnnaMarie thought that she had evaded the curse twice by sending your sisters away with their fathers, but it couldn't have been further from the truth."

It suddenly clicked for me. Their dads had died about the same time that my dad and our mom had. Everything that Hope had said earlier came full circle. The curse had allowed her to give birth to three girls and continue the magickal bloodline. This way, we would have to learn how to survive in the world without any support or tutoring in the magickal arts. The sound of an engine got louder, echoing around us, and I wondered if that was them. *Go away,* I thought to them, *Don't come here. Don't try to save me, save yourselves. He's completely insane!*

The engine faded, as though it had been turned off, and Richard, I refuse to call him grandfather, ran back over to the window to peek out of it, as though looking for them. He hissed his victory as he turned back toward me, and my heart plummeted. *They were here.* "I guess I do get to kill four birds with only two stones," he said, bringing up the fact that he had indeed killed Damien McGregor.

"How'd you do it?" I asked, trying to coax him into saying more. I had to find a way to keep him talking, not that I wanted the man to love me, but I couldn't take the chance that he would hurt either of my siblings. "He didn't look like he died violently when I found him that day."

"Ah, yes." He came in front of me and knelt again. "You almost caught me that day. I came back to the store to ask him one more time to give me whatever it was that he had for you, and he continued to refuse. He walked away from me." He paused.

"How dare he walk away from me?" he screeched as he jetted upward, his anger making him edgy.

"I had a dose of my potassium chloride with me, considering how hard it is for my body to produce enough potassium... I just got so mad at him, I lunged after him when he walked away from me." Richard had a mad look in his eyes, and I wished that I could get my other hand free.

I looked at him in confusion. "Why do you need potassium chloride?"

He laughed, but it wasn't a funny laugh, oh no, it was a laugh filled with hatred and anger. "Because when Mark died, I fell into the bottle." He paused, and I could see the tears in the corners of his eyes. "I didn't want to be without my child anymore. I just wanted another minute with my son. So, I drank myself to oblivion."

There it was, I thought, *that's how it all comes together.* Richard stopped abruptly as he heard a soft knock at the door and strode out of the room. I continued to work on getting the rest of my fingers free from my first hand, finally feeling the circulation returning to them, before I started working on the cord around my other hand. There's no way that I am going to try and escape from him with a cord still around my hand; it would be my luck that he'd grab the cord and I'd be trapped all over again. I could only hope that Hope and Sirona hadn't come alone. If we could all get out of here, then someone could come back and arrest Richard before his erratic behavior spread to someone else in town.

"Get in there," I heard him bark at someone before several sets of footsteps sounded in the hallway outside the room. "Go straight, right in there," he continued before I saw two people step into the room, and the air left my lungs in a rush.

Why did you come alone? I asked them silently, my eyes begging them, as both sets of eyes landed on me as they entered the room, blue-green eyes taking in my appearance and widening at the sight of me.

That's not good, I thought, they looked like they just saw someone who was completely torn apart, and I had to wonder how true that statement was. I felt torn apart, everything ached in a way that I'd never known was possible, but I was hoping that it was just a result of a possible concussion. Hope went to rush toward me, but Richard grabbed her arm in a harsh hold. "Now, did I say you could go over there?"

She yanked her arm out of his grasp and walked further into the room, her eyes speaking volumes as she continued to watch me as I watched her. Sirona looked around the room, as though trying to see if there was anything there that they could use to get us out of this situation.

"So, what's your plan?" they asked as their eyes landed back on Richard. "You're going to kill all of us in his guest house, and then what?"

He laughed. "I'm going to make it seem like a murder-suicide, of course! That way, there is nothing that is going to lead back to me. This will all be Lilliann's fault, of course," he said with an evil look toward me as he continued to push the other two people into the room and over to a chair. "Now sit down, and be quiet."

Dimly, I thought I heard the front door open again, but my attention was drawn away as he walked over to a table by the window and grabbed some cord from on top of it.

"Put your hands behind your backs," he demanded as he came up to them again. They glanced at each other briefly before complying. While his attention was entirely on them, I could hear the slight creaking as someone walked in the hallway outside of the room, before Alec's head popped into the room. I gasped, but quickly bit my lip as Richard turned around to look at me, and Alec's head disappeared.

"What's your problem, girl?" he demanded from me.

"Please, don't hurt my siblings," I begged him. He shook his head, completely ignoring me, before going back to his work of tying up my siblings. This time, I remained silent as Alec entered the room and walked up behind Richard.

Alec was tall, but Richard was taller. Alec took out his gun from its holster and whacked Richard across the back of the head with a resounding smack. Richard let out a roar of pain as he stumbled. Alec quickly moved backward. Richard whirled around, his eyes first seeing me out before landing on Alec. He glanced back at Hope and Sirona, who had moved closer together and away from where he had tried to tie them. He ran at Alec, who had his weapon still drawn but had been distracted by my gasp of concern, and his gun went flying as Richard knocked the gun out of his hand.

"I thought I told you to come alone," he growled, his eyes demonic as I caught a glance of them when he looked back at Alec. "Now, it is going to be even more people that I'm going to have to cover up for." He sighed as he straightened out. "Oh well," he threw a dirty look at Alec. "I hope you've said your goodbyes."

Alec laughed dryly and motioned for Richard to come at him. I was screaming in my head at Alec for being so reckless, but I dared not utter a single syllable in case it broke his concentration. Richard lunged at Alec.

Hope and Sirona ran around the outside of the room to get to me. I watched in horror as Alec and Richard fought until Hope and Sirona got to me and stood in my way.

"Oh my goddess, Lillie, are you okay?" Hope asked, as she took in my appearance, and again I had to wonder if Richard hadn't done something to me while I'd been out because she looked at me like I'd been beaten to death, even though I was still alive.

"I must look horrible," I said, going for levity with a tiny laugh, even though I wasn't feeling it. "Can you help me get my hands free? I think I almost got one free," I said, lifting my shoulders. Sirona went around and started working on the knots as Hope knelt and worked on the ones that held my feet to the chair. Soon, I was able to move my hands and feet without being stopped, and I breathed out a quick sigh of relief as I wiggled my feet.

"Why did you come?" I asked, looking at both of them as I stood up. "You should have just left me here and had Alec or the police come without you or something." Anger warred with appreciation, and I didn't know which way to go.

"Because," Sirona said, pausing for effect, "you're our sister and we're not ready to give you up yet." They pushed something into my hand, and my ring was revealed when I opened my hand. "Put it on," they demanded, "at least we can make sure you're safe while we're around."

I quickly snuck the ring onto my right hand, feeling power emanate from it as I did it. As soon as the ring was on my finger perfectly, it was a jolt of lightning, and a flash of wind rode me as the power settled.

"Oh wow," I mumbled and grabbed both of their hands as the power struck through me. Their eyes widened, and I realized that they felt the power of the ring as well. I felt energized as though a bubble surrounded me. It was an incredible feeling that made it feel as though nothing could happen.

So, the twisted old man pulling the strings… he's blood?" Sirona stated the obvious as they pulled their hand away. The effect was immediate, the power receded as though waiting for all of our touch.

"Yeah, why didn't you guys tell me that you'd met my grandfather when looking into our Mom?" I asked, although I focused the question on Hope, as she was moving away as well. We watched the two men fight, trying to figure out how we could help. I didn't want to leave Alec alone with him, even though I knew internally that he could handle it.

"I completely forgot," she said, "but when I heard his voice on the phone, I started to piece it together. I told Sirona on the way here."

Alec groaned as Richard punched him in the face. He stumbled back a few paces, and I ached to go to him and make sure he was okay. I may not be with him, and I may think he doesn't understand, but it doesn't mean that some part of me doesn't care. They continued to tussle, Alec randomly yelling at us to leave, even though I knew that I couldn't possibly leave him in this situation. A few punches and kicks were exchanged before Alec had the upper hand.

"So Alec was with you when you got the call?" I questioned, and they both nodded at me. "Why not just send the police here?"

"Because," Sirona interjected, "You're our sister and we were going to handle it our way." The way they said it made me think they meant with magick, which I was perfectly fine with doing, but then why bring Alec along? So I asked them.

"It wasn't much of a choice, he was there when we got the call," Sirona said as Alec fell to the floor, out cold.

"Alec," I screamed as he fell to the floor and started to go toward him before Sirona pulled me back.

"You can't," she said. "We need you."

I blew out a breath and nodded as Richard stood heaving in front of us.

"One down, three to go," he said with a manic laugh.

"Oh, no, you're not!" Hope said, stepping toward him. "You're not going to get away with this, Richard."

"You stupid girl," Richard said, taking a step forward. "You have no idea what I can do."

"No, you have no idea what we can do," Sirona said as they stepped forward. "You're done."

The fact that we stood together finally registered with Richard. His rage fizzled slightly, and his wild eyes darted from us to Alec's gun. He must have known we were witches, we had power, and we were stronger together. As he lunged for the gun, I took a step forward.

"No," I screamed again.

This time, a blast of wind blew around me, my hair flicking in the breeze as it threw Richard against the wall. The sound of breaking plaster as his head hit the wall echoed around us. Hope ran across the room to grab the gun from the floor. As Richard staggered upright, Hope hurled the gun behind us and seized my hand. I reached for Sirona, and the moment our fingers locked, the power surged—stronger, steadier. We stood united. I felt the protection spell wrap itself around Hope and Sirona.

"You're done, Richard," I said. "Just lie down and wait for the police to arrive, you don't have to fight with us." My voice echoed with the energies surrounding us. I felt invincible at that moment. "This could all be over right now."

"You're crazier than your mother if you think I'm going just to let you and your stupid sisters live," he said, blood dripping down his chin. "You don't deserve to live, you shouldn't be here, it should be Mark. He should be here!" His words ended in a screech as he ran toward us.

I closed my eyes, bracing for the impact, when something tugged at my mind. I peeked at Hope and then Sirona to see that they also had the same look of incredulousness on their faces. We looked toward Richard as one, our hands held together as we began to repeat a mantra that we had never seen or heard before. Richard tried to take a step toward us, but an unseen force constantly pushed him back, until the last word fell from our lips and he went flying backward, hitting the wall hard and falling limply to the ground.

I dropped Hope and Sirona's hands as I rushed over to check on Alec as soon as I was sure that Richard wasn't getting back up.

"Alec, Alec," I cried out, dropping to the floor next to him, my hand reaching for his face. "Are you okay? Answer me, please?"

I could feel the wetness fall onto my cheeks as I felt along his side to see if anything was broken, relieved when I felt him breathing.

"I'm calling the police," Hope said as Sirona gathered the cords around the room, went over to Richard, and started to tie him up. They weren't gentle as they worked, and I was grateful for it.

Alec groaned under me, and I scooted back to watch him as he came to. I was starting to ache and burn in places I hadn't realized were hurt.

"Alec," I whispered, placing my head near his on the ground, "Alec, please answer me," I begged, trying to calm myself down. "Just say something."

"Something," he whispered back to me, a groan soon following.

I gave a short snort of laughter. *Of course, you would try to make this into a joke.* I thought as I gave him a one-armed hug.

"You jerk," I said without any venom. "You had me worried there."

"Not as much as you had me," he said as he attempted to sit up. His movements were jerky and uncoordinated.

"What were you thinking going to the hospital to see Jo without someone with you?" he asked, a light line of fury underlying his voice.

"Honestly, I didn't. I just wanted to make sure that she was okay for myself." With a careful hand on his back, I helped him sit up straighter before standing up to offer him my hand. "Come on, let's get you into a chair and not on this floor," I demanded.

Alec looked at my hand as though it were leprous, not that I could blame him after my erratic behavior.

"Everything will be better once you're sitting up," I said with a straight face, even though he put pressure on my shoulders as I helped him up and across the room.

A dark pressure shifted through me, reminding me that Richard was out because of magick and Alec did not know of it, a pressure that I tried to ignore as I helped Alec sit down. The distant sound of sirens wailed in the background, and I looked over at my siblings as Hope hung up the phone and Sirona finished tying Richard up. Hope walked over gingerly, with Alec's gun in her hand.

"Sorry about that… I took your gun because Richard was going for it."

He nodded his appreciation as he sat down. Within moments, police swarmed into the house. I gave Hope and Sirona a quick jerk, indicating that I needed to talk to them. As the police officers came to check on Alec and put cuffs on Richard, they moved quickly toward me, and I took a step back from Alec.

"We all worked together to get him down," I said in a low tone as a police officer started to walk towards us. "It all went too quickly for us to remember what happened, but we worked together." It wasn't that far from the truth, and they both nodded as the police officer came up to us to get information.

We told the story from the beginning, filling in the pieces that each other had missed, until we were allowed to leave, with promises to come down to the station the next day to give a more official statement.

I walked out the door of the house, taking a deep breath in as I looked around me. Minutes ago, I didn't think that I would ever leave that house, and here I was standing outside. I could hear every noise as it resonated around me: crickets chirping, dogs barking somewhere, and the lights of the police vehicles splashing red and blue over the buildings where people stood at their doors, looking at us. Together, we walked out to the car where Poe sat in the passenger seat.

"Oh, buddy." I grabbed him, giving him a gentle love as I settled into the back seat. "I've missed you."

He meowed, purring in contentment as he settled into my lap. We headed back to the apartment in silence; the only sound in the car was the sound of Poe's purring.

* * *

The next morning, I woke up to the smell of breakfast cooking, and I wandered out of my room in a daze.

Who would be cooking breakfast? I thought as I drifted through the living room into the kitchen. Sirona stood at the oven, several pans laid out on the stove as they cooked. The wafting smell of bacon wrapping around them drifted through the apartment.

"Hot dang, that smells good!" I murmured as I stepped closer. Sirona turned around and glanced at me before going back to the eggs that they were working on.

"It will be done soon if you want to go get dressed," they responded.

I looked down to see that I was wearing one of my oversized shirts and not much else. I blushed as I rushed back out of the room into my room to change. Once I was dressed, I came back into the kitchen to see Sirona putting the food onto plates for each of us. My entire body ached in ways that I didn't think possible, but I refused to look in the mirror that morning, opting out of giving myself more anxiety.

"It looks even better," I complimented them as I grabbed a plate. "Where is Hope?"

"She should be back soon," Sirona said, as they grabbed another plate and we walked to the kitchen table. "We talked about it and decided it would be better for you, at least for a while, if we were both here with you to make sure that you're okay," she mumbled around a mouthful of food. "I went down as soon as the café opened this morning and told Linda about what had happened last night, and she was in complete agreement that you shouldn't be alone. We're moving in temporarily while we look for a place, and we have already made a payment to Linda to secure our stay here. So, no arguments."

"Wha-," I looked at them, flabbergasted. "Don't you think you should have talked to me about that?"

"You were the one who mentioned it to begin with," Sirona reminded me.

I'd woken up this morning convinced I needed to send them away. Not just for their safety—though that was part of it—but because I couldn't keep pretending that my presence wasn't costing them something. Everything about me felt like a fuse waiting to be lit, and they were too close to avoid the fallout.

Our mother's legacy had ruined lives before mine even started. Sirona's nightmares. Hope's chronic vigilance. All of our fathers—gone, one by one, like pieces in some cursed puzzle I was born to finish. If I hadn't existed, maybe none of it would've mattered. Maybe the curse would have ended quietly, buried with the generation before us.

And the worst part, the part that twisted in my gut like barbed wire, was that I had no right to feel broken about it. My childhood had been safe. Gentle. Filled with sticky-fingered birthday parties and school plays and hot cocoa on snow days. Janine and Bruce loved me as if I were a miracle, not a warning. And I had let them. I had been happy and taken care of until I found out during my senior year.

And then I became a ticking time bomb.

It hadn't been Janine or Bruce's fault.

While Sirona fought through terror with no explanation and Hope learned how to take care of everyone but herself, I was learning how to braid friendship bracelets and roast marshmallows. They were surviving. I was thriving.

So no, I didn't want to be the reason they hurt again. If it meant finishing this alone, so be it. It was the least I could do for them, and for the family I never got to know but somehow still mourned.

They didn't need me.

"Oh, quit with the pouty lip." Sirona said, "You're not getting rid of us. We're siblings."

"And you said you were the realist of the two of you, so you should have known that staying here meant that you were possibly going to be put into more danger," I said, biting into a piece of bacon, swallowing a hum of pleasure.

"So why would you be okay with moving in with me?" I questioned.

Sirona paused, their fork hovering in the air, as they listened to what I said. "I was wrong," they admitted, "but don't go telling anyone that because I'll deny that I ever said it. We are siblings, and we felt it from the beginning. I just wanted to deny it. I didn't want to think about getting to know someone else as a sibling when my own childhood was such crap. But -" they paused as they took the bite off their fork, "- I think that we are all going to do so much better if we get to know each other like siblings, which means living together."

The door opened behind us. Hope entered the apartment carrying a bag in her hands, and a suitcase followed her in. "I think I got everything," she started to yell, not looking at anything as she came in.

"The hotel is refusing to refund us the rest of the money for the week we paid for," she said, stopping abruptly as she noticed Sirona and me sitting at the table.

Hope paused in the doorway, bags in hand, eyes going wide as she saw us. "Oh—you're awake." Her cheeks pinkened. "I was hoping to have everything in before you noticed."

I couldn't help but laugh.

"I wasn't expecting this," I answered as she dropped the bag to the ground, seeing that we were eating, and grabbed the other plate from the counter.

"Do you guys really want to live in a small 2-bedroom apartment with me for the unknown future?" I asked, nervousness lining my words.

"Of course we do!" she exclaimed, sitting down right next to me. "Why wouldn't we want to live with our sibling?"

I rubbed my neck nervously, looking between her and Sirona. "Because I'm a complete mess. I'm in therapy and I'm coming out of a nasty relationship?" I answered honestly. "Why would anyone want to live with someone like that?"

"Because," they both answered, almost simultaneously. "You're our sibling."

Sirona continued, "Even siblings who grew up together are there for each other after a bad relationship. We're just going to be learning about each other along the way, comforting each other."

I smiled brightly at both of them. "I'm sorry that my grandfather," the word felt sour in my mouth, so I changed it. "I'm sorry that Richard almost hurt you guys."

"He didn't hurt us," Hope said, as she brushed a hair away from my face. "But he hurt you, and I," Sirona cleared their throat, "*we* couldn't stand the idea that you got hurt because you were alone. So, you're not going to be alone anymore." I reached across and pulled them both in for a hug, silently thanking the goddess that she sent someone, *no, my siblings*, to be with me on my new adventures.

"I'm so thankful that I have both of you," I said softly.

They rubbed my back as we basked in each other's embrace for a few moments, the magick swirling around us as though finally in harmony. As I released them, and we all settled back into our spots to eat, there was a knock at the door. I stood up.

"I got this," I said. "You both have done enough this morning."

Twenty-Seven

I walked over to answer the door, only to find Alec standing on the other side, looking almost as wrecked as I felt.

"Alec," I said in surprise, stepping outside and gently pulling the door closed behind me. "What are you doing here?"

He shifted his weight, rubbing the back of his neck—a nervous gesture I hadn't seen in years. "I came to check on you," he said. "You took off last night so fast, I didn't really get to see if you were okay. By the time we finished at the station, it was late."

I nodded, unsure whether to feel touched or uneasy. Part of me wanted to hug him. The other part remembered all the times I'd reached out only to be left waiting. "I'm fine," I said, the lie soft but practiced. "How about you?"

He gave a crooked smile. "Better than other things I've been through."

The unspoken weight of his past hung between us. I thought of all the times he didn't show up to school, nursing bruises no one dared to ask about.

"So, that guy… he's related to you?" Alec asked, careful but curious.

I laughed without humor. "Yeah. Unfortunately." I ran my fingers through my hair. "Not exactly the family reunion I wanted."

Silence fell like fog, thick and uncertain. We stood there, two people with a history too tangled to untangle in one conversation.

"You're going to have to deal with a lot now," Alec said finally. "Legal stuff. Court appearances. Let me know how I can help."

I offered a small smile. "Thanks." It was more than I'd expected him to say. More than I was ready to believe.

"Well," I said, gesturing back toward the door, "my siblings are probably wondering what happened to me."

He nodded and turned, but then paused halfway down the steps.

"Lilliann Luella King," he said, turning back to face me. "I know you've been through hell. And I heard what you said yesterday. That you've changed." He swallowed, eyes shining with something like hope. "Well… so have I. I want to be better. For real. Can we talk sometime? Maybe coffee. Or lunch. Just—give me a chance to show you."

The breath I didn't realize I'd been holding rushed out. "Maybe, Alec," I said quietly. "I don't know yet."

He nodded, this time accepting it without pushing, and continued down the stairs.

I stood there watching him as he walked away. In my heart of hearts, I hoped that this wasn't the end of everything for us, but at the same time, I just wasn't sure if I was the right person for him to be in love with.

Part of me wanted to call him back. To ask him what he meant by changed. To believe him.

But I couldn't move.

My feet stayed planted. My fingers dug into the doorframe.

Because what if he meant it and I still ruined it anyway?

What if I let him close, and all the things I've tried to bury came spilling out again?

I used to think I left people before they could leave me. But I guess I make it easy for them to go.

Maybe Alec had changed.

Maybe I had, too.

But I wasn't sure I could trust myself not to mess it up.

And worse—I wasn't sure I deserved it if I didn't.

Hearing him calling me by my full name, something he rarely ever did when we were younger, was just another example of how he had changed. He knew that things were different. That *I* was different, but he still came back. Was it really something I could do?

I left the tangle of thoughts at the door. I could pick them up again later.

My back hit the wood as I exhaled, and I forced my focus onto something lighter—

My siblings, sitting at the kitchen table, staring like I'd just walked out of a soap opera.

I tried to play it cool. "What?"

Hope arched a brow. Hope's brows lifted nearly to her hairline. "Was that Alec Becker?"

Sirona leaned forward with a slow, dramatic blink. "Do we need to get you a fan and some fainting salts? Because that was *definitely* a scene."

I huffed a half-laugh, toeing off my shoes before walking back toward the table. "You two are ridiculous."

"You're deflecting," Sirona said, reaching for their mug like they were settling in for an interview. "So go on—what did he want?"

"To check on me," I said, sliding into the seat across from them. "Said he didn't get a chance to see if I was okay last night."

Hope's hand froze halfway to her mouth, holding a spoon of cereal she was definitely no longer interested in. "Okay, but like... since when does Alec do emotional check-ins?"

"Apparently, since last night," I said.

Sirona exchanged a long look with Hope. "I told you he had it bad."

"You did not."

"I did! I said it when we left the hospital. Didn't I say that voicemail hit him in the soul?"

"You said—and I quote—'He looked like someone just stepped on his puppy.'"

"Exactly."

I rolled my eyes, but the corners of my mouth curled in spite of myself. "Look, I'm not saying anything is happening. He asked if we could talk. Maybe get coffee."

"*Oooooh,*" they chorused in perfect harmony.

Poe chose that moment to hop up on the table and plop dramatically between us like a seasoned gossip hound. He meowed once, loud and judgmental.

I looked at him. "Don't you start."

Hope reached over to scratch behind his ears. "You're not off the hook, by the way. *We* get to ask questions, too."

I raised a brow. "Do you? Because I have a few of my own."

Sirona smirked. "Fine. You go first."

I shook my head and gave a tiny smile.

"How about you tell me how you managed to get Alec to come with you to the house and exactly how you got there?" I asked, curious how they'd gotten there. "Because the last thing I'd remembered was being at the hospital, and my car is still there."

Hope laughed. "Funny, you should mention that…"

Sirona rolled their eyes, "She drove like a racecar driver heading for NASCAR's finishing line. She was a maniac behind the wheel."

Hope gave them a look before turning back to me, "Just because I happen to drive fast doesn't mean that I don't drive carefully."

I laughed. This sounded like it was going to be exciting.

Hope gave me a look that was part sheepish, part smug. "You left Sirona a voicemail. When you didn't come back and your car was still at the hospital, we freaked out."

"I tried calling you," I said weakly.

"I didn't have my phone on me," she admitted, brushing hair off her face. "Sirona found the message and we listened to it together."

"You sounded off," Sirona added. "Not scared exactly, but… like you knew something was wrong."

Hope nodded. "You mentioned Richard. Said he might come after us. That you saw him near Jo's room at the ICU."

I swallowed. "I wasn't sure if you'd believe me."

"Well, you don't usually leave voicemails," Sirona said, folding their arms. "That was a big red flag."

Hope leaned in. "We tried calling the station and asked for Alec. Some joker on the phone gave us a hard time, but eventually said he was out by

Westover End."

I blinked. "That's where Jo's cruiser was found." Remembering briefly hearing something about it last night through the dim haze of everything that happened afterwards.

"Exactly," Hope said. "We drove straight there. And yes—I drove fast. You're welcome."

Sirona rolled their eyes. "Fast is an understatement. Alec thought we were nuts until we played him your voicemail."

"Once he heard your voice…" Hope trailed off, her eyes softening. "It was like something clicked for him."

Sirona nodded. "We found your keys by your car, and suddenly he stopped being a cop. He became someone who cared."

Hope smiled. "He didn't want us going after Richard alone when he called us, but we convinced him. Sort of."

"Convinced?" I echoed.

Sirona snorted. "Hope told him to get in or get left behind."

Hope just grinned. "He got in."

That sounded like something that Hope would do. She was a do-or-die kind of person. She took charge of the situation each and every time I saw her with Sirona out and about, so I wasn't too surprised.

I swallowed. "And Poe? How'd he get there?"

"He practically clawed the door down trying to follow us," Hope said. "He knew something was off, too."

I glanced down to where Poe lay in the center of the table. He was zoned out, completely tuckered out from all of the activity and overfed from cans of tuna. I'm pretty sure we each had given him at least one can at some point between when we'd gotten home last night and this morning.

My heart swelled. It was nice to know that the kitten was ready to go to bat for me, even though he was a small puff of fur. I looked back up at my siblings through the curtain of my hair, not wanting them to see the tears that were close to falling.

"You two could've been seriously hurt."

Hope shrugged. "We weren't going to let him take you."

"I know," I whispered. "But still."

Poe stirred and stretched like he agreed.

Sirona reached across the table, brushing a crumb from Poe's ear before looking at me. "You don't have to carry it all, you know. We're here. For real."

I nodded slowly, not trusting my voice.

"And Alec?" Hope asked, more gently this time. "Are you gonna let him be here, too?"

I hesitated. "I don't know."

Sirona tapped the edge of their mug. "That's fair."

A moment of quiet settled between us, not awkward—just… full.

Poe gave a soft snore and flopped onto his side like a dramatic little prince. The sight made me laugh, just a little. Enough.

Hope pushed back her chair. "Well, I don't know about you, but I need caffeine and possibly a pastry the size of my head."

Sirona stood, stretching with a yawn. "Can we go to that weird bakery with the croissant-doughnut hybrid?"

"Yes, please," I said, my voice steadier than before.

They moved around me like a breeze, gathering their bags and keys and shoes. I lingered a second longer at the table, brushing a hand through Poe's fur, grounding myself in the rhythm of this new life—chaotic, imperfect, but mine.

Maybe I hadn't ruined everything.

I let myself take in the moment—this new life I hadn't planned for but had somehow walked into anyway. I was back in the small town I'd once tried to forget, living with the siblings I never knew I had until twenty-seven years after I was adopted. It would take some getting used to. I just hoped I could keep showing up, keep trying to be better than I used to be. I knew I'd spiral again—probably more than once—but right now, I just wanted to hold onto this feeling.

For once, I wanted to be happy. And maybe, just maybe, I was.

Bonus Chapter: Sirona

I was dead-ass tired. Not the kind you can sleep off, but the type that lives in your bones. We got in late last night, and the bed sucked anyway. The bathroom mirror in this cheap hotel wasn't kind either. My pixie cut was sharp and easy, espresso brown with a few silver streaks I'd added last week on a whim. I told everyone it was to mix things up, but the truth was, I was already planning something bolder for next time.

My eyes, blue this morning, with a stubborn hint of green, stared back like they were daring me to be someone else. For a second, I wished I could. But then… no. Because if I hadn't been me, I never would've found her.

"Dale," I muttered to myself. "Get it together."

I yanked on my Pink Floyd tee and jeans from Torrid and glanced down at my thighs. They still made me angry sometimes, not because of how they looked, but because of how people looked at them. Try growing up fat, brown, and queer in Colorado's white suburbia and tell me you don't come out fighting.

Hope was still half-dead in the other room. I should've gone for coffee without her. But nooo, I promised to wait.

"Oye, are you done yet?" I hollered through the door. "I'm dying for caffeine."

"Then go without me," she groaned, muffled by the comforter.

"You promised!" I flopped next to her on the bed and whined like a telenovela villain. "I drove through, like, four hours of tumbleweed hell to get here. I deserve a reward."

Hope groaned, her arm over her head, as I complained. "Go get it yourself," she said again, the weariness in her voice evident. "I just want to go back to sleep."

I looked down at what she was wearing. The orange two-piece suit was freshly ironed, and I realized that it must have been one that had been hanging in the back of the car. It looked good on her, bringing out the deeper hues of her blonde hair, and it felt like she was coming straight out of the sun.

"But you're dressed to go out," I argued, as I pulled on her arm. "Quite being a lazy butt and get up." She let me pull down her arm, glaring out at me as it fell to the bed.

"I hate you," she said flatly, no venom in her words, just our standard argument when we did something that the other person didn't like.

"No, you don't," I said with a slight giggle in my voice, "You love me."

"Nope," she shook her head as she struggled to sit up on the bed, and I scooted over so that she could sit up properly. "I don't love you at all when you force me to leave the comfort of my room to go get coffee this early in the morning."

"But the best coffee is first thing in the morning before everyone else gets to the store!" I argued, pulling on her arm to get her to come closer. "I promise, I'll be nice to you today and won't argue about the buildings we go look at if you go with me to get the coffee now."

She sighed, even as a small smile played on her lips. "Alright, alright," she finally agreed. "Let's go to that one coffee shop that we went to the last time we were here. I think the coffee there was the best." I sighed. I was hoping to go to the little restaurant on the edge of town, hoping against hope that the hot server would be there, but I agreed reluctantly. Knowing that it was the only way I was going to get her to agree to leave before noon.

"Fine, but we have to go to the Violet Bite for lunch then," I countered. "You know that their food was the best."

She shrugged, and I couldn't determine if it was because she didn't agree or if it was because she knew the reason I wanted to go there and didn't want to see me flirting with a girl. My eyes dropped to my lap. *She doesn't care that you are bisexual*, I reminded myself as the insecurity surfaced again. *Ella no es como la familia loca.* I stopped myself from continuing the thought. The family that raised me, took me in for the money of being a foster family, hadn't been the best, but they hadn't been the worst either. *They never left a mark on you*, I reminded myself. *They didn't leave bruises, but they made me feel small. Like my voice didn't matter. That's why I paint*, I reminded myself, *because sometimes color speaks when I can't.*

The other voice in my head said, reminding me of the fact that I'd hidden who I was for so long that I sometimes struggled with expressing myself verbally. *That's the reason why I paint*, I said back to the voice before looking at Hope again.

"Quit telling yourself that you're a bad person," she said, grabbing my hand from the bed. "You are an amazing person, and I love you." I smiled, glad for the reminder, but hating the fact that she could read me so well.

She always did that—said the right thing at the wrong time and made me feel like maybe I wasn't so broken after all. It pissed me off, mostly because I needed it.

"Shut up," I snapped, before standing up, not wanting to get all lovey-dovey.

"Okay, come on, let's get a move on," not saying it in a way to make her feel bad, but to get her to hurry up. She rolled her eyes as she stood up from the bed, and we walked together to the door. "Got the key, right?" I asked, not wanting to pay for another hotel key, if we were to forget it. She pulled it out of a back pocket that I hadn't seen and twirled it between her fingers.

"You mean this one?" Laughter reflected in her eyes as I rolled my eyes at her this time.

"Yeah, that one," I said and grabbed my bomber jacket from the hanger by the door. "I'm driving to the coffee shop," I said with finality, considering that the car keys were still in my jacket.

"That's not fair," she whined. "You drove in last night."

"Yes, but I'm the one who is going to pay for coffee this morning, so deal," I said as we walked out of the hotel and towards the car. It was a difficult decision, but we decided to leave my car in the city with our friends until we had a house to bring everything to. I missed my mammoth van. *That van got me through more states than my last caseworker when I was a kid.* The rental car was nice, but it wasn't the same.

I jumped over to the driver's side door, pushed her out of the way, and unlocked the doors before climbing in. After we both put on our belts, I turned the key and connected my phone to the stereo. The crushing tones of heavy metal belted out of the speakers as I backed out of the parking spot, and Hope cringed at the volume.

"Can we turn it down, please?"

"Hell no, this is the best part," I argued and turned it up.

"But it's like seven in the morning," she countered, looking around to see that not many other people were out and about.

"Don't see 'em, don't care," I replied and drove like a manic toward the coffee shop. The sweet taste of coffee was already making my mouth drool, without a single drop of it near me. I whirled into a parking spot as the coffee shop appeared before me. *Riverfront Coffee and Cream*, the sign read, and I sighed with appreciation. Now it was time to get my coffee on. Turning the key, the engine went silent, and I leaped from the car.

Hope got out at a more leisurely pace and followed me as we entered the coffee shop. There was no one at the register and I whooped with joy, without saying a single word aloud of course, as I headed straight for the counter. The woman behind the bar was an older African American who had been running the place for years, because I was pretty sure it was the same lady that I'd seen the last time we'd been here.

"What can I get you?" she asked as I scanned the menu.

"What's your sweetest drink?" I asked, glancing between her and the menu. "I need to jump-start the heart today." She laughed at my expression, and Hope rolled her eyes again. What can I say, I'm one of a kind.

She put something into the computer and then asked Hope what she wanted to drink. I didn't listen to a word she said as I looked around the building. It looked the same as it had five years ago, chalkboard menus with curling script, mismatched mugs dangling like charms behind the counter, and faded local art that still hadn't been swapped out. Someone had stitched a pothos plant into a dreamcatcher above the napkin station.

Total chaos. Total vibe. *I loved it.*

Hope nudged me, pulling me back to the present, as the woman stood there staring at me.

"Oh, sorry, did you say something?" I asked, feeling a little flustered that I hadn't heard what she'd said.

"Yeah, your friend here said you were paying," she gestured toward Hope, and I laughed.

"Friend? Nah, unfortunately, she's legally bound to annoy me for life." I exclaimed before pulling my wallet out and grabbing a card from a slot.

"Here you go," I said, handing it to her.

"Don't you want to know how much?" the woman asked, and I laughed again.

"Nah, just make sure that the drink is sweet and hot," I said as she handed the card back to me. She nodded and headed off to make the drinks.

"So, do you think we'll find her here?" Hope asked, scanning the people in the room. There were a few more people now waiting for the old woman to come and take their orders.

"I hope so," I said wearily, "I mean Brutus and Emily said that she had to be here. That's the last they knew about the location of our power source." I was sour about that. *Why did the last child get to be the power source?* I was so much older and wiser. Hope nodded, opening her mouth to say something, when the man called out our names and we went to grab them from the counter.

"Hey, thanks," I said, taking a sip of the drink and sighing as the blissful taste of chocolate and caramel swirled around my taste buds. She nodded, and we walked toward the door of the shop. I'd promised Hope that we'd go look at buildings, so there was no point in wasting time in the coffee shop. Not if I wanted to get to the restaurant to see that girl. "Well, let's get going," I said as I gestured her toward the door. "You first."

She started to push her way through when someone else was attempting to enter, and they collided. I snickered as I walked around them and headed to the car. *She hadn't wanted the coffee anyway,* I thought to myself as I went to the passenger side. I leaned against the side of the car and took another sip of my coffee, my eyes closing as I fell into the sickly sweetness of my drink. Vaguely, I could hear Hope talking to whomever she had run into as they profusely apologized. I sighed, my hand dropping down to the pocket where the keys rested, and opened my eyes to see Hope standing with another woman who, if I hadn't known better …a mirror image of her, the same jawline, same defiant tilt of the chin. My stomach clenched like it knew something I didn't.

I glanced away, surprise echoing throughout me as I contemplated whether or not we would have already found the third child of AnnaMarie. They chatted for a few more minutes as a deep sense of dread filled me. The air around them prickled, just a little too still, too sharp. My fingers twitched around the keys like they were warning me. Magick had a way of showing up when you least wanted it to.

If we had already found the third daughter of our mother, did that mean that something bad was going to happen?

The thought ran through my mind, knowing that Brutus had confided in me that our family was cursed and only evil could come from the joining of our sisters. Finally, when I could take no more of the agony that was filling my gut, I turned back and hollered at Hope.

"Come on, Hope, we've got things to do today," I added, impatiently tapping my foot, the sharp tips of my boots echoing against the pavement. The woman she was with laughed at my display. Displeasure coursed through me, *who laughs at someone trying to get the other person to hurry up?* I thought and gestured for Hope to hurry up. Eventually, she walked away from the woman and headed towards the car where I stood waiting. The girl turned and went into the coffee shop without a backward glance, and I sighed with relief.

"Do you think…" Hope started as she walked to the driver's side.

"No," I said flatly, not wanting to encourage her. "There is no way in hell that we would find our sister that easily," I said. Still, it couldn't be her. That'd be too easy—and nothing in my life ever was.

"I said I'd look at places, didn't I? So let's go."

Hope laughed, and I was pretty sure that she didn't believe a word that I'd said about the woman. "Come on," I dragged, "let's go."

"Oh, shush," she said as she started the engine. "I don't have coffee now, so you have to be nice."

"Actions have consequences," I said, sipping smugly. "You snooze, you lose."

"This sure is good."

She looked over at me, an evil glare planted firmly on her face.

"You suck," she deadpanned as she backed out of the spot.

"You know it," I said, taking another sip. "But I'll pay for lunch too since you lost your coffee."

"You'd better," she said and drove towards the Realtor's office that we'd looked up before coming. "Seriously."

Bonus Chapter: Hope

The magick floated around us, and I could feel it brush against my skin as we walked clockwise around the table. Lillie's ring sat in the middle, the blue wax dripping over it as the candle melted.

"Protect from harm," Sirona and I chanted together, our footsteps slow and meticulous, sending our energies towards the ring.

"Protect from harm," the words were repeated as we reached our sixth turn around the table. As we stopped, we stood facing each other and clasped hands over the table, pulling the energy into the confined area.

"The keeper of this charm," we chanted together, ending the spell and forcing the magick into the ring. It vibrated against the table as it was overloaded by the positive energies and intents that we sent toward it. Sweat dripped down my back, as though I'd run a marathon, making me feel exhausted, and yet I was more alive than I'd ever been before I reached for the ring at the same time as Sirona, our fingers meeting in the middle right above the ring. I could feel the magick running along our skin.

"Oh, my goddess, do you feel that?" I asked them, my eyes catching theirs, more blue than green at that moment,

"It's like electricity running along my skin." They nodded, and I let them grab the ring as I stepped back and blew out the candles. The room went dark when the last flickering light of the candle went out, and Sirona reached out for me.

"Hope, are you still here?" I could hear the panic in their voice.

"Yes, Sirona, I'm here. Are you ready to go back?" My tone was light and breezy, the complete opposite of theirs. I was determined to get back to the apartment without getting caught outside of the house again, so I was ready to attempt another teleportation.

They must have nodded their head because there was no answer, but I could hear them bumping against the table as they walked around it to where I stood. Their arm reached out blindly, trying to find me, before latching onto my arm.

"Are you ready now?" I asked again, as they pulled themself closer.

"Yeah," they whispered, and I could hear the nervousness in their voice. "Are you going to do the teleportation again?" Their voice was edged with distress at the idea of being pulled through space again, but I grabbed their hand resting on mine and squeezed quickly.

"I am, but it's going to be okay," I said, and I started thinking about the apartment. I tried to think of the most minor details so that when my magick started, we would land in the right spot. "Do you have the grimoire?" I asked as the first tingling of my teleportation hit me, something that I was starting to recognize now.

"Sí, I got it," their voice was rough, "Is it starting?"

"Yu-" My word was cut off as we disappeared without another pop, and the secret room faded from view.

We landed with another pop and almost broke the coffee table as Sirona started to fall backward, the sounds of sloshing coffee in the mug we'd left behind loud in the apartment. I grabbed them as the grimoire fell out of their hands and pulled them toward me. I didn't want to break the coffee table, even though it wasn't our place to rent; heck, we weren't even technically living there.

"Are you okay?" I asked as they finally found their footing and stood without any wobbling. They nodded, and I turned to see if I could find the ring, as I was sure that they must have dropped it in their tumble.

"What are you looking for," Sirona asked, and I looked at them and smiled innocently.

"Nothing," I smiled wider.

"No," Sirona deadpanned, "What are you buscando for?"

I laughed nervously, "I was looking for the ring."

They looked at me and rolled their eyes.

"And why would you be looking for the ring?" They asked as they held the ring up, moving it back and forth between their fingers. I rubbed my face, wiping my hands over it, as I looked back at them.

"I assumed you had dropped it," I said in a gentle tone, avoiding any accusations that might upset them. "But, obviously, I was wrong," I said with a smile.

"Yeah, right," Sirona rolled their eyes again, "I wouldn't have 'dropped' it if it was for your stupid power making me feel enfermo each time you drag me into it." *Oh, it was on like Donkey Kong.*

"My stupid power?" I said, distraught. "My stupid power allowed us to go make that charm for Lillie. We just found our sibling, Sirona, and you think I want to lose her? It's crazy to think that we grew up without each other and lost so much time. I'm not letting anything come between us now. I understand that my power can be challenging to handle at times, but we need to achieve what we need to. I really value our relationships, and I'd never want to mess things up." I demanded. "So, I'm sorry that 'my stupid power' makes you ill, but at least it is useful."

Sirona looked like they were ready to rumble, and I prepared myself for a good tussle; we'd done it a few times to get out our frustrations. Usually, it involved a good amount of hair-pulling and slapping before we were able to pull ourselves together. But then, they took a deep breath and stepped back.

"Look, I'm sorry, okay?" They said, looking out the window, "I just don't like feeling like the world is being pulled out from under mis pies. It's very discombobulating to be standing completely still one moment and then suddenly appear in a different place. You've got to understand that."

I took a breath and walked over to them, hugging them, as I nodded. "Yes, I get it," I agreed, "but you've got to admit that at least I was able to control it the last two times, that must mean that it is getting better."

I tried to put a positive spin on it. They nodded and we separated, the ring still in their hand. I glanced over at the TV to see that the time said it was close to ten o'clock at night.

"Shouldn't Lillie be back by now?" I asked, suddenly aware of how silent it was in the apartment.

Sirona paused, head tilted, as they listened to the apartment as well. "You're right, she should be here. Give her a call," they demanded as they walked toward her bedroom to put the ring on her dresser. I reached into my pocket for my phone, only to find nothing there. *Oh no, where is my phone?*

My panic levels started to rise.

What if I left it at the house?

We could get into a lot of trouble. I followed Sirona into the bedroom, pausing at the door, as they placed the ring down in the center of her dresser.

"Umm, do you know where my phone is?" I asked.

"What do you mean, 'do I know where your phone is?'" Sirona narrowed their eyes at me. "You should have your phone with you."

"Well, technically, yeah, I should have my phone," I said, agreeing with them, "however, I can't seem to find it." I bit my lip, a nervous gesture I'd had since I was a kid.

Sirona's eyes widened. "Well, let me call it." They reached into their pocket for their phone, only to realize that they didn't have it on them either. That's when we both remembered that her phone had fallen earlier, and we headed back out into the living room.

"Where did I drop it?" They demanded, looking at the chairs as we came to the seating area.

"I think it fell on the floor if I remember correctly," I said, and got down on my hands and knees to look under the coffee table. My long hair fell in waves around me, blocking my view, and I paused to push the strands behind my ear before continuing. Sirona fell to the ground by me as we looked under the table and then around in front of it.

"Could it have fallen under one of the chairs?" I asked, my voice growing thicker and deeper with frustration. Sirona moved to the chair by them, and I headed for the couch, feeling around under it until I felt something.

"I got it," I said, even though I hadn't brought it out yet, and Sirona hurried over. As I brought out what I hoped was their phone, I held my breath, worried that I'd said it, and then it turned out that it wasn't it. However, the fear was needless, as when it emerged, it was indeed their phone, and they were quick to pick it up and touch the screen.

Their brows furrowed, and I frowned in concern as I sat up and leaned back against the couch. "What's wrong?"

"Lillie called and left me a message," Sirona said, showing me the notifications on her screen. "She's never left me a message since we met."

That's true, I thought to myself as anxiety crept in like a thief in the night. Generally, Lillie leaves the voicemails with me if she isn't going to make it to one of our meet-ups.

"Listen to it," I demanded, my phone forgotten in my concern for our sister. Sirona nodded as they opened up their phone and went to their voicemail. They put it on speaker as Lillie's voice echoed around us.

"Hey, Sirona. I hope everything's okay…" She trailed off for a moment before continuing, "Anyway, I tried calling Hope, but she didn't answer. I think I know who killed our grandfather, I just don't know why yet, but I have a bad feeling that he may come after you guys next." We looked at each other, dread filling our gazes,

"But, you remember that Jo found the name Richard when we were looking through the book log? Well, the old man who was at the coffee shop this afternoon, the one I asked if you had seen, was here when I arrived at the ICU. Coming out of a room a couple down from Jo. I just thought it was really odd because he's a tourist, so why would he be in the ICU?" We could hear her take a deep breath as she continued, "But he paused when he saw me, and I called out to him, using the name Richard when he walked by me. He totally stopped for a second. He had to be the one to kill McGregor." We could hear her pick up the pace now as she realized that the message would be cut off soon, "Anyway, he's wearing a blue button-up shirt, has these Greek cheeks, peppered grey hair, and is so tall! If you see him, call the police. I'll leave their number for you here in a second. Tell them you need to talk to Alec, okay? I'll be home soon, visiting hours are over in like ten minutes," She rattled off the number to the police station before hanging up.

I could feel the sweat pool at the small of my back at the implication of Lillie not being home yet. The call was over two hours old, there was no way that she would have stayed at the hospital after visiting hours, and she would have contacted one of us if she had decided to go over to the Violet Bite or something.

"Do you think -" I trailed off, not wanting to say it out loud, even as internally I whispered to myself... *that Richard took her?*

"Nah, there's no way that -" Sirona stopped, not able to complete the sentence, knowing as well as I did that something terrible had happened.

"I think we should call the police," I said finally, getting up from the floor, only to be faced with my phone lying face up on the couch.

I closed my eyes, shaking my head, at the realization that I should have seen it earlier when I'd been reaching into my pocket for my phone. I grabbed it off the cushion as Sirona got off the floor next. There was a notification that Lillie had called me as well, but there was no voicemail, and I realized that she must have left the voicemail on Sirona's phone because she didn't want to keep calling us back.

Sirona nodded their head and listened to the voicemail again, this time I dialed the number as Lillie read it off. When the voicemail ended, I called the police station and put it on speaker as Sirona approached me. I could dimly hear the scratching of nails against a door, as the rings continued to sound out around us as we waited for the station to pick up the call. Someone finally answered, and I was quick to ask to speak with police officer Alec.

"Do you know which Alec you need to speak with?" The male voice on the other end asked, and I looked at Sirona with wide eyes. The terror reflected in their eyes at not knowing his last name.

"Umm," I stuttered, not knowing how to answer.

"I'm just joshing ya," the guy said with a guffaw. "There's only one Alec on the police force here. Can I tell him who's calling?"

I sighed with relief and watched as Sirona visibly relaxed as well. "Tell him that it is Hope and Sirona, Lillie's siblings, on the phone."

"I didn't think Lillie had siblings," the man said in surprise.

"Yeah, neither did she," I said with a short laugh. "It's a long story, but I need to speak with Alec. Like right now." I tried to place the importance of the call into my voice so that the man wouldn't take any more time.

"I gotcha," the man said in understanding, obviously thinking we were calling for a different reason than we were, but now wasn't the time to figure out what he thought we were calling for. "I'll get him on the line."

There was a brief pause as the man put us on hold. The scratching continued, and Sirona rushed away to the kitchen to let Poe in through the door while I waited on the phone. The man came back online as Sirona came back with Poe in their hands.

"I'm sorry, darling," the man drawled, "but Alec is out on Westover End picking up a cruiser." Our eyes were drawn to each other as it dawned on us that Alec had found Jo's cruiser.

"You said, Westover End," I clarified, thinking of how we would get there. Several houses in that area had been for sale that we'd toured earlier in the month.

"Yup," the man agreed, "but he shouldn't take too long before coming back to the station. Do you want his num-"

"Thanks, I'll head out that way to find him." I cut the man off in a rush, as I grabbed my purse from the couch, and Sirona walked back into the kitchen to grab the apartment key off the counter before I hung up the phone.

"Are you ready to go?" I asked as I came into the kitchen. Sirona held up the apartment key and nodded.

"Where are you going?" Poe asked, still clasped in Sirona's other arm.

"To find Alec," I said, "we think Lillie's been kidnapped." Poe dropped out of their arm, hair-raising.

"What do you mean, 'kidnapped'?" He demanded.

"It's too long to explain," I said, "just come with us." Sirona went to open the door before stopping abruptly in front of me.

"Ow," I said, as my toes throbbed from being jammed into the back of their shoes. "What are you stopping for?"

"Her protection charm," Sirona said simply as though it was the best explanation in the world. I nodded and moved out of the way as they went to grab it from the bedroom. Poe looked up at me like I was walking in slow motion. Sirona came back from the bedroom, and we all took off through the door and down to the car we'd rented.

"I'll put the directions in to get to Westover End, you drive," they said as we separated to get to the doors. I unlocked the car and hopped into the driver's seat while Sirona waited for Poe to get in. When everyone was in, we drove off.

* * *

Several minutes later, we arrived at the entrance to the small gated community called Westover End, where we saw two police cruisers parked outside the gate. I slowed down as I came upon them, rolling my window down.

"Is there an Alec here?" I asked the two gentlemen who were standing between the cars.

A rugged-looking man, with shaggy brown hair and olive skin, smiled as he walked over to me.

"I'm Alec Becker, how can I help you?" He asked in the deepest voice I'd ever heard. My heart skipped a beat, and I wondered what his connection was to Lillie because a voice like that could stop hearts.

"Yeah," I stuttered, "Umm," shaking my head, I tried again. "Lillie is our sister, and we think something's happened to her."

A look of complete confusion washed over his face before vanishing, his police persona sliding into place in a second flat.

"What do you mean?" He asked, looking around me to see that another car was waiting to pass, "Why don't you pull over to the side of the road there, and I'll come over?"

I nodded before pulling away and parking at the spot he'd pointed to. He spoke briefly with the other police officer, waving to the car that had been waiting before walking over to it. Sirona told Poe to be quiet as he walked toward us, having just finished telling him about everything that had happened that day.

"So," he said as he leaned against the back passenger's window, "You think something's happened to Lillie?" His voice changed a little when he said her name, "And you're her sisters?" His eyes betrayed the doubt that he kept from his voice.

"Yes," I said, clearly getting annoyed that I was going to have to repeat myself. "I think," Sirona coughed next to me, and I clarified, "We think that something has happened to her. She was supposed to come back to the apartment after seeing Jo, but she's not back yet, and she left us a message."

I gestured toward Sirona to give me their phone. They handed it over with a problem, continuing to pet Poe as they sat next to me. I handed it to Alec after pulling up the voicemail. He hit play and listened, a variety of emotions sliding over his face until the message ended with her telling them to find him if they saw Richard.

"Okay, explain yourselves." He said, pushing away from the car, and knelt at the window so he could look me in the face.

"Hey, Alec," the other officer called out, "I think I found something." He turned toward him and then back to me.

"Don't leave," he ordered us, "I need to go check this out, and I'm keeping your phone as insurance that you won't leave." I nodded, hoping to reassure him, and watched him walk away.

Mmm, that man had a figure. I thought to myself, and Sirona slapped me in the shoulder.

"Stop ogling the man," they said, "Don't you think it's odd that Lillie said to find him specifically? Maybe he's her ex or something." I paused and turned around to look at them.

"You're right," I said, "but I got eyes, don't I?" I laughed at their expression before turning off the engine to wait for him to return.

Minutes later, Alec returned to the car, a book in his hands as he knelt by my window again.

"Do you know anything about this?" He questioned, holding the book up for me to see. I took a glance at it, only confirming that it was indeed the same one that Lillie had picked up during our first adventure to the house. Jo and she had poured over for hours trying to find someone who could have killed the bookstore owner, our grandfather.

I quickly nodded, and Poe jumped from Sirona's lap to mine, his head popping out of the window toward Alec. Alec dropped the book down, looking down at the kitten and then back up at me.

"Isn't that Lillie's kitten?" He asked, suspicion clear in his voice.

"Well, duh," Sirona said from beside me, "we were just at her place. Did you not hear Hope tell you that?" Their sarcasm was going to get us into trouble if they didn't rein it in. I gave them *the look* before looking back at Alec.

He tilted his head and looked deeper into the car to see Sirona. "And you are?"

"I'm Sirona Santos, pronouns them/they/theirs, and I'm Lillie and Hope's sibling through our biological mother," they stated matter-of-factly and reached their hand around me to offer it to Alec through the window. He gingerly took it before things started to click into place.

"Aren't you the ones that Lillie met when she first got here, and she was kinda nervous about?"

I shrugged. "You could say that," Pausing, I tried to think of how to explain how we set each other's radars off when we first met. I gave Poe a quick rub on his head before continuing. "It was more along the lines that we recognized each other on the spiritual plane, and she wasn't quite in tune with it yet." I went for the diplomatic response.

He laughed dryly, pulling his hand out of the car, "So you all are related?" I nodded again, "Okay, I can see some similarities," he admitted, "but why didn't you tell her when you first saw her?"

I sighed, "I didn't realize that she was our sibling at first; she was the one to put it together, actually. She got the information about her biological parents from her mom and dad and then asked us if our mom's name was the same."

He nodded, "That sounds like Lillie Bell," he said with a sigh, looking down at the book. "Anyway, what does the book have to do with all of this?" He demanded, and I took note of the little adorable nickname he had for her.

"If you look in there, there is a man's name, just a single name. Richard. Well, I think Lillie found him. I gestured to the phone that was in his front pocket now. You heard the voicemail. Alec, she hasn't come back to the apartment yet, and we're worried." He nodded, tension running along his shoulders at the thought that she wasn't back yet.

"Let's go to the hospital to see if she's there, and we'll go from there, okay?" He said, grabbing the phone out of his pocket and handing it to me. "I'll drive in my cruiser and you can follow me," he reiterated before standing up.

I nodded and started the car up, doing a U-turn when I saw him enter the cruiser. The other officer waved at him as he started the engine. Alec opened his window and said something to the other officer, nodding his head. He began to pull away, and I followed closely, but not too closely, behind him. Eventually, we arrived at the medical center, which was closed to visitors.

I looked around the nearly empty lot for Lillie's car before seeing it, and I drove toward it in a hurry.

Why is her car still here?

The thought rolled like thunder around in my mind as I pulled into a spot nearby. Alec parked outside the main entrance as Sirona and I popped out of the car with Poe. Poe walked delicately across the blacktop toward Lillie's car, his ears back as though he was already feeling bad juju around it. I looked over toward where Alec was before shaking my head and walking to her car.

Sirona followed Poe as they walked to the car, making sure to keep him in sight while still feeling out the air.

"Do you sense anything?" I asked them both, wondering if there might be a way for us to determine what had happened. They both shook their head, and I sighed, my anxiety was at an all-time high, and I wondered if I was ever going to come down off of it.

There was the sound of crunching pebbles as Alec came over to us as we neared the car, our eyes darting everywhere, trying to find Lillie.

"Do you see anything?" he asked, and Sirona was quick to pick Poe up from the ground before he reached the car. "I tried to ask security if there were any videos out here, but they said there was nothing to record in the parking lot, so I'm afraid we're out of luck there."

He sighed, and I could hear the frustration roll off of him in waves.

"So we'll have to see if there is anything suspicious here by her car."

"Would a set of keys be suspicious?" Sirona said it in a way that suggested they intended to be sarcastic.

I looked over at them to see that Poe was holding a set of keys between his teeth that Sirona had taken away before Alec looked at them.

"Yeah," he said as he walked toward them, "a set of keys would be highly suspicious." He took them from Sirona and examined them. "Do you recognize the keys?"

"Yeah," I said, fear now coursing through me. "Those are Lillie's keys."

He cursed, the keys gripped so tightly in his hand that I was sure that they were going to leave a mark. Then a sound echoed in the silence of the early evening light. I looked toward Sirona, silently asking them if they had their phone. They shook their head, and I looked at the car. I'd left my phone in the car as well in my haste to get out and look at Lillie's car. I ran toward the vehicle, the sound of Sirona's ringtone getting louder with each step. I jerked the passenger side door open and grabbed her phone from the seat.

It was Lillie.

"Hello," I swiped across the screen before putting it on speaker. "Lillie, is that you?"

"No, not Lillie." The voice on the other end stated, sounding vaguely familiar. "But I'm sure that you already knew that, right, Hope?"

I took a step back in shock, almost dropping the phone.

How could he know who I was? I thought. *He was calling Sirona's number.*

"Is this Richard?" I asked, trembling, trying to place where I'd heard the name before. It wasn't just from the book.

"Of course, it's Richard. Who else were you expecting?" He said with such an air of arrogance about him that I wondered if he was rich.

Call me a money troll if you want, but it sounded like someone who was used to getting what they wanted whenever they wanted.

"Why did you take Lillie?" I demanded, anger now flashing through like a tidal wave. "What does she have to do with this?"

"She has everything to do with this, not that she'll be around much longer to be a nuisance to me anymore. You're next on my list. You and your sibling. I'm done with your family." I spared a glance to see that Sirona had a fire raging in their eyes.

"Where are you?" I asked, trying to sound pleading. "We'll come and give ourselves to you if you'll spare her."

"Now, why would I give her up? You're more than welcome to join me, though," he said with an evil laugh. "I'm at where Damien lived with thoughts of me every day, even though Damien refused to give me what I needed, even though I gave him the house he lived in, I'm going to get my revenge. Come, find me, and come alone." He hung up without another word, and I dropped my hand to my side, the phone falling with it, as Sirona rushed at me with Poe.

"What is going on here?" Alec demanded as he stepped toward us.

"I don't know," I said, only telling a partial lie. The voice was familiar, but it was so clear to me that I knew it.

If he was done with our family, that meant that it was someone who knew we were witches, and there was no way that I was going to tell someone in the law enforcement department that it was because we were witches that this was all happening. He'd lock us up instead of going after the real person, meaning that Lillie could die.

"But I don't think we have much time."

Alec reached for his walkie, but Sirona held out a hand to him, "Don't. If you call for reinforcement to his house, he'll probably kill her out of spite. Let us go."

Alec cursed and looked back and forth between the two of us. "Do you think I'm going to let you do something erratic? There is no way that I'm sending two unarmed people into a potentially life-threatening situation."

"It's not like you have much choice," I said as I gave Sirona's arm a quick squeeze. "Let's go." They reached down to the ground and picked up their phone before turning to the passenger side of the car.

"Now, hold on a minute," Alec demanded as he took a step toward us.

"You can either come with us, or you can try to arrest us, but either way, we are going. Besides, we aren't going to let you call for reinforcements either, especially when our sister's life is on the line. So, are you coming or not?" Sirona said as I walked around to the driver's side door.

Alec blew out a huff of air.

"I need to drive there myself," he argued, pointing out that he would need somewhere to put Richard once he was arrested.

I laughed, "Are you wanting to set him off? What if he can hear two cars?" I said, thinking of things from a different angle.

Alec groaned, not liking the idea of only being in one car, before he reluctantly agreed, or so I thought.

"But then, where am I going to put him?" He demanded, trying to make sure that he still followed the letter of the law.

I shrugged, not really sure, and he sighed again.

"Let me follow you guys closer to the house, and then I'll get out and get into your car when I'm closer, deal?" He offered, trying to make a compromise, so that he was still agreeing to the one car but making it so that he had his car closer to where Lillie was. I sighed, thinking of all the extra time that it would add to the drive. Lillie was in danger; there was no time to have a petty argument over a car.

"I don't have time to argue with you, Alec. I need to get to my sister. Either you are coming with us, or you can come and find us." I stated with finality as I got into the driver's side.

He started to walk toward the passenger side door, clearly not happy about coming in one car before Sirona cut him off.

"Nope, that one is mine, lawman, take the back," they said, handing him Poe as they opened the door.

"Get to know Poe while we drive." They laughed manically as they got into the car.

As soon as all the doors were shut, I revived the engine before running off into the night.

About the Author

Jillian E. Thompson creates captivating cozy mysteries that offer readers intrigue and comfort. Her stories combine small-town charm and suspense with a flair for crafting compelling characters and puzzling whodunits, keeping readers coming back for more.

Jillian has always been passionate about storytelling and writing in various genres, from mystery to poetry. Her cozy mysteries, however, have become her signature, reflecting her love for the genre's balance of warmth and suspense.

When she's not plotting her next mystery, Jillian dedicates her time to special education advocacy. With over a decade of experience in the field, she is currently pursuing a doctoral degree. She is committed to supporting educators in fostering inclusive learning environments.

At home, Jillian lives with her husband of 18 years, their two children, and a lively household that includes four dogs, a kitten, and several reptiles. Balancing family life, writing, and education, Jillian brings creativity and heart to everything she does—on and off the page.